Eva

București, 2019

Oana Babagianu | **Eva**

Eva

Oana Babagianu

Bucharest, 2019

Printed at Artprint

Strada Sulina, numărul 26, 5th District, Bucharest
Postcode: 040576

Contact address: Mitropolit Dosoftei, numărul 14,
5th District, Bucharest

ISBN: 978-973-0-29606-8

Chapter 1

Happiness and suffering are a part of us. We are born with them. Every person on this planet has them when they take their first breath. They come as a whole and, steadily, one of them leaves room for the other, as our lives develop.

We cannot choose our place of birth, our names, our relatives. Nor can we choose the way our parents decide to raise us, or the education we receive or, even less, the lifestyle we adopt during our first years of life. Some of us are born lucky, in more open-minded, more lenient families striving to guide us towards anything that is beautiful and good. Others of us, don't – there is the rest of us who start off on the wrong foot and must fight for a bit of lucky which may save us from an unhealthy and less fortunate environment.

Even so, the destiny which every one of us holds is unique. We are unique and come to this world for a purpose. Some of us need a while to figure out what their purpose on Earth is; however, there are others who fail to ever find it.

We are born with a burning desire to learn. We learn how to walk, eat, love, hate, do good or evil, make mistakes or how to fix them.

We learn to have priorities, to choose our priorities and the way to rank each of these priorities. We learn to accept, we decide what we can't tolerate / accept and how to draw conclusions.

When we come to this Earth, we know nothing about ourselves, about those around us, nor about the functionality of any physical or non-physical item surrounding us. We learn it all, absolutely everything. We grow with love or hate, we decide what is good and what is bad and we make mistakes, willingly or less willingly, which may impact our entire lives.

Sometimes, we need to break away from the things and people we love. Even if it goes against your heart, even if leaving them behind is something that hurts deeply, you have to go. You need to close the chapter, say Goodbye or not, and not look behind. It is painful to give up on something which meant so much to you, up to that particular moment. Decisions can be made quite easily, however it is the accepting part that doesn't come so lightly. The feelings of guilt, frustration, desire … they are all mixed.

Sometimes, we need to give up, sometimes we are asked to give up, while other times, we just want to give up. All three actions are different, however, they basically share the same content.

We often undertake to finish something without realizing that that something may be hurting us. We stop considering that it is not what we actually wanted or it does not have a positive impact on us, but instead, it just brings about frustration and unhappiness – and we continue to immerse ourselves in achieving a goal that does not lead to anything good.

As I've said before, we can't choose who are parents are. We must love them, worship them and respect them. At least, until the time we are able to realize what is good and what is bad and until we are able to spot the difference between mistake and ill-faith.

The memories of my childhood are few, but significant. My mother, named Kristina, was always wearing long, ankle-bound dresses, tight shirts and a scarf twisted to look like a braid. She was always wearing two golden-blonde ponytails. Her few grey hairs were visible on the sides. Ever since I was a child, I remember my mother holding prayer books, icons, the unmissable candle and the strong desire to teach me as many prayers as I could learn. Every Sunday, she would dress me up pretty and take me to church with her. Even though she was from a lower social class, everyone would say Hello to her and respect her in that holy place.

- Mom, why doesn't dad ever join us for church? You've seen our neighbor, Maria, how she is accompanied every Sunday by her mother, father and grandmother.

- Dear girl, every family is different. And it is not always that which you see from the outside is the true reflection of what is happening on the inside. Your father, Ivan, is less of a believer than we are. You must continue to pray to God, for yourself, as well as for your father, who has lost his faith.

I have never heard my mother badmouthing her husband, namely my father. Even though the sadness was visible in her eyes and her cheeks flushed with rivers of tears, she would always remain a strong and positive woman.

We had a small house, located on the edge of the Necşeşti village, in Teleorman. The kitchen was at the other end of the garden, along with the bathroom, and the house was made up of a living room, a bedroom and a closet. There was just one stove, half of which was placed in the living room, and the other half, in the bedroom. I was always trying to help my mother carry the wood and stick it in the stove, but she would always say to me: "Play! Childhood is for games and fun, not for household chores." At the time, I failed to grasp how right she was. I wanted to grow up and cook food, wash, fire up the stove and tidy up the garden. My only toys were a brown bear and a yellow animal book. Mother had managed to take them from someone in the village and they seemed something extraordinary to me. I would store them by the window and refrain from playing with them, except dust them and speak to them from a distance – for fear not to break them. Instead, I would find something to do with a pencil, old dishes and I would often ask my mother to five me some used clothes for me to cut them up and stitch some clothes for my little bear. What's funny is that I never named "my friend, the bear". Even though I would speak to him on a daily basis and tell him what I wanted to do, where I wanted to go and what I wanted to change, I never called him a particular name.

- Eva, please stay in your room, I'm just going to peel some potatoes and cook something up, mother said, with her forever-gentle voice.

- Yes, mother! Are you making chips?, my face was all smiles, as if I was about to eat strawberry and chocolate – however, at the time, potatoes were a delicacy for me.

- Yes, I am. Would you like anything else?

- Do we have any chicken?

- No, we haven't got any. Only double cream.

- Chips and double cream then, mom. Please shout when you want me to come and eat.

She smiled and pulled the door behind her. I would always run to the living room window, to watch her make her way to the kitchen. I would admire her, I loved every little thing about her.

My eyes immediately moved in the direction of our ramshackle door. The sound of the door handle, whenever my father would open the door, is ever-present in my head and brings about mixed feelings. I knew him by his eyes. I knew if he was coming from the marketplace, where he had a booth and was selling whatever my mother was growing in the yard garden, or if he was coming from the tavern. If I saw him waggle, I would run straight into the small closet in the house, which was not heated, I would cover my ears with my hands and would pray to God for it to pass quicker. I knew what was to come, I would rewind the string of events in my head and I would cry silently, for fear of not hearing me.

- Eva!
My heart was pounding even harder whenever he was calling my name out.
- Come out already, or I'm coming to get you and it won't be pleasant!
I would wipe the tears from my cheek and came out, looking shy, from my retreat.
- Yes, father.
- Where is your mother?
- In the kitchen, she's making..
- I couldn't care less about what she's making!! I want her to pour me a *ţuică* *(translator's note: a Romanian hard liqueur)* and bring it over!
- I'll go now! Let me just put something on…
- Forget about that! Go now!
- But I haven't even got any slippers on…
He darted at me and, with his large hands, he grabbed my shirt and pushed me towards the door:
- Just go like that! Now! Hurry up!

I took off barefoot, treading the snow without any shoes on, tears in my eyes. I used one sleeve to wipe my nose, and the other, to cover my freezing hand. When I opened the kitchen door, my mother burst into tears.
- Mom, father wants…
- Yes, dear, just stay next to the stove and warm up. I'll go.
She took off her headgear to wrap my feet, which I felt numb due to the snow I had walked through, and she placed her coat on my shoulders.
I was all gathered on a chair next to the stove, while I was watching my mother leave again, now heading towards the house, with a piece of bread in one hand and the *ţuica* in the other. I was watching the hot pan and was rapidly wiping my tears off. I didn't want to cry anymore, I didn't want to make her suffer again even worse. I wanted to be strong for her.

My mother could have taught me to hate my father. She could have badmouthed him to me or tell me how much she hated him. I knew she hated him, I could see it in her eyes and I could sense her mood change whenever he would walk through the door. But she never did. Every time I asked a question, she knew exactly what to answer. I was, I think, about 4 when father hadn't come home for almost a week. I remember my mother every day and preparing the bags to be taken to the marketplace. Money was tight, so we had to eat only homemade bread with cheese and onion. I wasn't complaining. What was, however, hurting me was my mother's pain.

- Mom, where is dad? It took me quite a while to ask her. And I kept thinking, over and over, whether I'm doing the right thing or not, whether I can change something or it would make her feel even sadder.

- Eva, why don't you ask me something that could help you grow up instead, help you gather information, develop. There are so many things that you need to learn. Stop wasting your time and thoughts on useless things.

Useless things? How could seeing your mother cry every day be deemed as a useless thing?

- But, mom, your eyes are so sad. And whenever you're sad, I'm sad, too. I wish I could change something! Anything! Just to bring a smile on your face.

She took me in her arms and kissed my forehead.

- My sweet child, my only joy shall be when I see you moving as far as possible from this place. I want to see you settle down, with lots of children, as far away as possible from the bad things having infested this world!

- Like the princesses in the stories you often tell me? On a white horse, with a prince, in a castle?

- Yes, honey, exactly like that.

- Can you tell me another story?

- Of course! Once upon a time…

Whenever my mother was telling me stories, it meant the house was peaceful. That he, my father and her husband, was not around. She would hold me in her arms, next to the stove, and would repeat the same story until I would fall asleep. Sometimes, she would mix up the story, probably due to the thoughts in her head, but I would open my eyes and correct her. I loved falling asleep at her chest and hear her voice. It was comforting. And I felt as if I was comforting her, too, whenever she would look at me and smile.

Mother was already starting to worry. Father had never been missing from home for more than one week. Now, it was almost three weeks. She dressed me up in street clothes, got her dark blue top coat and we left the house in a hurry. She would usually check the windows, the fire, the kitchen… this time, however, nothing mattered. We exited the house and she would swiftly pull me behind her. I didn't ask where we were going, but I knew it was related to him. It was spring and I was happy I could enjoy the blooming trees and the roadside flowers. Even if I was only admiring them with my eyesight, it made no difference. I wouldn't get the chance to see the village too often. Mother was always busy with household chores, while father… father was almost never around. I was starting to feel sad about him not coming home. Probably, all my prayers and requests addressed to God were not fulfilling. But I could not comprehend why mother was so upset! Why would you go out and search for your husband when you clearly know that, whenever you find him, you would not get anything else than cursing, beatings, reproaches and other nasty things?

- Mom, do you love dad?

I can still remember the look in her eyes, at that particular moment. I felt like I had my heart in my boots. From a gentle and calm woman, she had turned into a lioness, ready to strike.

- I am really sorry, mom! I didn't mean to upset you!

- My sweet child, you a darling little girl who will grow up and become a woman. Love is ephemeral, it comes and goes. In some homes, it stays longer, in others, less. On the other hand, respect must be eternal! There will come a time when you will need to choose a man and you must then consider my words: do not take any interest in beauty, money or wisdom! Always look for a man who will cherish you, love you and move mountains for you! Because nothing, absolutely nothing is more important than peace of mind.

- What is peace of mind, mum?, I probably shouldn't have interrupted her, but I was still a child.

- Peace of mind means ease, safety and contentedness. It is a time when your soul is filled only with light, without any darkness.

She would have probably proceeded, but we reached some large gates, where she rang the bell and asked me to be nice while she would have a conversation.

- Can I gather flowers while you speak?

- Yes, you can, but don't wander off!

I wouldn't have anyway, because I wanted to hear what was going on. I couldn't tell her that, but I was worried about her and about father.

- Maria, I'm sorry to bother you! Ivan hasn't returned home for about three weeks now. Do you know anything about him? Or perhaps Cornel knows. I'm worried that something may have happened to him.

- Come inside, Kristina, perhaps my husband knows something about it. I have no idea, just that he stopped coming to the marketplace and we all thought you had nothing to sell.

- The bags are ready, I'm already starting to worry. Don't worry, I'll wait here, so I can keep an eye on Eva, too.

I gathered a bouquet of flowers. I didn't know whether to give it to this lady, Maria, for helping my mother to stop being sad, or to give it to my mother.

- Kristina, Maria silently shouted at her, I asked Cornel and told me not to tell you, that we should stay out of it, but from what I understand, he got together with auntie Geta's daughter and he's at the tavern, drinking the day away with her. My husband had also told him to…

- Thank you, Maria! Do you know which tavern?

- Aunty Geta's.

- The one next to the school?

- Yes, that's the one.

- Thank you so much.

- Kristina, you never heard this from me! Otherwise, my husband will kill me!

- Don't worry, Maria! I could never hurt you, when you helped me out!

In my childish mind, I decided to give the flowers to Maria (of whom I would later find out that her marketplace booth was right next to my father's). I felt she had done my mother good having told her where she could find my father, just that… at the time, I failed to understand exactly what it was about and that sometimes, it is better to hold your tongue than do more harm.

Mother grabbed me by the hand and we left for home. She was silent all the way to the house. She didn't cry, either. As opposed to any other time, I could not read her. I sang her a song, picked a flower for her, in a rush, from the side of the road – she failed to make any gestures.

When we got home, she made the fire, put some bread and jam on the table, next to me, and said:

- Be good and stay inside the house. You are not allowed to go out. Wait for me here until I return! Do you understand?

- Yes, I do… my answer came, and I was scared now more than ever. Not once had she left me alone in the house. I don't know what I was more scared of: the fact that I was alone or that my mother had left. What if she wouldn't come back?

I was on the porch, gazing at the door. It was raining heavily. I was trying to count the rain drops, but I failed to. I felt uneasy and I didn't know exactly what was happening. Where was my mother? Where was the unrest in my soul? I was hungry, too, but that wasn't of much importance. I would say to myself thinking that I could have been starving for days, only for my mother to come and hold me.

Could she love father more than me? Could she have left me and went after him?

I had so many questions in my head as if I could not think straight anymore.

I could hear children laughing on the street. I snuck next to the door and started gazing through the fence beams. There were a few neighbors running through the rain and laughing. And what a laughter it was! I wish I could have been laughing with them. They were chasing a ball and splashing every puddle on the street; they were having great fun altogether. I felt a push. I wanted to go out there and make friends with them. After all, I was a child nearly five years of age, who wanted to play. I missed playing, I missed friends, I missed childhood. More than that, I was now missing my mother.

I was already wet to the skin, but I couldn't let go of the fence. After a few minutes, the ball ended up near the fence, at my feet.

- Come out and play! Why are you standing there? There's three of us, if you join us, we can have two teams. Come one!

My heart was jumping with joy, as well as fear. However, after a few seconds, I was out on the street.

I felt free. I was screaming, running, playing. I was kicking the ball and felt like flying. I was jumping up and down in every puddle and was all smiles. My hunger, my desire to see mother, everything was gone.

In the meantime, the rain stopped. We were all wet, but we couldn't stop playing.

- Eva!!! I froze up and for all the joy and happiness filling my heart, I burst into tears. You unfortunate child! Come here!

- Father… please…

I didn't have time to say anything else. He grabbed me by the collar of the shirt with an inexplicable hatred and took me inside the house while swearing all the way. He threw me to the floor like a dog. I had my knees folded up to my chest and I was shaking. I don't know whether I was shaking of cold or fear. Or both.

- Where's your mother?

- She went looking for you. I was shivering and shaking and I could barely breathe.

I tried to get close to the stove which was barely warm and I remember falling, face down, on the brown blanket covering the bed, following the powerful strike I had received from him, my father. I could not understand what I had done wrong. Why was he so upset? Because I had played outside? Because I had not stayed in the house? Why?

- I'll kill you! Both of you! I'm living with two idiots! What's there to eat?

I couldn't make a sound. He was finally home after three weeks and all we got were badmouthing, beatings and cursing.

- Are you deaf? What's to eat? And he was coming towards me again, but I managed to run to the other corner of the room so I could try to escape. Where do you think you're going?, he shouted at me, and I saw him pull out the belt from his trousers.

At first, I didn't know what he wanted to do, but then I could feel it. The first strike was horrible, somewhere on the backside. I could feel the leather belt sticking to the wet clothes. I covered my head with my hands and started praying. Mother had told me that whenever we pray, angels can hear us and they defend us. But no one was defending me now. I was taking one strike after another, until I couldn't remember anything. I couldn't sense any pain or fear, just hate. I hated him with all my heart and the last words I heard were: "Your mother never taught you to do anything!" I sank into a sea of thoughts and prayers. I was praying for time to pass quicker, for God to give me strength and recover.

I was lying on the floor and watching the window. A huge sun was out, the sun after the rain. I could also see a few branches of the blooming tree next to the house. I don't know if I realized what was happening to me, why I was there. I was wondering whether all fathers were like that. What if my friends outside also received beatings due to having played in the rain? Had they gone out with fear in the hearts, too? Were they lying on the floor, like me? What is normal? What is wrong? While I was asking myself a million questions, the door opened and I saw my mother covering her face with her hands and dropping down to the floor, next to me.

- My sweet child… my daughter… the apple of my eyes! She was crying and screaming, at the same time. I could feel her pain from the way she was holding me in her arms.

I stopped crying. I was happy to see her, to have her by my side and that she returned home. I could have withstood all the beatings in the world, but I couldn't have been able to withstand losing her.

She took the wet clothes off me. When she saw my reddish body, streaked from belt strikes, she couldn't take it anymore – she got down on her knees and started screaming:

- Why, oh God? Why are you making me go through all this pain? What have I done you wrong?

- Mom, don't cry. I'm just happy you're here. Please don't leave again!

She must have held me in her arms for quite a while. I could feel her tears running down and the way she was sighing was only making my heart ache even more. Physically, my pain was gone and I wanted her pain to be gone, too. But, at the time, I couldn't understand that spiritual pain is bigger and deeper than any physical pain. I didn't know that when your heart is upset, nothing else matters. It was like an inner disease devouring her slowly, but surely.

- Where is he? Where is that bastard?

The hate in her eyes told me it would not end there. I could already see him beating my mother up too, and the thought was killing me. What I did not know up to that point was the number of beatings and cursing my mother had concealed from me until then. The number of times she had been kept starving for days and locked up in the closet. The number of times she had been abused, physically, as well as verbally. I didn't know too much back then. I knew and I felt she wasn't feeling right, I knew mother was sad, but what I didn't know was how much she had endured from the very first day he had decided to marry her.

I could now see why mother was sending me away for days to stay with our neighbor, Vica, an old lady living two blocks away. She didn't want me to see all these things. She didn't want me to grow up among fights, to suffer and gather hard feelings which might have had an impact on me in the future.

Chapter 2

Auntie Vica was always teaching me how to write and read. Her house was quite small, full of pictures and paintings. She was now all alone after both her children had moved to America, never to return again. She would always tell me that my mother was like her child and that she loves both of us very much. She would never speak of my father. At one point, I started to think she didn't know him, but I could just now understand why she even refused to say his name. I remember she had taught me plenty of poems and songs. She had quite a library, with plenty of books.

- The more you read, the further you will get! Reading helps develop your mind and knowledge. By reading, you can travel with your thought to places you didn't even think existed. You can imagine anything. You can decide on what is right and what is wrong. Always read! Never let a book out of your hands! That was the advice my favorite auntie kept giving me.

Until I started to learn the letters, I would always ask her to read to me. Her tone was warm and her voice, charming. I loved eating pancakes made by her on holidays and listen to new stories. I would always imagine the look of the houses mentioned in her stories, the way princes and princesses are, and I would imagine having a crown of my own and sitting on a chair similar to a throne. I didn't realize, at the time, how much these things were developing my imagination, nor how good it was for me to be away from the troubles at home. What I didn't know was that, whilst I was happy and learning all kinds of new things, my mother was hurting, crying and enduring things no woman on this planet should need to endure.

I don't know what happened between mother and father on that particular day. I just know that mother had improvised a bed in the kitchen, next to the stove, and that I fell asleep there. Father did not even come by to see if we had any wood or not, not to mention any food. I just saw him walk by the kitchen with a bottle in his hand. I was so scared! I kept thinking he would barge in and we would be forced to endure the same horrific events. I closed my eyes and waited for him to pass by. I slowly opened my eyes and looked straight at the door handle. It was unmoved. We were lucky. My mother must have probably realized how scared I was.

- My daughter, I promise you will never go through what you went through today. It was my fault, I should not have left you alone.

- Mum, but why is father so mean? Did he beat me up for playing with the children, outside?

- Any child should play, you haven't done anything wrong. He is a man who has lost his way. Pray, Eva! Pray for peace and health, nothing else. Come on now, time to sleep!

- But I'm cold…

- Come and let me hold you, I'll warm you up.

And she did. I fell asleep in her arms and I woke up the next day, my mother holding her hand against her jaw and eyes pointed towards me. How many hours had she spent there? Perhaps she didn't even sleep.

Fear, hate and malice. That was the picture of the house every single day. I felt love on the part of my mother, but it was all gone whenever father would show up or his name was spoken.

I was just getting ready for my first year of school. I was so proud of my uniform and the backpack mother had bought me from the only shop in the village selling school materials. There was a town around 40 km away, called Alexandria, but it was almost impossible for us to get there. Sometimes, mother would ask a neighbor to buy some things for us from Alexandria.

I already knew how to write and read – all thanks to auntie Vica. I was sad I couldn't see her anymore. She had passed away a year before. But she had promised me she would always watch upon me from the Heavens and that she would take care of me. So, when I left for my first day of school while holding my mother's hand, I knew auntie Vica was watching me from up there, and I smiled.

It was a small school, intended only for the primary classes. Every year, a new class was being set up. Children from the village, as well as children from another 3-4 adjoining villages, would join. I would soon find out that my teacher's name was Lola and that I was to spend four hours a day along with other 15 children. We were, all in all, nine girls and seven boys. Every one of us was holding a bouquet of flowers which, in turn, we would hand to the teacher while she was greeting us with a traditional "Good Luck".

- Welcome! Please sit at a desk, wherever you desire.

She was wearing a black dress with white dots. Her hair was dark and her eyes, the same. She was thin and tall. I remember being anxious at remaining just us and her and beginning to discover the magic of the alphabet.

My mother would say Hello to one or two ladies, but I didn't know anyone. I sat at the second window desk. I was so curious to see who would sit next to me. Ultimately, a girl sat down – she was crying.

- Mom, don't leave me here! I want to go home! Please! She kept holding on to her mother's dress and, tears in her eyes, she kept begging her not to leave her alone there.

I failed to understand why some children were crying when coming to school. I was just so happy. I couldn't wait to get to know everyone and play during the recesses between classes. I knew it would be a beautiful stage in my life, and the thought of staying away from home for a few hours would make me even happier.

- What's your name?, I inquired my desk mate enthusiastically.

- Irina…

- Irina, don't cry! We'll play together and you'll love school.

She wasn't minding me too much, nor did she have too much confidence in my words. Her mother must have tried to convince her of the same, too.

- Don't you want to know my name?, I kept speaking to her, as I desperately wanted us to be friends.

- Yes, I do.

- My name is Eva. I'm seven and I love mathematics. Look, if you're interested, I'll show you how to finger-count.

I managed to stop her from crying. Much to the surprise of her mother, she was no longer sad when her mother left. We continued to play and make calculations until Mrs. Lola started speaking to us.

- Please be silent, children! From today onwards, we shall be spending a few hours a day together. Please don't be late for class and behave. No speaking over one another and, whenever we want to ask something, we raise our hands. Alright?

- Yes! We replied as one.

- Today, I'm going to ask you to introduce yourselves, one at a time. After that, we will play a little game, and in two hours, you will go home. Real school starts tomorrow!

We had, on every desk, a cut-out chicken made of yellow paper. As we were stating our names and age, Mrs. Lola would write them down on that little chicken which she would then stick on our chest. We had to keep the chicken on all week, during classes. That made it easier for her to learn our names, and for us, too, to know each other.

I have no idea how those two hours went by, time really flew. I was happy. I felt at ease and I couldn't wait to return to school. When mother came to pick me up from school, I jumped straight into her arms and said:

- Mom, I love you! I saw how happy she was, too. She was happy for me and I believe that any parent, seeing their child on their first day of school, feels a certain level of fulfilment.

Chapter 3

I loved school and I managed to steadily rank among the top three in my class. I loved the teacher. I admired her a lot and, anytime I had the chance to, I would ask her plenty of questions. I didn't know whether or not I was bothering her, although I think I was born with a special sense of reading people's facial expressions, and whenever I saw I was crossing the line, I would run off as quickly as possible while also apologizing. I think she liked me a lot, because whenever there was a parents' meeting, I was offered as example. I can only imagine how happy and fulfilled my mother was feeling. I was her only joy and I only wished I could make her even prouder.

At home, things were getting even worse. Father was quite aggressive. I could no longer feel the beatings – they started to seem like nothing out of the ordinary, but mother was getting weaker by the day. She seemed very ill and I began to worry. Her suffering were not the beatings and insults from father. She was hurting on my account. She would always say to me that she couldn't take it any longer, that she didn't want to see me go through that again and that she would do anything to salvage me from this suffering. I wasn't listening, as for me, nothing else mattered than being with her. With beatings, with screams, with fear – I could take anything, however, I could not accept knowing that I let her alone in the presence of an animal. Only an animal could do what he was doing. The amount of hatred and malice he was carrying for me and mother, it was nothing like I had ever seen anywhere else. At the same time, however, he didn't want to depart and leave the two of us alone or let mother leave with me. He was obviously ill. At one time, mother even attempted to gather some luggage and take me away! Where? I have no idea. It wouldn't have mattered either! I can still remember, though, throwing a broom at us, outside the house!

- You miserable women! Get back in the house! Where do you think you're going?

- Let us go, you animal! You're better off without us, and we're better off without you!

- Leave? You think you'll ever be able to escape from me? I am Ivan! I'm your man until you pass away! And if you try to leave again, I'll hang your daughter from a beam and I'll put you in the grave! You got that!??? Then, he grabbed mother by the throat and I felt like she couldn't breathe any longer.

- Enough, father! Leave her alone, please! Please, father! I got down on my knees in front of him and I was begging him, crying. We're not going anywhere! Please, father!

I don't know whether it was my prayers that made him let her go or he was just afraid not to kill her. Mother was barely breathing. Her face was reddish, but she never shed a tear.

- The day will come when you will leave this place, Eva! I will not rest until you are out of this hell! That's my only wish before I pass away – to see you as far away as possible from this cursed place!

I know mother loved me more than anything else. She would have given up her life for me. I remember her spending her last pennies when I asked "How much is an ice cream?". I didn't dare ask for one, but I dared asking that question while passing by a shop, during a hot summer day. She asked me whether I wanted an ice cream and I replied negatively. However, she read the unspoken desire in my eyes, went and spent all the money she had left in her wallet in order to see me happy. And that was just a drop in the bucket, compared to all the other things my mother did for me. As, most certainly, any mother would do for her child.

Childhood has marked me in several ways. It taught me a lot of things, showed me what was good and what was wrong. It made me able to withstand pain. Physical, as well as spiritual pain. I learned to stop crying. I was taking some of the beatings without even shedding a tear. I got to a point where I could look my father in the eye and confront him. He would get even madder, but it was in vain! I had got to a point where nothing else could make me suffer. The only thing I was vulnerable to and which could have had a large impact on me was losing my mother. To me, mother was Heaven on Earth! I thought the world of her and I knew that, if she was no longer there, I would have fallen. Just by looking at her I knew we would make it and that we would get over all the bad things. It was merely about time, though.

I was in the 5th grade when a white Logan pulled up in front of our door. The three of us were inside the house. I was reading for school, mother was weaving and father was drinking his ever-present *ţuica*, in the kitchen.

- Good day! Are you the Guţău family?

- Yes, we are, please come in! What can we help you with?, mother answered shy.

- We are from the Child Welfare Protection Authority, and the gentleman is a Police officer. Following complaints by school staff, we came here to investigate the state of your child, Eva Guţău.

I saw mother more broke down than ever. I ran to the other room and hid behind the door. What would they do to me?

- Please, gentlemen, don't take my child away! Please, she is my only reason to live.

- Madam, we are not here to do any harm. We just want to make things right. If the child is abused, by yourself or your husband, we'll need to carry out a few procedures and place her in special care. It is one of the many other complaints we received and we must, at this point, take action! Is he your husband, Ivan? We will need to have a conversation with both parents and, separately, with the child. Where may we sit?

- Please join me in the kitchen.

Mother was crying her eyes out and she didn't know what else to do. She was more desperate than ever. She welcomed the guests to the kitchen while taking her wooden cross off her neck and started praying.

I don't know how the conversation started, but after I saw them having entered the kitchen, I snuck outside and sat by the window in order to hear everything that was happening.

- It is my understanding, Mr. Ivan, that you abuse your daughter on a daily basis. Is that true?

- Officer, how I choose to raise my child is my problem. Whenever I give her a beating, it is not for free. Who are you, to come into my house and tell me what to do? Who called you? This hag of wife of mine? And all of a sudden, he stood up, raising his fists to my mother.

- Mr. Ivan, sit down right now or I will be forced to handcuff you and take you down to the Police station. I said NOW!! I think the entire village must have heard the words of that Police officer.

- Gentlemen, if you decide to take my daughter away, can I go with her? Please! I am living in a hellhole here, anyway. He is a drunkard. He doesn't know anything, apart from drinking and beatings. He's been traumatizing this child ever since she was born. Ultimately, I will do anything for my daughter to escape him. I'd rather stay and take the beatings, as long as my daughter is safe! The violence, insults and cursing won't be something she misses! I'll go anywhere, make any statements to anyone! It means that this is how God intended, for you to end up on our doorstep and save my child from this hell! Please, madam, mister, help me!

My mother wanted to give me up? How could she tell them to take me away from her? Not a chance! I would have rather endured beatings every single day, just to stay home! Home, with my mother.

- You crazy woman! How can you say that about me? You've ruined my entire life! Take them both and leave me alone!

- No, no. Mr. Ivan, you seem to miss the point; they are not the issue here. It seems that things are quite obvious. Do you admit to having abused your child several times?

- No, madam… what is your name?

- My name is Elisabeta and I'm with the Child Welfare Protection Authority. Please answer the question.

- Well, I just did! No! I did not abuse my child, I educated her! You might understand that if you spare the rod, you spoil the child; there is no way around it. You mean to say you don't sometimes beat your children?

- We are not here to discuss whether or not I am beating my children up! We came here to save a child!

The Police officer swiftly interfered in the discussion, probably in order to prevent father from saying any other foolish things:

- Mr. and Mrs. Guțău, please tell me if any one of you is currently in work.

- I am not, officer… mother replied with a trembling voice.

- What would she know how to do, this one? All she does is babble on!, father interrupted her.

- Please be silent! Please, Mrs. Kristina, go on.

- I only help with the sowing and seeding. Ivan goes out and sells in the marketplace. This is what we live off from. We have a booth there, and whatever he makes from the sales on the day – half of it goes for his booze, while sometimes, he brings the other half home. Other times, he just keeps them for the days when he has no booze money.

- You would know! You know it all! You stupid woman, wait till it's just the two of us again!

- You can beat me up as much as you want, I don't care! I just want to know, gentlemen, what will you do with my child?

- First of all, we will need to talk to the child separately, too, and after that, officer Dan shall decide what happens next with regard to himself, while I will make the decision in the child's best interest! Now please, we would like to speak to Eva alone.

I couldn't even move. I knew mother would open the door and see me propped against the window wall. I couldn't care less, I just wanted to stay with mother.

- Eva, honey, what are you doing here? Come to mother, I need you to speak to the gentlemen, please!

- Mom, mom, please, mom, don't let me go! I don't want to leave your side! I hugged her and started crying. I don't want to, mom, I don't want to!

She took me in her arms and sat me at the table. Father was murderously looking at us. I felt shivers just thinking of the moment when the unexpected guests would leave the house, and we would be along with him, again.

- Eva, we will need to have a small chat, just the three of us: you, me and this nice officer! Are you alright with that?

- Yes, but I don't want you to take me away from my mother! Please! I beg you!

I threw myself at Mrs. Elisabeta's feet and while the officer was asking my parents to step out, I was praying to God not to separate me from my only joy, my mother!

- Does your father physically and verbally abuse you?

I was silent.

- Eva, you need to talk to us, otherwise all three of you will need to go to the Police station, where it may be worse than this. She then went on to explain all the procedures, of which I couldn't understand anything anyway.

- Yes, I am! I am abused by my father, but not to the extent that I would want to leave home! I'm already used to it. I don't feel the beatings and I'm not crying any longer. You can ask my mother.

- Has your mother ever hit you?

- No!! How can you think that?

- We don't, but we need to ask you.

- My mother is the best person on this planet! There is no better mother than her. And, no matter what happens, I don't want to be away from her. She always takes me to school, she always picks me up from school. At school, I am among the top three in my class. You can ask all my teachers.

- I don't doubt that, you can see you're a nice child. Eva, my dear, please take your clothes off, except for your underwear and socks.

- Why would I get undressed? Mother told me never to take my clothes off to anyone, particularly with a man present.

- Unfortunately, you will need to. Mr. Dan is the officer in this case. Both he and I need to draw up protocols and state everything that we saw. He will be my witness and I, his.

- Please… please…

- Look, he will turn around and only look at you if you have marks on your body. How about it?

- Well, I have some…

- Please, Eva, let's do things the easy way! Please take your clothes off, so we can finish this quicker! There is no point in dragging the matter. Come on! Put your clothes here, on the table, it won't take long.

In fact, I wasn't bothered about someone seeing me naked. I was mostly ashamed of the marks on my body and, secondly, I was afraid that, when they saw the marks, they would take me away from my mother! I had no choice and started to strip. My whole body was shaking and I could only think about the worse. But what could I have done? How could I have changed the situation? I had no power whatsoever – neither over these two people, nor over my parents. I was in a desperate situation. When would this all eventually end?

I first took my pants off and I saw Mrs. Elisabeta screwing her eyes. She said nothing. But when I took my shirt off, she put her hands on her face and started crying.

- Dan, turn around, please! You need to see this!

Was it that bad, though? Was it just me not realizing it?

- Oh God, my child, how could you withstand all this? It is my duty, as Police officer, to carry out the arrest Mr. Ivan Guțău, with immediate effect!

Arrest? I couldn't understand what was happening. Were they arresting father? What struck me was that, even at this time, I wasn't happy. Probably, some part of me still loved him. I wished it would just be me and mother, but I could not wish him harm, either. He was just a man having lost his way.

- Get dressed, Eva! We'll go together.

- Where are we going? I don't want to go!

I couldn't grasp what was about to follow. I saw father being escorted to the Police vehicle, called by Mr. Dan using his radio. My heart was aching for him. Where were they taking him?

- Are you taking him to prison?, I asked, with a shy voice.

- No, not yet; for now, he will just be remanded in custody. The relevant bodies will decide what happens next.

Mother was not crying, she was looking at the door, lost. I don't know if she was rejoicing, but what I do know is that she was such a good person that she would never build her happiness on someone else's troubles. I'm sure she was relieved, even if not for long.

- And now? What will you do with my daughter?

- Your daughter has been abused. And not just a little, the abuse was severe. You should have come to us and file a complaint. How could you withstand all of these? Have you never thought about the pain you care causing your own child?

- I was afraid, madam, I was afraid that he might do even more serious harm… Why else would you think that I didn't? I was so scared…

- Eva, please go inside the house and take whatever you want with you, we are leaving together!, Mrs. Elisabeta said, on a calm tone.

- What?!?, mother and I shouted simultaneously.

- Where would we leave together? I'm not going anywhere!

- Where are you taking my child? What will I do without her? I'm coming with you, I'll go and prepare a set of clothes for both of us.

- Mrs. Kristina, it seems that you don't understand. Eva is coming with me and she will placed in foster care.

At that point, mother effectively fell off her feet. Mrs. Elisabeta went on:

- We can't leave her with you any longer, first of all, because of beatings and the treatment she was subjected to, and secondly, due to the fact that you are not in work and don't earn any money. I am terribly sorry, please understand so that we don't need to use force.

I was dumbstruck. I couldn't say anything. Why is it that because of a drunk and violent father, both I and mother have to suffer? They were taking me away from the only person who was offering me peace.

- Madam, please, I beg you! I'll do anything you want! I'll go to the marketplace and make the sales. Please don't take my child!

- The decision has been made! We will notify you of her new foster home within 10 working days. You will have the chance to see her every Friday and, if things improve, you may take her home two weekends a month.

- What kind of soul do you have, doing this to me? It is the greatest pain, taking a child away from their mother, the greatest pain...

And I couldn't hear her any longer. They put me in the white Logan, without baggage, without a soul, without the will to live. I saw mother lying on the ground and screaming. I couldn't make out what she was saying, but it must have been awful for her.

I was silent all the way. They attempted to make me say a few things, but it was in vain. I couldn't care where they were taking me, I only cared about how long I was meant to stay away from my mother!

Chapter 4

The trip was about one hour long. I didn't know where they were taking me, in what city, for how long... I knew nothing. I cried almost all the way through the trip. I cried in silence, I would wipe the tears off my eyes as quick as I could, so that I wouldn't let them see me suffer. I felt the hate for them and I would have done absolutely anything to disappear. I could imagine mother crying in the house and that made me feel even worse. Even the thought of not going to the same school was destroying me. Why all these? Where had I gone wrong?

Eventually, we arrived in front of some large, white gates. After blowing the horn twice, a man came to open to gate. I didn't look at him, in fact, I didn't turn my head at all. I saw a large building ahead. Over to the right-hand side, there was some kind of a park with a playground: a rusty slide, three swings moving with the wind and a trampoline. They all looked deserted and sad. I started to feel scared. I had all sorts of thoughts going through my head and I felt like shaking.

- Eva, please calm down. Come on, you will be better off here than at home. Come out of the car, we need to go inside.

How would she know I'd be better off than at home? How would she know what is "best" and what is not for me? Who gave her the power to decide all of this? What kind of soul must you have to separate a child from their mother?

I jumped out of the car and followed her. I had no luggage. I hadn't eaten for several hours, even if having been asked about wanting to eat. My stomach was aching, but I doubt I could have swallowed anything. I was feeling ill, I was scared, I was nervous…

- Good evening, Mrs. Elisabeta! What do we have here? A young lady?

She was a very fat woman. I was looking at her boots and I could see they were unzipped due to the fact that her foot was too large. She was wearing a short, red hairdo, with grey roots. She had a back-zip skirt on, which looked lop-sided on her, for which reason the zipper was almost at the front, at that point, and a blue striped shirt. She approached me gently and took me in her arms. It was one of the fakest hugs I had ever received. My hands stood still, I was a statue, just waiting to see what was going to happen. I couldn't see any children. Where were they keeping them? Where would they take me?

- What is your name, young lady? I'm Anna and I will be here for most of the time. Come one, we need to fill in a sheet and afterwards, you can go to your room.

I was dead silent. I couldn't make any sounds. My mouth was glued up and I couldn't think of anything. My mind was focused only on my mother.

Eva, you need to speak, Mrs. Elisabeta tried to encourage me. It will be much harder if you close up. This is the situation, at the moment, and we need to adapt to it. Both you and us. Come on, sit down and talk to Ana!

- Madam, go home, I'll stay with her. I'll register her and allocate her a bed. I'm here, don't worry!

- Alright, Ana, then I'm off. Take care of her and we'll see each other later. Eva, remember, the first night is the most difficult… it will certainly get better after that. I'll see you tomorrow.

Bag over her shoulder, she left. She left me there like rubbish, like I was a delivered good. Nothing mattered to her. Perhaps this lady was doing it on a daily basis. Perhaps, her job was to take children away from her parents and take them to foster care. I was on the agenda today. She took me, brought me and delivered me! Check! Tomorrow probably it was going to be the next child.

- Name and first name? Ana's voice was completely changed since Mrs. Elisabeta had left.

- Eva Guțău.

- Age?

- 12.

- How did you end up here?

- I don't know.

- What do you mean, you don't know? You're not a 5-year-old. Tell me what happened.

I instantly burst into tears.

- I want to be with my mother… please…

- Do you know what? I haven't got time for slobbering. If your mother had kept her head on her shoulders, you wouldn't have been here. You should not be crying after her and just be happy you escaped. Just be grateful that you are here, otherwise what would you have done, sleep rough?

- My mother is the best person on this planet and…

- I understand!, she cut me short. I don't need to know details about her. Right, I will put down whatever I like, then. What grade are you in?

I wanted to leave and ran towards the door which, to my surprise, was code locked.

- Listen, little girl, what do you think you're doing? She didn't even bother to stand up. Sit down and don't cause me any trouble, or else! Again, what grade are you in?

- 5th, I replied, leaning against the door.

- I said sit down on the chair!! She screamed so loudly that I thought my ears were about to explode. Now!!!

I realized I was making her angry. And I didn't want to start all over again with the beatings. I had no way to escape, so I sat back down and I started praying in my thoughts. By doing this, I felt closer to mother.

- Have you got any spares?

- No, nothing. I could barely speak, tears flooded my face. She stood up and went over to the cupboard at the back of the room.

- Underwear, socks… - she was speaking while taking out package after package - …pajamas… Don't you even have a sweat suit?

- No, none.

- Why would they be sending you here like that? Do they really think that they can get rid of you and we're left to give you everything? Some parents…

I felt like someone was thrusting and twisting a knife in me. I could imagine smacking her over the head. How could she speak like that about my mother? She didn't even know her and was already seeing her as an irresponsible mother. How would she know that my mother crawled in the dust only to prevent me from being taken away? How would she know that mother would have done anything in her power to keep me by her side? All she knew was to bobble on and on and make accusations as a consequence of her frustrations.

- Here you go! I got you one of each, we'll see about the rest tomorrow.

She gave me a pack of clothes to hold, and on top, there was a towel and a pair of sneakers. I think they were three numbers larger, but I couldn't care. I took everything and awaited new instructions.

- Come on, let me take you to your room! Tomorrow morning, you'll wake up with the rest of the girls at 7.00 AM and have breakfast. They will then be going to school, but for you, it will take a while to get you registered. Make your bed and come down to the kitchen. You can help us out in the kitchen or the laundry. We'll see tomorrow, depending on the jobs needed to be carried out. Do you understand?!

- Yes… I was looking at her and couldn't believe the serenity in her voice.

We ascended two floors. Stairs were cement and were provided with a blue railing. Double-glazed doors were used to separate the stairs from a large hallway. She discreetly entered a code, while making certain that I wouldn't be able to see it, and proceeded before me.

Come on, what are you waiting for? Room 8 is yours. You will share the room with… she started skimming a few papers she was holding… with three other girls: Dana, Raluca and Alexandra. You will get to know them better and even become friends. We are all friends here and don't cause any problems. Is that understood?!

- Yes!

And, all of a sudden, I found myself in front of room 8, with an opened door, with Mrs. Ana asking me to come inside. I couldn't see anything from the hallway, except for a large brown wardrobe. I had my heart in my boots, so I counted to 3 and entered the room.

- Girls, this is Eva, she will be your new roommate! Come on, show here where to put her clothes and tomorrow, take her down to breakfast with you. Is that understood?!

- Yes!! They all replied in one voice.

She didn't say anything else and left. She left me in a room with three strangers. There were two bunk beds, four altogether. Two of them were by the wall, the other two, by the window. Eventually, one of the girls broke the ice which had left me stranded in the middle of the room.

- You can put your clothes in the wardrobe, at the lower left-hand side. And this is the free bed, pointing to the top bed next to the window. If you need to use the bathroom, it is down the hallway, on the right. Showers are on the left-hand side, toilets, on the right-hand side.

I didn't even know the name of the girl having just shared these instructions with me. And, to be honest, I couldn't care less. I put my clothes where I was told and I just kept the towel. I took it with me to the bathroom.

I didn't take a shower, I didn't even wash my face. I locked myself in a toilet and sat on the floor. I cried a lot, so much that I felt I was short of breath. I would stop and start over again. I could only think about my mother and the nights I had slept wrapped around her arms. I didn't realize how warm they had been, until now, when I was alone in a cold bathroom in a foster home.

I heard the door open and someone came next to the door I was leaning against. I couldn't see who it was, because I had my back turned to them, but I couldn't care.

- Eva? It's Dana. It was the same voice having explained where to put my clothes. Please, come out! I know it's difficult, especially at the beginning, but you have me. I had no one during my first night here. Come on! I promise I'll sleep with you in the same bed, I promise. If an attendant comes in and finds us in the bathroom, we will be in trouble. Please open the door.

After several minutes of plea, I stood up and opened the door. Dana held out her hand to me and pulled me back to the room.

- Put your pajamas on and come to bed. I'll hold you and it will be easier.

I looked at her and didn't know what to think. We were more or less of the same height, meaning she could not have been much older than me, but she seemed quite mature. I was amazed by how a child of my age was trying to take care of me. It did me good, though. I snuck into bed with her and let her cuddle me. As I was looking out the window, I could see the sky. I was praying and I could imagine my mother looking at the sky, just as I was, and that we were communicating through the stars.

Chapter 5

The night went by quite slowly. I felt my soul was empty and it seemed as though I had no tears left to cry, either. I was failing to explain myself how I ended up from my small and cozy room in such a cold bed. I couldn't understand why I had to pay for my father's mistakes. Why was I being held accountable for the fact that he was a heartless and violent person? After having endured so much over the years, why did I need to endure an even greater pain by ending up in a foster home? I could never imagine how a foster home looked like. Nor was I aware of where children without parents would end up, I had never asked myself such questions. The hell of forgotten children was my home now!

I had almost no sleep. I would dose off, but quickly wake up because of the fear. I was so scared. When I saw the sunrise, I realized it was not long before I had to face the reality of my new life. I had Dana by my side. She did hold me in her arms all night, though. Although she inconvenienced me sometimes, I didn't want her to return to her bed. It was good to have her there, I felt like I had someone familiar next to me, even though I had only met her a few hours before. I didn't even know exactly how she looked, but I could feel the warmth of her soul and the suffering. I knew it hadn't been easy for her either, otherwise she would not have been able to understand what I was going through during my first night there.

- Come on, girls, wake up! Let's make our beds before Ana comes in. I didn't know whose voice was that, but I would soon learn that it was Raluca – the room's officer and the home's spy. She always knew what was going on and she could obtain anything that was required of her. She was 14 and she ended up there after having lost both her parents in a car accident, when she was just 4.

I got up, too, and followed them to the bathroom. On the hallway, I could see groups of two, three or four girls coming out of every room. I was lost in space and all I could do was to hold on to Dana's pajama and follow her. I even followed her into the toilet.

- Please, let me stay with you!, I whispered slowly, so that other girls wouldn't laugh at me.

- Come one! We need to hurry up.

While Dana was brushing her teeth, I was lying in a corner of the bathroom. I didn't have the items needed for the morning toilet chores, so I started counting. I couldn't believe that over 20 girls would fit in such a small bathroom. There were only five sinks and there was a queue at each them. It was all timed, so that no girl would spend more time. It was obvious who "was making the rules" and who was obeying them. It was about attitude, stature and, more importantly, priority. Those who were washing up first were most certainly senior and their message was: "don't mess with me!" I didn't make any sounds, nor did anyone ask me anything. They probably didn't even take any notice of there being a new soul in the room. Or perhaps I wasn't even the only newcomer, perhaps other girls had been ripped apart from their mother and arrived there the day before.

Within 30 minutes, we were all downstairs. I was the only one without a uniform. I entered a large dining room where, much to my surprise, there were plenty of tables. Within two minutes, the room was full. We were no longer 20 girls, we were 60. Age 2 or older. I was still in shock and still couldn't believe I was there. I sat at the same table as my roommates and was waiting for new instructions, but no one was saying anything.

- What now?, I whispered.

- Now, we wait for the kitchen to open. When they open those windows, and Raluca pointed straight to the backside of the room, we go and take our food. You can't take more than one piece of each. One loaf of bread, one teaspoon of jam and one apple. Sometimes, we even get eggs, depending on which room prepares breakfast.

- What do you mean by which room prepares breakfast?

- Well, the girls on the 2nd and 3rd floor take shifts. Around once every two weeks, our turn comes to wake up at 04.30 AM and prepare breakfast for everyone. We have a cook with us and she tells us what to do. That's when I'm the fullest because I eat as much as I want to out of everything. There are still around nine days and our turn comes. You'll like it!, Dana tried to cheer me up, but it was in vain.

Everything sounded so bizarre and strange that I still couldn't fully figure out what I was doing there. I didn't want anything to eat from them, I wanted my mother's meals. Oil-fried bread and sugar on top was the best breakfast.

The windows opened and, much to my surprise, no one crowded up to get food. Only three older girls got up, who went there first, while everyone else was still sitting.

- These are the "bosses", Dana began to explain to me. They get to take the first meal rations, they get to choose their clothes and so on. You shouldn't mind them and you should stay away from them. Raluca has a somewhat alright relationship with them and we sometimes get an advantage. I couldn't get close to them, even if they paid me to. They are too stogy and tend to get on my nerves. When they sit on their miraculous chairs, that's when we can go and grab our food! They don't like to be disturbed… poor old them. Oh, God, I can't stand them!

Dana's frustration and anger were clearly visible in her body language and sight. Raluca was looking at them with admiration, but the other girl was looking down.

- What's your name?, I dared ask her.

- Her name is Alexandra. Raluca replied, as if she was the one I had asked. She is a bit quieter, she's an extraordinary girl, but doesn't speak too much. Don't nag her, let her start speaking to you.

It was not my intention to nag anyone. I just wanted to know the name of one of the girls with whom I was to share a room for God know how long.

- I understand. I won't bother her, I just wanted to know how I can call her out.

- Alex, you can call me Alex! The child raised her head and started talking to me. And you're not bothering me, don't worry. Welcome to our hell! Prepare for the worst!

- My God, Alexandra, shut up, don't scare her on her first day!, Raluca tried to quiet her down. Best encourage her and help her understand how things work around here. Relax, Eva, you have us and it will be a lot easier for you than it was for us. Surviving here is not easy, but it's not impossible, either.

They continued to contradict one another, but I wasn't focusing anymore on what they were saying. I had no way of telling which of them was right. All I had to do was to wait and see for myself how difficult it would be to live in my new "home". After about half an hour, a buzzer rang.

- That's it, we're off to school! Take care of yourself, Eva, see you in the afternoon!

- Dana, what should I do know?

- Don't do anything. Sit here, on this chair, and wait.

- Wait for what?

- They will come and let you know what you are supposed to do today. In a week or so, you will probably start school, too, perhaps we are lucky and you will end up at the same school as me. I have to run, see you!

With her backpack on, she started rushing towards the door leading to the main entrance. I looked around and there was no one else. Did that mean I was the only newcomer? That frightened me even more.

- Eva Guțău?

- Yes, that's me.

An old lady, with grey hair, stuck her head out the window.

- Come here, child, I'm going to ask you to help me gather whatever is left on the tables and wash the dishes afterwards. Have you had your meal?

- No…

- Why not? You need to eat. Otherwise, you will fall ill! These people here don't have enough money for medicine, so don't do anything stupid! Go on, eat! She handed me a plate with one fried egg and one piece of cheese. I'll sit with you while you eat, alright?

I couldn't believe that someone in that building was speaking to me so gently.

- Thank you!

- Don't worry about it. How old are you?
- I'm 12…
- Did you come in yesterday?
- Yes, yesterday evening.
- Oh, yes, you're right, I haven't seen you at dinner. You must have come in late.
- I don't even know what the time was when I arrived. May I ask you something?
- Yes, child, ask me whatever you want.
- Do you know how long I need to stay here? My mother is waiting for me at home.
- Dear, I have no idea how long you will be here, but what I know, is that once you are here, it means that something went wrong in your home or your parents are dead. If you say that your mother is waiting for you at home, it means your chances of spending less time in this place are higher than they would have been had she no longer been alive. I could answer tell you that you'll be here for one month or your entire life. I wouldn't know, my dear!

I started crying loudly. So loud that I think everyone heard it. I could barely breathe because of all the sighing.

- Stop!, and the old lady took my hands while speaking. In here, you have to be strong and not cry! Only weak people cry in front of other people, you must show them that you are strong! The older you are, the quicker you will get out of here… trust me… alright? I will be here for you as often as I can. What you mustn't do is cross the line and understand when to shup up and when to speak. That way, you won't have any problems. Let's go to the kitchen, I'll tell you a few other things, too. Take your plate and you can finish eating there, we haven't got too much time.

- Alright, madam… what is your name?
- Geta, call me auntie Geta!

Yes, I was even more certain now that she was a clear reminder of auntie Vica. I had a new old lady by my side. I began to think auntie Vica had sent her there to take care of me. Once, she had promised me to watch over me from the Heavens and I think she hasn't forgotten about that. She was now by my side, at a time when I really needed someone.

- Thank you, auntie Geta!
- What do you keep thanking me for?
- For everything! May I hug you? I didn't even wait for her answer and I jumped straight at her, placing my arms around her.
- Oh, you crazy little girl… Let's get some job done, all we did today was hug!

She gently placed her hand on my neck and we both started walking towards the kitchen.

In time, Dana would become my best friend. As we were of the same age, I had the sheer luck of being registered in the same class as her. I can honestly say that school was my joy again. It was the place I was taking shelter in and I ended up spending plenty of time at school. I would register in all activities and spend many hours in the library.

At the foster home, it was terrible, from all points of view. I would get very little to eat, almost no clothes and whenever I needed medicine, I had to ask one of the "bosses" or turn to Raluca.

Raluca was fine, a little fake sometimes, but she wasn't causing me any trouble. She was pursuing her interests and wanted very much to spend time with the girls who were turning the wheels in there. I never liked them too much and I made it clear. I left them alone and they, in turn, ignored me. There was just one time when we had a dispute, when one of them came over to me and said I had to give her the jacket I had on me, because she loved the color more. I think it was more of an excuse, just waiting for me to retaliate. I didn't, though. I took the jacket off, handed it to her and said: "Here you go!" She took it and left. You could see the amazement on her face because I had shown no fear, no desire to befriend her. I had been crystal clear.

Mrs. Ana was an "ass-kisser" – that's how I liked to call her. She would do anything just to make a good impression with the directors. She would behave very badly with children. I heard she was beating some of the girls, but she never got to lay a hand on me. Probably because I didn't give her too many reasons or because our paths weren't crossing too often. I found out later on that she was sleeping there, too, because she had in turn been abandoned by her parents and grew roots in there, and she was now working for the organization. You could clearly see she was having many mental issues, things which should have been controlled and solved, as she was working with spiritually impacted children. No one thought about checking this Ana and she was spouting all her frustrations and hatred on other innocent girls.

There was one lady psychologist who would come in once a week and would talk to some of us. Normally, she would have had to speak to every one of us, upon every visit, but it wasn't that important to her. She would sometimes call us to the office, have us sign some papers and, after ten minutes, she would leave. Very rarely would I hear about her sitting down and talking to us, as she should have. Not once did it happen to me, though. She would just call my name out, say "Sign here!" and leave. She would hand out to us all sorts of printed fliers which would all end up in the waste basket. She would hand them out to us and tell us that this would have been our debate for the day, but that we would better understand by reading them individually. She was unconscious because she was obviously not thinking about the younger girls who couldn't read. The entire system was wrong, from the doorman to the director! No one cared about the faith of these innocent souls who hadn't ended up there as a consequence of their will.

Three months had already gone by and I knew nothing about my mother. She hadn't come to see me, I had no idea whether she was still alive or not, whether she forgot about me… nothing! I tried to make some inquiries, but no one was helping me, they would always say:

- If she comes to see you, we'll let you know!

I had already lost all hope of seeing her soon. I knew she wouldn't have left me, it was just about the formalities. Perhaps she didn't even know where they had taken me. I had auntie Geta, who was filling in for my mother, whenever she could. She was my ray of light during the storm. I would hug her on a daily basis, and she would kiss my forehead. I was really close to her and felt like she loved me, too. She would always give me a chocolate, a croissant, whatever she had… But that's not what mattered to me. I knew she was there and that gave me some peace and quiet.

Chapter 6

It was already December and snow had started to fall. I loved watching the snowflakes while lying in bed. I loved seeing the white blanket cover the entire yard, it gave me a feeling of peace. It was about to be the saddest Christmas I had ever had. I didn't know how things went around here during this time of the year, but I could not think of anything nice. Our room was not at all adorned, we only had an artificial Christmas tree at the entrance of the foster home. From what I had understood, during this time, many people remembered the children in foster homes and would send out all sorts of gifts: clothes, sweets, books. Unfortunately, everything we were getting had to go through a filter – there were about two-three broads checking all the bags and, after they took whatever they wanted, for their children or relatives, they would share with us whatever was left. There was also an order for picking the gifts. It was all on preference, equality was missing even on the part of employees, who obviously should have been objective. Whenever someone more important would come in, they were all smiles. I hated seeing them gather all of us in the dining room, caress our foreheads and passionately kiss us. I failed to understand how they could be so fake and hypocrite. The little girls were enjoying their kindness and were even taking advantage of such rare moments, in order to sit on their laps. Some of the visitors were impressed by their attitude and I could hear them say:

- How lucky these children are to have you here, by their side! I heard it is horrible in other places. Congratulations on a job well done!

Without any sense of regret or common sense, they were feeling excellent upon hearing that. They were feeling important and wanted to show, at any cost, a little love by caressing some of us.

I remember a lady coming, and she brought Santa Claus with her. That was a time when we were all happy and the joy on our faces was visible. We were all gathered around him and singing carols. He gave us gingerbread and juice. He wanted to spend the day with us at any cost. Apart from toys and plenty more things, he brought us a very large television set. He asked to be set up there and then. Therefore, the ladies at the foster home had no opportunity to take it home. We were all watching cartoons and were mesmerized at the size of the screen. I liked to visiting lady, I would have wanted to perhaps go to her and hug her. I haven't. I analyzed all her moves from a distance. I would say to myself that that would be me, one day, and that I would go to plenty of foster homes in the country. I could see the sadness in her eyes. Although she was happy then, as a consequence of the joy she was bringing us, her soul concealed a sad story. I never managed to find out what had happened and why she was there with us at the time, but it didn't even matter.

When she stood up and put on her raincoat to leave, the sadness got to me. I would have wanted to ask her to take me with her, make me work, do anything, just to be able to escape the gutter I was in. I knew that was what most of the girls were thinking about, because any of us would have wanted to leave, grow up in a family, have someone to offer them love. She came to each of us and shook our hand. When my turn came, I hugged her. I could no longer shade my feelings and my desire away and I started crying.

- Eva!! Go back to your place, right now!, one of the broads shouted.

- Madam, let her be, she hasn't done anything wrong... she spoke gently... what's wrong, my dear?

- Nothing... I just wanted to hug you... I miss my mother!

I saw her burst into tears straight away and she held me in her arms even harder. She didn't say anything else, she just stood like that for a few seconds. I could spot the hatred on the faces of all the women in that room. I knew something bad was waiting for me after that lady would have left, but I didn't care. After saying her goodbyes, she started giving each of us 50 lei. She asked every one of us to go and buy something for ourselves. It was the first time we received any money in there. We were all so thrilled and were already beginning to forget that the lady was about to leave and making plans what to buy and where we would hide our money.

The lady barely left when Ana made a sign. No one was to leave the room, for the time being.

- Stay here, we still need to talk. As you well know, you got a lot of clothes and toys from Mrs. Savu. You've spent quite a few hours with her and, since she was a nice lady, as usual, she also brought you a television set, which you can enjoy! You were really lucky and also received money! However… we will gather this money and we will do something with it to improve the home!

- But… the room raged, and a large-scale chat was starting to develop amongst ourselves. Why would she take the money we got?

- No *But*! Come on, each of you, leave the money on the table as you walk by! We have so many things to buy, how would you know?! You don't have a clue! You won't be able to use the money, might as well we use it for something useful. Do we understand each other?! I don't want to hear anything else! After you leave the money on the table, go straight to your rooms!

None of us was brave enough to place the money on the table first.

- Hey! Have you gone deaf? Come on, left to right. And faster, I haven't got all day.

She had taken away all our joy and happiness. Apart from the fact that we had to put up with every second in there, that we accepted her stealing all our gifts and only buy us expired food… Ana was now taking away something we had received ourselves. Some girls were crying, others were used to it, it didn't matter anyway. When I got next to the table, she shouted at the back of my head:

- Eva! Leave the money there and go sit on the chair! After everyone leaves, we have some things to discuss.

- Why? Did I do something?

- I'll show you what you did!

I was looking at her and couldn't believe the amount of hatred flowing through her body. I did what she had instructed me to, what else could she want from me? Was the amount of damage done not enough for her? She had to twist the knife in a little bit more or it wouldn't be complete.

Auntie Geta was sweeping the floor around the area and she looked at me, eyes full of pain. She made a signal to me to shut up and be nice. I knew she was the only employee there with a bit of mercy and humanity left in her, when it came to all of us. The rest, they were savages.

- Right, miss Eva. What was that?

- That, what?

I felt my head flying towards the right hand side and I could barely open my left eye. It was that hard that she had slapped me.

- You have the nerve to ask me that? You spoiled brat! Where do you think you are, hugging that woman and telling her that you miss you mother?

Barely had she finished the sentence that another slap came, on the exact same spot. I felt my face burning up and I didn't even want to raise my head from the ground.

- Ana, leave her alone, she hasn't done anything wrong!

- Who are you, Geta, to tell me what's right and what's wrong? Do you want me to give you a good beating, too? I saw her walk over to her, a poor little old lady…

- Why do you pick on her!?!? Come beat me up, but leave her alone, she's a helpless old lady!

I saw Ana more puzzled than ever. She was gazing back and forth, at me and at auntie Geta. She didn't know which of us she would strike first and the evil in her was pouring out from her nostrils. I saw her tighten her fists and walk over towards Geta. I covered my eyes. I was afraid to even watch. Much to my surprise, she only grabbed the broom from her hands and said:

- Get lost or I'll give you a beating you'll remember! Now! Disappear!

Geta covered her mouth, after which she started praying. She was slowly heading towards the door, but her eyes were still pointed towards me. I then saw Ana coming towards me, pounding the ground as if I had the possibility of running anywhere. I had reconciled with the thought and was just waiting for the pain to strike.

- You little weasel! I'll show you what happens when you talk back to me!

She used the broom stick to beat me up until blood was pouring out of my nose. I was lying on the floor and I could see auntie Geta crying at the door. Ana was the devil in disguise. I think she felt a sick pleasure while hitting me. She would smile cheekily with every blow she was handing out. She felt no remorse and it seemed perfectly normal to her. I was used to it anyway, I wasn't shedding any tears and was just waiting for it to finish. After she got tired of humiliating and striking me, she dropped the broom next to me.

- Come on, get up and go to your room! I don't want to ever hear you talk back when I'm speaking! Let this be a lesson to you, and if not, I have other methods, too!

She left, shaking her hands. After having wiped the floor with me, she was finally satisfied! She loved spilling the frustrations and dark shadows of her soul on me, on us, the weakest!

- Come on, little one, get up! Let's go to the kitchen and I'll stop your bleeding.

- Auntie Geta, you're so kind to me! Thank you! I'm fine, don't worry about me. Nothing is forever, it all fades away. Next time, don't say anything to her, I was really frightened she might hurt you!

- Please stop talking, dear!

It had been a "wonderful" Christmas Eve. I spent my time in bed, without being able to roll over to one side or the other. When Dana saw me, she burst into tears, too. My eyes were blue and my body was all reddish from the strong beating I had taken. Any normal child, on Christmas Eve, would make all sorts of wishes a child would think of. I was praying to God to send my mother and to get out of there! I didn't want toys, food or anything else… I just wished for a miracle to happen so that I could escape from that place. I could only imagine Santa Claus going down the chimneys of houses and making other children happy. Why could I not have been one of those children?

The time spent in there was a nightmare, from all points of view. I ended up hating every door handle, every corner and every breath of air I was taking. I was feeling as if any drop of will and ambition were abandoning my mind. I had been living with the thought of escaping that place and that was my motivation, but I had lost all hope. There were always young families coming in and looking for a child to adopt, but none of them were interested in girls of my age. And they were right, who would adopt a child who was halfway through to adolescence, full of problems and frustrations? Most of the time, they would introduce all of us, but we all knew that, once we were passed the age mark of 5-6, we would never be so lucky as to walk out those doors holding the hands of our adoptive parents. I was happy when I saw that little girls were being adopted. Even though I wished I had been in their shoes, in my mind, I would still wish them all the best in the world. I was glad for them, at least, to escape the hell of abandoned children and to create their own life stories elsewhere.

There were some girls who were taken for a certain period of time and brought back. It was probably due to the negative impact the days spent in her had on us, that none of us was no longer fully functional! We certainly did not realize that, nor did we want to believe or accept it, but something strange was happening. The violence, malice and hatred flooding our souls would leave scars for life. The weird thing is that, whenever a child is left without parents, whether due to them passing away or not, it is obvious that some damage is done. There are some psychological phenomena impacting the brain, as well as the behavior of a poor child. Without sufficient time available to recover after the initial shock of losing their parents, the child ends up in a foster home, where it gets even worse and more painful! Most of the times, the people working there are just savages. They have no idea what it means to offer affection, love or just not offer anything. Perhaps, even without realizing it, they create even deeper wounds in the poor innocent souls who did not end up in there willingly. In addition to all the emotional shocks and lacks, most of them reach that place with other forms of abuse, too, be it even verbal! And that is how you start creating an individual who begins life with a handicap!

Just as life is made up of good things and bad things, man must also share moments of sadness, happiness, smiles and tears. But what happens when children are not taught how to laugh? What happens when, for them, joy only exists in things that are way too small and, moreover, they grow up in an evil environment, and they end up believing this environment to be a normal one? Who would ever be able to tell those little creatures, later on to become adults, that the normal environment is not the one they were experiencing every single day, but that normality is when the balance hangs more towards the good than towards the bad?

By growing up in an environment where you are always told that nothing you ever do is appropriate and where you are always sanctioned for whatever bad things you are doing, we were impacted. All of us! I would notice this every single day as I would look at the behavior of my "house" mates. The fact that we were lacking affection was obvious in our conduct and particularly, the way in which we were integrating at school. Most classmates were kissing, hugging, we had no idea how to do that or perhaps, we were not able to any longer. We were acting like robots. Whenever a teacher would caress me, I felt shivers on my spine. It seemed incredibly nice and I was longing for such moments, even if I failed to admit it.

I could see parents reprimanding their children in front of the class whenever they would get a bad grade or display inappropriate behavior. However, during the days to come, the same parents would also be able to display love. I was always dreaming about my mother coming to the school gate, one day, and hugging me. I would be asking myself, several times a day, what she would be doing at those particular times. I knew she was struggling to get to me. I could imagine her working really hard to save up some money and get me out of there. I wouldn't imagine it being soon, but I knew it had to happen one day. There were days when I would deceive myself, thinking that my time between these strangers was coming to an end soon. There were also days when I thought I would never leave that place. But every time, no matter what I was thinking, I would encourage myself by saying that, one way or another, God will take care of me!

- Eva, I'm in love!, Dana whispered to my ear during one of those nights when we were both reading while in the same bed.

- What? Right… I don't believe you!... How did it happen?

- Yes, I am! Andrei, in my class, left a note in my desk today. Can I show it to you?

- Of course you can! Show me now!

She jumped right out of bed and headed towards her purse. She took the note out and brought it back with her.

"Dana, I dared write you this note because I really like you. I can't wait to come to school and see you again. Thank you for existing".

She had butterflies in her stomach, it was obvious! We were both so happy. We grabbed each other's hand and started jumping up and down in bed. We both had long smiles on our faces and would chant: "Love, love, love!"

- What happened, girls? Raluca had just walked in and was watching us in amazement as we were fooling around.

- Nothing! We both replied in one voice, just as if we had agreed on it beforehand.

- It can't be nothing! You must have a reason for jumping up and down and rejoicing as you were! Please tell me…

I signaled Dana not to say anything. Not that Raluca could have harmed her in any way, but I had already learned that the less people know about your personal life, the better. Had she told her, perhaps we would have given birth to other discussions and interpretations.

- Raluca, give us some privacy, please! Come on, don't be bad, I said, while trying to put my arm around her neck.

- You are the bad ones… I always tell you everything!

The hell you are, I thought! Do you actually expect us to believe that? But Raluca proceeded with her whining.

- So, you can't share your happiness with me now?

- Alright, I'll tell you…, Dana began to speak – naively, as usual!

- Dana, let me tell her, please! I glared at her, perhaps this time she would understand that she needed to keep quiet. Look, Raluca, I'll let you know… but you have to promise not to tell anyone.

- I promise! You know you can trust me! I'm your friend! That's what she kept telling us, but she could never keep anyone's secret to herself. I knew the things I was about the tell her would eventually be known to anyone.

- When I left school today, I saw a cute boy and I smiled to him.

- And?

- And that's it! What more would you want?

- So what? Is that why you and Dana were so happy about? For smiling to a boy?!

- Yes, of course. If that's not enough for you, then let us enjoy it. And next time, don't ask us anything else because we won't tell you.

- No, no! Come on, don't be mean! I thought it was more than just that! But if just one smile makes you happy, Eva, than I'm really glad for you! She left satisfied to have learned something.

- Eva, why did you tell him that? We should have told her the truth. Now, all those monkeys will laugh at you, that you're happy just for smiling to a boy. I don't want that…

- Dana… Let them do whatever they want! Today is your happy day and I want to share your happiness. No one needs to know about those notes of yours. Come on, we need to have you write a note back to Andrei and leave it in his desk tomorrow.

- No! No… no…, she instantly blushed… how could I write him a note? No way!

- Come on, I'll give you a hand!

I jumped out of bed, took a notebook and a pen and placed them in her hands.

- Don't be silly, write something back, write what you feel…

- I have no idea what to write! Oh, come on, Eva, all these silly ideas you have. I'm not good at writing. I'll just write thank you and that's it!

- You can write whatever you want, I'm really upset now! The poor boy, he fell in love with an ice woman.

- "Ice woman"? Right! Come on, don't be upset and stop falling for that! Let's both of us write it...

- Is it nice being in love?

- Yes, it sure is... I feel my stomach ache, even though I'm not hungry. I always think about him and I can't wait to get to school and see him. I can't take my eyes off him and we smile to each other. He's really handsome!

- I'm so happy! I hope I will be able to fall in love, one day...

- That day will certainly come! Come on, tell me... what do you want me to write?

- What do you mean? Just write whatever you feel!

Half of that notebook must have ended in the rubbish bin, nothing either one of us was writing was enough. It was Dana's first love note and it had to be extraordinary!

- Dana, I know! I've come up with the greatest idea ever!

- What idea? Come on, share already!!!

- I'll make up a short poem for you, two-three verses. Would you like me to?!

- Yes... come on, please, this is the greatest idea ever!

- Alright! Let me focus and you can have it by morning!

- Right... I'll let you be, then! I know you'll make up a super poem. Thank you, Eva! She jumped all over me and started kissing my face. I think these were the "love" effects.

Then, I started thinking, writing, erasing, writing again and, eventually, I got something.

"Be it scream, laugh, love or cry,
Hide my pain, so much I try,
When you smile, it's like I fly,
I can only think of eyes thy.

As the day comes, I gaze at you,
I pursue,
I stand true,
How is it that you're here, too?

A sky of suffering you spared me,
You had my heart running wild,
And in my stark life, behold:
There you were, the best you could be!"

I left the poem next to her pillow and eventually went to bed. I had written all night, it was already 4 AM and I only had two hours of sleep left. But I wasn't sorry. I would have done anything to see Dana happy!

Chapter 7

I had already been there for over two years. No one had come to see me, I didn't know anything about mother and I had lost all hopes of ever seeing her again. I had sent a few letters home, but no answer came. We hadn't had a phone at home, before I left, and I didn't know the phone numbers of the neighbors. I had tried over and over to find a way to get home, at least to visit, but no one wanted to help me out. I ended up thinking that my mother had died and, not only was I not notified, but I also missed the funeral. Such thoughts were hurting me and I had, in time, gathered so much pain inside. I could not comprehend why there was no one able or willing to offer me any information and, as mother did not reply to any of my letters, I thought about the worst. That is, if she was still alive. From the day I had been put in the white Logan and had arrived at the foster home, I had received no news of my father, either. It was like they both disappeared or had forgotten about me.

In school, things were progressing sensationally, I was learning really well and the teachers only had praises for me. I would always take part in different competitions and I had gathered a few diplomas in my room. Books were my place of refuge and I would spend hours in the school library. I had befriended the librarian lady and we were always debating the new novels, writers or different events. I didn't have an explanation as to why such a learned and educated lady was working there, on such a low income.

- Mrs. Lisa, how many years have you been working here for?

- Well, Eva, I can't even remember! Anyway, I came here long before you were born... I've been here for 33 years.

- 33 years in the same place? How is that even possible?

- Honestly, I have no idea either! She then started laughing, staring me in the eyes, and continued. But I do love spending my life between books and children. It's amazing!

- Do you have any children?

- No, unfortunately not! Perhaps God did not want me to have children. That is why I have you, you are all my children. God punished me, on the one hand, but rewarded me, on the other.

- So, we can safely say that you are our mother, of us all! Especially ours, the children in the foster home.

I saw her sadden and she could hardly hold her tears back.

- Yes, I am especially your mother! Eva, life is not always as sad as you think, you know. You will see that great, cheerful moments are yet to come... all you need to do is be patient and pray.

- When? When will those moments come?

- They will come, you'll see! Trust me, I'm older and wiser. Nothing lasts forever and I see a great future in store for you. You are an amazing child and, at one point, you will take life into your own hands, you will know exactly what you are meant to do. All you need is patience, just a little bit more patience.

- It seems to me that nothing is ever going to change and that I must embrace my fate, just as I have during these past years! That's that! I didn't even have tears left to cry, I was so relaxed about the subject and I truly believed what I was saying.

- It will change! Mark my words. You will soon get to high school... have you thought about the road you want to start on?

- I have no idea... I just know I want to become a lawyer, I want to defend helpless people against the evil ones.

- It's very important to know what you want to do and reach straight for it. And I'm happy to see that you already have a goal. Make sure you follow it and don't give up until you've reached that goal! It won't always be easy, but you will see that there is something to learn from every event. I'm sure that the years spent in the foster home have also taught you something...

- Yes, I learned not to have any feelings, be always careful and be scared of my own shadow!

I probably didn't realize what I was saying at the time, but I couldn't find any positives to living in a foster home. Nor could I see the light at the end of the tunnel, as the well-wishers around me kept saying, that I will have better days.

Dana and Andrei shared a lovely relationship. His parents had accepted her quite easily and she was already a part of the family. Even though they were regular people, they seemed quite attached to their son and, ultimately, to Dana. Not many families were willing to open their arms to "foster home offspring", but it seemed that there were still some nice left people on this planet. She would spend plenty of time at their home, as Andrei's mother would come and pick her up on her own signature. Usually, until you turn 18, you are not allowed to leave the foster home without someone having to sign for you, you were supposed to have adult supervision. However, after the age of 16, things would become easier. Firstly, because the directors were trying to get you to find your way in life, because, once you reached maturity, they were entitled to throw you out and, apart from that, one less child in the home was like a blessing to them. Not too many girls age 16-18 were left, but the ones still there were starting to take advantage of an amazing freedom, with the hope of something coming up and them ending up leaving the nest.

We had barely turned 16 and already we were transferred to the school in Alexandria. We would take the bus every morning and return every evening. One day, I asked Dana to help me – namely, to ask Andrei's mother to get me out on her signature so that I could leave the foster home from Friday to Monday. I had already been working part-time for a year now, at the coffee shop by the school and I managed to gather some money. I dreamt of one day opening my own coffee shop, but I knew the road ahead was long and tough.
- Eva, I've spoken to my future mother-in-law, she laughed subtly, and she promised me that on Thursday, when she's coming to sign for me, she would also fill in the papers for you. She just asked me to tell her where you want to go. Or perhaps, you want to sleep in the same bed as I and Andrei? She continued laughing even harder.
- Stop fooling around. I'm in no mood for jokes!
- Wow, you've become really serious lately. Come on, tell me, where do you want to go?

- Thank her for me and tell her that I appreciate everything she is doing for me! I'm off to look for my mother!
- What!? Have you gone mad? I'm not letting you go alone, I'm coming with you!
- You can't come with me! Stay with your boyfriend and his family! No use wasting time!
- There is no argument about it! I'm coming with you! But have you got any idea how to get there, how long the trip would take?
- Yes, I've spoken to a gentleman who always comes in for a coffee at the coffee shop and he says he owns a taxi company. He said he would help me out, I just need to pay him 200 lei for the diesel. I shared with him a little bit of my story and he was impressed. He said he would assign a person from his company and that he would drive me wherever I needed to go. I have to see how I can get to Necşeşti and perhaps, I may not even come back.
- Eva, don't be silly! Even if you find your mother…
- Not IF I find her, I cut her short, WHEN I find her!

- Right! You will definitely find her, but you need to come back! You can't leave me alone now. We need to return, take life into our own hands and fulfill our dreams. In the meantime, I'm coming with you, make no mistake about that!

I couldn't talk her out of it. Andrei also tried to persuade me to come with us, but it already seemed too much. I had no idea what was to follow, what I would find out and I was certainly in no mood for audience. Even if I never told her this, I was happy to hear Dana say that she was coming with me. And I appreciated her gesture quite a lot. Not being alone on such a day meant the world to me.

On Friday evening, I slept over at Andrei's house, with a plan to leave on Saturday morning. The gentleman at the coffee shop made good on his word and sent a car in front of the coffee shop, at 6 AM. It was a black Fiat, quite small, but I couldn't care. Andrei accompanied us to the car and helped us put our bags in the trunk.

- How are you, my friend? What's your name? He reached across to the driver to shake his hand.

- Hello! I'm Johnny. How many of you in the car?

- Just the girls! Please take care of them! And, if you have any problems, here is my phone number. He had it written on a piece of paper, which made me think his plans had long been drawn up.

- Relax, nothing can happen! We're going to Necșești and wherever else we may have to, alright? Who's going to give me the money?

- I am! I reacted hastily. Look, I can give it to you right now!

- Good! See you! And he raised the car window.

I waited a little for Dana to say goodbye to Andrei. They kissed a hundred times, like we were leaving for a month. But I didn't say anything, because I was the only one anxious to leave and I had to understand that it was how people in love behaved.

I couldn't eat anything that morning. I had barely swallowed two mouthfuls of water. I knew it was a decisive day for me and I was a little scared of what I was about to find out. I was having all sorts of thoughts. It had already been five years since I had no word of my mother and she hadn't looked for me, either. The option of her being dead was out of the question, but I had another riddle popping up in my head: "Could it be that she didn't want to see me anymore?".
I don't know what would have hurt me most, losing her or knowing that she didn't want me anymore?

A Jewish proverb says that: "God couldn't be everywhere, so he created mothers." "Mother" is always among the first words a child will say. And it is most certainly one of the most familiar words on the planet. The connection between a mother and her child is the definition of dependence. Beginning with the time of conception, she holds the child in her womb for nine months and carries him/her everywhere. Spiritually, a mother "carries" her child for her whole life. "You will be my child until I pass away, even after that" – mother would always say to me.

The feeling of peace and comfort felt while in the arms of your mother cannot be found anywhere else. Of course, in this lifetime, there are mothers who stray from this path. There are lees to every wine! However, I refused to think that my mother would be part of that group of irresponsible and uninterested mothers. I couldn't believe she had left me to suffer in a care home, at such a young age, without even a phone call, a letter, for her to come and look for me or just send me a message. Something must have happened, and I had to find out what. This was the purpose of my travel and I had no plans to return without answers, irrespective of the actions I would need to carry out to find those answers.

- Eva!
- Oh, Dana, you scared me! Why are you shouting?
- Because you didn't even hear us! We were talking to you and you… you're looking out the window ever since we left. I know you're stressed, but please, just talk to us, time will fly faster if you do.
- Alright! I was in no mood for their jokes and laughter, but I had no choice. And still, who was this boy and why was Dana giggling so much with him?
- Look, Johnny holds stock in the "Zales" club in the city. He said we should go back to his place when we return and we can get in for free. Right?!
- Of course! It will be my pleasure! I have plenty of friends. You'll love it. Especially you, Dana, you seem more lively. You, Eva, on the other hand, seem a little bit under the weather and you will soon realize that life goes by and you won't even know what happened!

I didn't even know what to say. I pinched Dana's leg really hard, perhaps she would return to reality because she started talking nonsense. She signaled me to leave her alone, and I did. I had too much on my mind at the time and couldn't really focus on the idiocies she was making up. I just left her to carry on. I knew it was just a fling and that she sometimes loved showing off. At one point, I fell asleep and woke up horrified.

- How much more do we have?
- Around 30 minutes. Eva, you know, I've been thinking. Perhaps I could stay with you and take you back on Sunday evening. How about it?

What the hell was going on? Either I was going crazy having silly thoughts, or this boy really did have a big heart and wanted to help me find my mother.

- Well… it depends on how much extra it will cost, because I still have no idea where I need to go and I will probably have plenty to run around.
- That's fine… you take care of the gas and a place to sleep. Don't worry about other money, we're all people! We should help each other!

I was truly amazed by this boy, but still, perhaps my ability to read people did not fail me this time, either. I didn't know what to do, whether to accept or not. Overall, it would have been a lot easier with him around because I could travel. But now, I was starting to feel guilty for not taking Andrei with us, too. I had turned down the poor boy and I was, again, in the position of having with me an extra person, apart from Dana. It was late and I couldn't use too much of my energy, as I had other more important things to do.

- Johnny, please, may we stop to go to the bathroom? I don't think I actually needed to go, but it was more the feelings that were overwhelming as we were approaching my village.
- Sure, right not, at the gas station.
While he was filling up, Dana and I went to the bathroom.
- Did you see how nice he is?
- Who?
- God, Eva, what do you mean "who"? Johnny!! He's a really nice guy and has so many connections. I really believe he can help us in many ways.
- Dana, have you gone out of your mind? You're crossing the line, come on now. Stop trusting people so easily.

- Well, I'm tired of you being so pessimistic and negative. Can't you at least once be more open and gullible? Why are you always discouraging me and can never let me enjoy myself?

- Alright, Dana, go ahead and enjoy yourself! But please, understand that I can't think about that right now.

- Well, I do understand you, unlike you, me!

- I apologize, you are right! I will rely on your words and give this boy a chance. You never know! Sometimes, the first impression may be misleading.

- Thank you!! She hugged and kissed me. Come on, you will surely get to meet your mother today!

- I sure hope so!

We returned to the car and I felt my palms sweating, knees shaking and my stomach shrinking. I was starting to recognize the streets and the surroundings. We were approaching the village of Necşeşti – my childhood village. When I saw the church I used to accompany my mother to, located at the entrance of the village, I felt like throwing up. I felt so sick that we had to stop and pour some water on my face. I just couldn't control myself. All sorts of feelings and memories had overwhelmed me and I felt I was losing my footing. I don't think I was ready to learn anything bad.

- Eva, are you alright? Shall we wait or shall we proceed?

- No, no! I'm fine! That's it, we're going!

We got back in the car and I didn't even know where to go, where to ask them to take me. I would have wanted to go home, but most certainly, I would have stumbled upon father. I didn't know our neighbors too well, either… We could have gone to the school.

- Which way? Poor Johnny was waiting for me to point out the route, but I was so lost in space that I didn't even know what to say.

- Go straight, we're going at my home, first. Do you want to stay with me or shall I guide you to a bar and I'll come back to you?

- We're staying with you!, Dana replied while grabbing my hand. She must have noticed, too, that I wasn't feeling too well.

It wasn't long before we ended up in front of the house. So many memories were going through my head. Although I hadn't had a fantastic childhood, there were plenty of nice stories to tell. The door was chained from the inside. That meant that either no one was home, or they were inside, but failed to unlock the door. I pressed the door handle and stepped in the yard, right foot first. I was really superstitious and was hoping that it would help me find my mother in the house, by the stove, weaving. I slowly approached the house. Dana and Johnny were following close by, without making a sound. I was afraid or, perhaps, just scared. I was all shaking and I didn't know what to do first. I went to the window and saw that the lights were off. Eventually, I tried to open the door. It was locked. It was becoming clear that no one was home. I went to the kitchen, because I knew the place where they were hiding the house key. Unless they changed the location, in the meantime!

When I opened the kitchen door, I froze. The mess was unimaginable. Rotten food was lying on the table, there were plenty of unwashed dishes, the stove was black and the smell was unbearable. I took the key (luckily for me, it was still there) and I came out as quickly as I could.

- What happened?, Dana inquired from the front door.

- Nothing. I just took the key.

I could barely speak. I signaled them to wait for me at the front door. I wanted to be alone when going into my house after so long.

When I opened the door, I burst into tears. My little teddy bear was lying on the window case. I took him in my arms and slowly leaned down against the wall. It was all dusty. I was crying so loud that I could barely breathe. All the pain I had gathered during the previous years must have burst out at that point. I don't know what hurt most: that mother wasn't there or just the need to unburden. The house was basically the same, just dirtier. There were clothes all around, plenty of empty bottles and a backgammon board. Father loved to play backgammon and he must have gained a partner… or perhaps a lady partner.

After several minutes, I stood up and slowly headed towards the bedroom. What a mess I found there, too! My mother's absence was obvious. I went to the wardrobe and looked for some of her clothes. There were none. Where had this animal taken my mother? What had he or someone else done with her? I pushed everything away and eventually discovered a while bag full of her clothes and mine. I took one of her shirts and felt her smell. It was her smell, the smell I had been missing for all those years! I got down on my knees and I started screaming even louder while holding her shirt. I was shouting as loud as I could, I was calling my mother out and hoped she could hear me.

- Eva, what are you doing here, Eva? Dana had walked through the door, but she burst into tears, too. She sat down next to me and hugged me.

- Why, Dana, why did they take my mother? Where is she now? Mother! Mother, why can't you hear me?

- Eva, please, calm down! We'll find her! Don't worry, we will! Come one, let's get up and go!

- I don't think we'll ever find her! They must have killed her! Can't you see all her clothes are gone from her own home?

- Stop talking nonsense! Come one, let's get up and go! We will eventually find her!

I couldn't stand up straight away. I held to calm down in order to be able to move. I wiped by tears off and gathered the little strength I still had left in me to proceed. I took the teddy bear and mother's shirt and I came out of that wretched house, without looking back. I had promised myself never to return there again. I put the key back in its place and headed for the car. I was torn and started to lose all hope.

- Where shall we go now?, Johnny asked. He was destroyed, too, the poor boy, of what he had seen. I don't think he was ready to see me so broken and he was probably starting to regret the decision he had made to stay with us.

- I don't know… give me a few moments, let me think…

None of them said anything else. Johnny quickly disappeared from the house front thinking that probably he would help me recover a little. He was driving on the streets of the village and wasn't looking at me at all, not even in the mirror.

- I know!, I shouted instantly. Let's go to Maria! She was a friend of my mother's. She must know something as, back then, she knew every gossip in the village.

- Alright! We'll go wherever you say, just let me know which way it is.

We went in circles for a while, until I realized how to get to her house. I recognized the house by its size. It was one of the largest houses in the village. When I saw those tall stairs again, visible from the street, I remembered the visit I had paid her with mother when father had disappeared from home. I wasn't nervous any longer and I just wanted to find out the truth. I came out from the car and rang the doorbell. Much to my surprise, there was no answer. I opened the front door and went up the stairs. I started pounding the door.

- Who's there?, a manly voice shouted.

- It's me, Eva! Open the door, please!

- What's wrong, girl? Why are you pounding the door? Is there a fire? It was Cornel, Maria's husband.

- Good day! Excuse me, is Mrs. Maria at home?

- Shouldn't you first introduce yourself, young lady?

- You're right, I'm terribly sorry! I'm Eva Guţău and I'm here to have a word with Mrs. Maria, if possible.

- Ivan's Eva?!

My God, this man was in a chatty mood today, while I was tormented by the question of finding out what had happened!

- Yes, it's me! Better yet, Kristina's Eva!

- Weren't you in a foster home?!

Was this really the time to ask questions? Was he not going to spare me the part where he wanted to find out more about me? They were known to be such a family, though. They loved getting into a person's life and find out as much as possible about them, in order to have as many stories as possible to share with the entire village during the Sunday sermon.

- Yes, I was and still am! And that is precisely why I don't have too much time to spare, as I need to return quite soon! Could you please ask your wife to come out?

- Yes, of course! Come inside and I'll call her out… She at the back, feeding the animals. Sit down at the table and I'll call her straight away! Would you like something to drink?

- No, that's fine! Thank you anyway!

He went to the backyard, filled with amazement. I don't know whether it was the shock of seeing me, or perhaps he was puzzled about how his wife would tell me what had happened to my mother, or even the fact that my return to the village would, for him, be "exclusive news" he would sell to the neighbors as soon as I left. Irrespective of the reason for his amazement, I couldn't care too much about that and I was really anxious to see Maria and speak to her. I was already starting to wriggle my foot. I wouldn't normally do that, as it seemed quite a rude gesture, but I was no longer able to control my body. How long would she need to come from the backyard into the house? A few dozens of seconds, most certainly. But they had to gossip a little bit and express their views probably with regard to what they were to tell me.

- Eva, my dear girl, how are you? Mrs. Maria appeared, dressed the same as a few years back – a red, knitted vest and a pair of black, tight pants.

- Good day, madam! I'm fine, thank you! How about you?

- I'm alright, dear! I'm just doing some household chores. Would you like something to drink?

- No, thank you! I don't want to take up too of your time. I do, however, need your help!

- Of course… Tell me, what can I do for you? What a hypocrite, of course she knew why I was there for.

- You know, ever since I was placed in the foster home, I wasn't able to learn anything about my mother. Would you be able to tell me anything about her? Her whereabouts, perhaps?

My heart started pounding, like it was about to explode. I was nervous and I saw the look on her face changed. She seemed amazed that I didn't know anything. She couldn't believe it was her the one who was meant to give me the news... bad news, apparently...

- Mrs. Maria, please tell me where my mother is...

She continued to keep silent and I couldn't believe she would let me go through this nightmare. I started crying and grabbed her hands.

- Please, madam, stop tormenting me. I've been tormented enough. Please... tell me, where is my mother? Is she dead? Madam, please, tell me... is she dead?

She also started crying and continued to gaze straight into my eyes.

- Eva, my dear, you sweet child...

I didn't interrupt her and kept looking at her, waiting for an answer. She was crying, caressing my face and continuing to tell me how sweet and wonderful I was.

- Damn it!!! I shouted and stood up. I don't care how extraordinary of a child I am! I've travelled all this way and I've been waiting for this moment for so many years, and I'm not expecting you to stare at me like a crazy woman and not tell me anything! What kind of heartless woman are you? Just tell me that she's dead and that's it!!

- Eve... she stood up and started coming towards me.

- Tell me! I grabbed her by the shoulders and started shouting even louder. Look into my eyes and tell me if she's dead!!!

- Please, calm down! She's not dead! Kristina is not dead! Sit down!

I felt my heart aching even harder. If she wasn't dead, she must have definitely forgotten about me. I put my hands on the table, lowered my head and started crying even louder.

- Please, let me get you a glass of water, just calm down.

She slowly caressed my head and waited until I stopped crying. She gave me some water and a towel to wipe my face. After a few minutes, I got braver and started asking again.

- Then, where is she now? If she didn't want to see me, at least I can see her from a distance...

- Eva, stop talking like that...

- How am I supposed to talk, then? It's been so many years that I've been waiting for her to come and see me! Now, I find out that she's not dead and my heart aches even harder! What could I have done so wrong for her not to want to reply to any of my letters?

- Eve...

- No Eva! Do you have any idea how many letters I had written to her? Hundreds! Every night, all these years, I dreamt about coming here and looking for her... and this is what I find out!

- Eva, please shut up! Listen to what I have to say!

- Listen to what? How long am I supposed to suffer? How long my heart should be aching? Why is God so keen on tormenting me?

- Eva, Kristina is in the hospital... I felt my blood freeze up. I felt extremely bad for what I had said for the previous minutes. I was an idiot!

- In the hospital? The tone of my voice was completely changed.

- Yes, unfortunately... she's in the hospital. On the day they took you away, she passed out in the yard. A neighbor found her and called the ambulance. They took her to the clinic here, in the village, but later on, they urgently carried her to the main hospital, in Alexandria. We all thought she was dead. However, one day, I went over with Cornel to see if we could find out anything else about her. We knew the poor woman didn't have anyone and we decided to take care of… well, what we thought would be a funeral, at that time. Much to our surprise, when we got to the hospital in Alexandria, they said she was not dead and that we could find her at the "Speranța" hospital in Bucharest. For the moment, we were really happy, but when we got there, we realized that "Speranța" was a different kind of hospital.

- What kind?, I interrupted without even realizing.

- A mental health institution!

God, when will the suffering end?

- Unfortunately, when they took you away, Kristina suffered a shock, and that shock led to the loss of memory and the triggering of a disease. I can't remember the name of the condition, but I can tell you that your mother doesn't react to almost anything and she seems most often absent. She doesn't even know her name, nor where she is. She doesn't recognize anyone.

- How do you know? Have you seen her?

- Yes, I have! Once every two-three months, on Sunday, we are going to see her. We get her a few things… try to speak to her… but it seems in vain… she is no longer our Kristina!

I was drowning in tears and my eyes were stuck focused on a corner of the room. I couldn't believe what was happening to me.

- Eva, my dear, if you need anything, we're here for you.

- Thank you… I could hardly speak. Could I see her?

- Yes, of course. Tomorrow is Sunday, you can go. Visiting times are every Sunday, 8 AM to 8 PM. If you went to see her now, I would be peaceful, I haven't been to see her for a while. Or, if it's alright with you, we can go together!

- No… I'd rather I went alone, if you don't mind. May I please have the address? Thank you so much for everything that you've done… one day, I will make it up to you.

She wrote down the address on a newspaper bit. I hugged her and thanked her again. She insisted I stayed there to sleep overnight, but I already wanted to head over to Bucharest. I wanted to be there first thing, the next morning. I couldn't have wasted any more time. I returned to the car and briefly told Dana and Johnny what I had just learned, then I asked them to head towards Bucharest. I also asked them to leave me alone, while also mentioning my thank you for them being there, but that I needed peace and quiet. I had gone through too much for one day and I could no longer speak.

The fact that I could barely see her the next day was driving me crazy. It felt like time was standing still and the whole universe was plotting against me. In a way, I had managed to calm down a little because I was very close to finding her. I knew she was alive and I was particularly happy to be able to hug her again, at least once.

I was sitting on the backseat of the car. Dana was at the front, with Johnny. They inquired a few times whether I wanted anything, whether I needed them to stop the car, but I just waived at them, signaling that I was fine and that they should leave me be. The trip took about two-three house by car, during which time I would be bathing in my thoughts, recalling moments from my other life – the one where mother was by my side and loved me. I couldn't believe how one single day can change one's life. Not only your life, but the life of the people around you. I still couldn't understand why mother and I had to pay for my father's mistakes. Where was the justice? Why did we get punished for him being a drunkard and brutal savage? I knew my childhood wasn't perfect, that I was far from normal for a child of my age back then, but my normality was there – in my house, with my parents. Some people took all I had left and threw me in a place of horror. They took me away from a terrible environment just to send me to an even horrible one. At least, at home, I had my mother, who could offer me peace, love and protection. As much as she could, but it was sufficient for me. They tried to save me from my father and managed to completely ruin my childhood, my feelings and my thinking – namely, my entire life. They took away my smile and ease and replaced them with fear, malice, frustration and scare. In a foster home, no child can learn anything good. All they learn is to defend, hate and despise. They get no consolations, no hugs, not even nice words. So, who are these people pretending to help you when, in fact, all they do is hurt you?

- Eva, do you know any hotels in Bucharest?, Dana asked loudly, managing to almost frighten me. Where will we sleep?

- I have no idea! I've never been here before! We definitely need to find something cheap. We'll go as close to the hospital as possible and check in at a motel or something similar.

- Alright. Come on, don't be sad, it will be fine! The poor girl, she was willing to try and encourage me, but we both knew that once mother ended up in there, she was far from fine.

- I'm trying to…

- Lie down on the backseat and try to get some sleep. We don't have long to go and you definitely need some sleep, even if just for a few minutes.

I lay down, but couldn't sleep. I was looking at Dana, admiring her charming smile. She was all smiles and talking to this Johnny guy as if they had been childhood friends. She was a positive person and, no matter how upset you would be, you would loosen up just by looking at her. I was quite surprised when I saw his hand slowly move towards Dana's leg. I couldn't understand why this was happening. Or I was saying to myself that I had perhaps lost track of the conversation and that it was just a friendly gesture. I didn't ask any questions and I returned to my own thoughts. My brain was being oxygenated using previous memories. When a phone rand, I jumped, startled. It was Andrei. He must have been calling to see how we were doing.

- Andrei, we're fine! We're on our way to Bucharest, not long to go now. Eve's mother is there, she admitted to a hospital… she slightly turned towards me and I saw her pitiful look. We're staying at a motel overnight because she can only visit her in the morning. I'll call you later and give you some extra details. She hung up and continued to speak, but this time, it was with me. He's worried and he asked me to tell you that he is spiritually supporting you.

- Thank you!

I could hear, like in a dream, Dana telling Johnny about her relationship with Andrei. I was surprised to hear her say that she was bored, that she wanted more, but that he couldn't understand that. Why hadn't she perhaps told me all these things? Or at least to Andrei. He was a fantastic boy and I think he deserved to know the truth. Or perhaps it was just another one of Dana's moods and I had nothing to worry about.

- Look, a motel! We still have about 10 km to Bucharest and I think it would be best to stay here overnight and leave tomorrow morning, around 6 AM, and get to the hospital early. How about it, Eva?, Johnny asked, feeling tired after all that travel.

- Yes, let's go in and see if they have vacancies. Shall we get a triple room?

- No, I think it would be better if we took two rooms, I would feel more comfortable.

- Alright, whatever you say.

We gathered whatever we had left in our vehicle and entered the motel which, by the looks of the entrance, seemed to be more of a shop. It was just the large, red sign saying "Mozi Motel" that confirmed me that we were in the right place. Reception was in a small shop, with plenty of products on sale.

- Good evening, how may I help you?, a young lady welcomed us. She was wearing a push-up shirt, two ponytails and chewing on gum. Her round and large earrings were hanging from her ears and, once in a while, the young lady would cross them using the pen in her hand. I was starting to see Johnny go all to pieces and I couldn't explain why men would get so hasty whenever they spot a bit of vulgarity.

- Good evening, we would like to book two rooms until tomorrow morning.

- I haven't got two rooms, I only have one, with two double beds. They are somewhat separated by a wall, but they are still in the same room. You have a toilet and sink in the room, and the showers are down the hallway. Is that alright?

- It should be fine, yes. What do you think, Johnny?

- Yes, that's fine for me, I just want to lie down as soon as possible! I have had enough driving for one day!

- Alright! How much for that, please?

- 95 lei.

I looked in my bag and all the money I had were 267 lei.

- Would it be possible to have a small discount, please? We are leaving at dawn tomorrow, at 6 AM!, I asked the lady, somewhat ashamed.

- Miss, listen, the regular price for the room would have been 110 lei, but seeing that it's late, I already gave you a discount and offered you the room for 95 lei. And I could see her play with the pen in her hair, sometimes even with the earrings, sometimes even placing it next to her mouth.

- Alright, I just asked.

- And I answered. So, do you want the room or not?

- Yes, we'll take it! I was too tired and upset to be able to go into an argument with her. I was also feeling bad towards Dana and Johnny and I wanted to see them get some rest as soon as possible.

We went up a small staircase, following in the footsteps of the receptionist. We stopped in front of room number 8 and she unlocked the door for us. It was a sensationally small room, with two beds separated by a wall. On the right-hand side, there was a curtain concealing the toilet. The room had no windows, just a skylight on the ceiling which seemed to open with the help of a stick.

- Showers are down the hallway, to the right. Towels are on the bed; if you need anything else, just give me a call. OK?

- Yes, we will! Thank you!

- Excuse me, please, Dana eventually decided to ask, where may we get something to eat?

- Downstairs, the shop. If you are after cooked food, there is a small restaurant just across the street. Anything else?

- Nothing, thank you! And I was slowly heading towards the door, perhaps I could make her go away faster as she was already starting to irritate me.

She first fitted her shirt, just to make sure that her breasts were quite visible, and she closed the door on her way out.

- I'll go and get something to eat and until then, you can have a shower and rest.

- Eva, but I can go, Dana said.

- No, no, please! I need to get some air, too. I won't be long! Would you like me to buy anything in particular?

- No, just something to eat; I'm starving. Johnny, do you want anything?

- Buy me a beer, please, if you can. It helps me fall asleep faster.

I exited the building and sat down on the curb. I stuck my head between my hands and was trying to imagine what the next day would be like. In my mind, it was quite vague and I had no idea what it would be like. I started praying and watching the sky. I was wishing for another miracle. God had already given me one my keeping my mother alive. But I needed one more, I wanted so badly to find my mother well and for her to recognize me. That was my greatest fear, that she would look at me and would have no idea who I was.

I gathered myself and stood up. I had to be strong and hold on, irrespective of what was to happen. I entered the small shop at the reception and I took a few things off the shelf. The vulgar young lady was pursuing me with her sight, probably for fear that I would steal something. I didn't even look at her again, I placed everything I had gathered from the shelves next to the cash register and was waiting for her to calculate the total amount due.

- 28.70 lei.

I handed her the money, took the bag and headed for the room. There was no noise, they must have already fallen asleep, so I decided to open the door gently so as not to make any noise. When I stuck my head in, I saw Johnny on top of Dana, kissing her passionately, and he had his hand under Dana's shirt. I was dumbstruck and couldn't believe my eyes.

- Eva! Dana quickly jumped out of bed and ran towards me, while my eyes were stuck on Johnny, who was arranging his clothes and ghastly wiping his mouth. Eva, please don't be upset. That's how I felt… I feel quite attracted to Johnny and my relationship with Andrei is no longer what it used to be.

- But, Dana… I could no longer speak. My day had already been a difficult one, but I couldn't deny that Dana had let me down.

- Please, Eva, you have to understand me! You are my friend and, just as I understand you, I beg you not to judge me.

- Of course I'm not judging. The choices are yours and, irrespective of whether I agree with them or not, I respect them. You know best what you have to do and I don't think this is the right time to talk. I'm going to take a shower.

I took the towel by the side of Johnny's feet and rushed to the bathroom. I was in shock. I couldn't understand why she was choosing to do things that way and, particularly, why she would give up her safe relationship back home for a boy she had barely met. I got under the shower and I left the water running all over my body for several minutes. I curled up under the water jet and I started to cry. I was gripping my feet with my hands and I felt my whole body, head and particularly, my soul ache. It was a horrible pain for me not to be able to comprehend how I ended up in this mess and it seemed as though I would never be able to escape this chaos unleashed in my head. I remember my mother singing to me and that made me cry even harder.

I heard the door open and, in a few seconds, Dana stuck her head behind the shower curtain. I was already on my feet.

- Eva, I was worried. I came to see how you were.

- I'm fine, Dana! It was too hard a day and I dread thinking about tomorrow.

- I know! I'm here for you! And I do apologize if I managed to upset you even more.

- You haven't! You know I'm your friend, whatever happens! I just want to know why you never told me about the fact that your relationship with Andrei is no longer what it used to be!

- I wasn't too certain of it and I never realized exactly what I wanted. So, I preferred to keep quiet and suffer in silence.

- And now, you are certain that Johnny is what you want? You've only known him for a few hours, Dana… can you trade in a certainty for something completely unsure in such a short amount of time?

- Eva, now is not the time for you to think about what I want to do. But yes, I feel that what I am doing is the right thing and all I ask of you is not to judge me!

- I won't judge you… your actions are yours and yours only! Just that, from now on, I'd rather you told me if you have any problems. Alright?

- I promise! Come on, just come out of the shower and let's go to sleep, it's late and tomorrow, we're off early in the morning. Tomorrow is not going to be an easy day!

I got dressed and walked towards the room. Down the hallway, Dana stopped me and hugged me.

- I love you, Eva, and I promise you that, no matter what happens, I will love you for the rest of my life!

- I love you, too!

Her hug and words were a sign that I wasn't alone and that she was there for me. That gave me strength and all I wanted now was for time to fly and for me to get to my mother quicker.

- How shall we sleep?, Johnny asked when we both entered the room.

- I'll sleep in the bed next to the door.

- Eva, do you mind if I sleep with Johnny? Her question left me dumbfound, but I chose to reply unmoved.

- No, suit yourself! You can sleep in the rear bed, and I'll stay here.

- Thank you!

I didn't even know what to think about first. The fact that Dana was so ignorant and that she was in bed with a man whose surname she didn't even know, mother, myself or the coming day? I lay down in bed and covered myself with the blanket. I placed the pillow over my head and started praying again. I could hear them giggle, kiss, and the squeaks of their bed were creeping me out.

- Take your clothes off, I want to see you naked!, I heard Johnny whisper. They must have thought I couldn't hear them, or that I was asleep or perhaps they didn't even care too much about what I thought.

- Shhht… quiet down, I don't want her to hear us, please!

- She doesn't, don't worry. Come on, take your top off!

I heard her top fall on the floor and I could sense the hormones dancing in the atmosphere. I could hear every kiss and every movement.

- Do you want me? Come on, do you want me? How much do you want me? Johnny was talking as if I wasn't even in the room.

- Yes, I want you! I want you so badly! I want you in me now!

The bed was squeaking louder and louder. Dana was making all sorts of sounds and, by the way she was breathing, I realized she was having one orgasm after another. Johnny must have wanted to show her how manly he was and he would strike her, making her scream even louder.

That's exactly what was missing from the picture, a live sex scene!

I felt relieved when the bed stopped squeaking and I heard them get up and wander through the bad I had brought from the shop. After a good romp, a beer was a true blessing for the alpha male. I was really happy to hear them say "Good night" and go to bed.

I knew I wasn't going to fall asleep and all I wished for were for time to fly even faster. I wanted nothing more than to hug my mother.

During the few hours left of that night, I twisted and turned restlessly in bed. I had set the clock alarm for 6 AM, but I was already dressed and ready to leave at 5.30 AM. I searched for my cigarettes in the room and I told them I would wait downstairs. I was longing for a coffee, so finding a coffee machine at the motel entrance really made my day. It was quiet, hopefully it was not the quiet before the storm. I could see plenty of lights on the horizon and it seemed that everyone was just waiting for a start. I would sometimes see a person walking by, some more pensive than others, walking head down as if speaking to themselves about all sorts of problems. I sat down on the curb and lit myself a cigarette. The morning coffee was the best thing about the start to the day. I was looking at my white trainers, trying to count the number of holes the laces were going through. My mind wanted to refuse to think about how that day would be and what else I was to find out. It seemed that nothing could damage me and, in a strange way, I felt that my mother would recognize me and that we would find a solution to living together again. I was willing to quit school, take up even more work… I could have done anything just to be able to have her next to me. I had missed her too much lately and my greatest wish was to get back those moments I had spent away from her. I would have wiped the slate clean and start a whole new life along with the only being that truly mattered to me.

- Eva, are you ready?, Johnny interrupted my thoughts. Shall be take something to eat?

- Yes, we should! There must be a shop somewhere on the way! I took every eatable thing from this shop last night.

- Alright, then, let's go! It will take about 45 minutes to get to the city center. Do you have the address?

I handed him the address Maria had given me. The hospital's name, "Speranța" *(Hope)* was fueling my expectations. I imagined the look of the hallways, stairs and rooms. I could imagine my mum in a large, cream-colored room, with huge windows and plenty of flowers. I pictured her reading. I would imagine her reaction when she saw me. What would be the first thing she would tell me? My body was shaking and I couldn't hold my emotions under control. I couldn't find the strength to control myself. The uncertainty, hope, worry, emotion… they all made me feel lose control and shake unimaginably.

- Eva, what's wrong with you? Dana reached over the seat and grabbed my hand. Your hands are very cold and you're shaking. Do you want us to stop?

- No, no! We're not stopping! We're going to my mother! I want to see my mother! And again, tears started to flood my cheeks.

- Not long now, just have a little more patience. And stop crying. Do you want her to see you crying? You finally found her and you must show her your happiness. Please, Eve… you're strong, you need to calm down!

- I wish I could… but I can't… it's like I'm powerless. Do you think it will be alright? Will she recognize me? I had become weaker than ever. I could see the surprise on Dana's face, too. She hadn't seen my like this before. She jumped between the seats and came to sit with me at the back. She hugged me fiercely and laid my head in her lap.

- Please, try to ease up, if that's what you need to do, but I will have to calm down! I can only imagine how hard it must be for you, but that's not the Eva we all know and, least of all, your mother knows. Snap out of it and show us that happiness on your face when you get to see her. I can imagine how difficult this must be, but please, you need to get a grip on yourself. Please!

I snuggled in her arms and was trying to hold my breath so as not to sigh so loud and so often. I was saying prayers in my thoughts and was waiting to stop shaking. Dana was rights, I had to be strong and appear before my mother with a smile on my face!

When the car engine stopped, I could feel my heart pounding even harder. I was still lying on Dana's feet.

- Are we here?, I asked, almost whispering.

- Yes, we are! Do you want to stay in the car for a few more minutes?, Dana inquired, while signaling Johnny to get out of the car.

- No! I want to go!

- Hold on! Listen to me for a minute! Eva, you must be strong and prepare for whatever is about to come. It can all turn out really well, or really badly. In any case, you must be happy to have found your mother and accept it as it is. Please, I need you and I don't want to see you like that anymore! Promise?

- Promise what, Dana? I exhaled, pulled away from her arms and jumped right out of the car.

- Eva! Please!

And that was the last thing I heard on my way to the great, white doors of the "Speranța" hospital entrance.

I was running so fast that I was feeling out of breath. I could see the name "Speranța" written everywhere in white, yellow characters and all I wished for was to find my mother already.

I entered some large, sliding doors where, before me, the "Reception" appeared, in large characters. In the room, there were many ladies dressed in white and wearing bonnets. Some were talking with persons from the outside, others were talking on the phone or filling in all sorts of papers. I didn't know who to ask, who to inquire to and all I could do was try to calm my breath down because it was already running wild. I tried to approach one of the ladies, but she discreetly signaled me to wait. While explaining something to a gentleman, she signaled a young lady holding a notebook to inquire what my business was there.

- Hello, my name is Claudia, what can I help you with?

- Hello… well…, I started stuttering and could no longer find my words. I'm here to…

- Do you have a medical issue? She grabbed my hands and pulled me over to a chair. Stay here! Breather slowly and please calm down! After feeling better, perhaps you could tell me what happened.

- I came to see my mother, I was told she is admitted here.

- I understand. Could I please know her name and yours, so I can check and come back with the information required? Alright?

She handed me a paper which I was meant to fill in with all sorts of data, however, I only wrote my name and my mother's name. It was sufficient and there was no point in wasting time with nonsense.

- Please help yourself to water, tea or coffee from over there, she said as she pointed towards a table in the corner of the room, until I go and check. Alright?

- I'm fine, thank you, I'll just wait here.

- Perhaps it would be better to have some water... And she left towards the large Reception at the hospital entrance.

I was looking around and could only notice sad-looking faces. Once in a while, I was blessed with the image of an old man smiling and hugging his children or grandchildren. I kept looking at the large stairs and I could imagine my mother coming down on them. Had time changed her? Was she looking older?

- Miss Eva!

- Yes, yes! I'm here!

- Your mother, Kristina... and she started looking with a lost figure through some papers.

- Is she dead?!

- No, no! She's not dead, she's in room 3018, 3rd floor, ward C. Would you like to be escorted to her room? Or would you like to wait for her to be brought downstairs, in the cafeteria? How will it be?

- Well... I don't know... I've never been here before. I'd rather go and see her immediately, if that's alright, of course!

- You've never been here before? Hmm... I take it you're not aware of Mrs. Guțău's condition?

- No... I slightly lowered my head, feeling ashamed, even though I had no reason to.

- Right, let's just have a seat then and afterwards, I shall call a nurse to take you to her room. Your mother was transferred here after having been treated at the Horias Hospital. She had a stroke. When she arrived here, she was in a pretty advanced state of amnesia, in addition to depression, stress and anemia. All of these have led to a loss of memory. We hope it is just temporary... Otherwise, she seems healthy!

- Healthy? How exactly does she seem healthy? I started crying and punching the edge of the chair.

- Miss Eva, I'm going to have to ask you to calm down. All I meant was that, from a clinical point of view, except for the memory part, we've managed to get her back on her feet. I'll wait for you to calm down and I will personally accompany you to her room.

- Please, madam, I want to see her as soon as possible! I'm going to settle down on the way.

- Are you sure?

- Yes, absolutely!

She stood up and I, immediately after. We walked together towards the elevators at the rear of the room. She pushed the 3 button and looked at me, as if she was asking me whether I was ready or not. I nodded my head in agreement and entered the elevator, which seemed to move quite slowly, floor by floor. When the doors opened, my heart was the size of a pea and I knew I was a few steps away from my mother. I had been waiting for this moment for so long, and now, that it was actually happening, I still couldn't believe it. I had goosebumps and my ears were whistling. We were passing by other rooms and I could see, on every door, a little window barely allowing to see on the inside. 3015, 3016, 3017... and 3018. We eventually reached her room. The only thing standing between me and my mother was now a door.

I entered fearfully. I didn't know what to expect. I stood in the door for a few seconds, eyes shut and fists clenched, as if attempting to encourage myself to enter and look inside the room. I saw a bed with a green blanket, a small painting and a little table with an armchair turned towards the window. Mother was sitting in the armchair. I could see her ankles.
- Kristina, someone is here to see you! The nurse's voice truly frightened me.
She failed to display any gestures. She was lying still in the armchair, her back turned towards me. I wanted to see her face, her hands... I would have loved to hug and kiss her. But I was so scared.
- Come on, you can go sit next to her!, the nurse slowly pushed me from behind.
I plucked up my heart and decided to steadily approach the armchair. My entire body was shaking and my mind had come to a standstill. I held my hands on the arm of the chair and, all of a sudden, I took a step forward and ended up on the right-hand side of the armchair. It was mother! It was truly my mother! She was weaving something white. Her eyes were unchanged, just like her hands. Her hair was now grey and her wrinkles were clearly visible. I placed my hands on my face and started crying.
- Mother!, I screamed in pain and of a desire to love.
She raised her sight, placed her hands in her lap and stared at me. I was drowning in her eyes and couldn't believe it was sitting in front of me. I bowed to hug her and wrapped my hands around her neck. She had no reaction whatsoever. I strengthened by grip around her and kissed her on the right cheek.
- Mother, it's me... Eva, your daughter! Please, say something! And I continued to endlessly kiss her hands. Please, mother, speak to me! I missed you! I longed to see you!
I started speaking to her, kiss her, on the hands, on the cheeks, on the forehead. I missed her smell so much. I started telling her what happened to me and where they had taken me. I would, at times, stop and look at her. I loved watching her. I missed her so much that I did not want to lose sight of her for one second.
They let me stay with her for about two hours, but it only seemed a few minutes to me. They brought food to her room and I tried to persuade her to stand up and eat with me. Again, no gestures. I don't know whether she was as shocked as I was, or that was just her general condition. I couldn't care about anything during that time, except the fact that I was by her side.

Pain may not be expressed too much in words. Nor in tears, probably. When you hurt, you feel like every part of your body is dying and you continue to sink in a dark void of which you feel you may never escape. They say nothing last forever, but I believe pain can. Its intensity may display different levels, but there are instances where pain never goes away.

Seeing my mother in that condition, I realized I loved her even more, I felt infinite love and the desire to asset my feelings, now more than ever. At the same time, I felt I had lost my purpose in life and had no idea which road to take. It was as if we were living in parallel universes and all I wanted for us to be part of the same universe again. But how?

I came out of the hospital and began to scream. I fell on my knees and reached for the sky, as if asking for a miracle. I felt the need to get the evil out of me. The sun was in my eyes and floods of tears were pouring down over my cheeks. I gave way to my feelings, the crying, the anger… I knew I had gathered too much inside me in all these years and that hadn't helped me at all. I could no longer hold anything back. My heart had filled with negatives, but now, when it seemed that I was losing my mother, I realized that nothing of which I thought it was difficult actually was. The physical loss of the most important person in my life was truly a catastrophe. Mentally, I had tried to prepare myself for such times, but spiritually, I failed. I was confuse, sad and stricken. I displayed my suffering crawling and screaming. I was pulling my hair and all I wanted was to die!

A circle had formed around me and people were looking mesmerized. Such idiots! They were turning my pain into a comedy. I gathered all the power I had left in me and stood up.

- What the hell do you want? Why do you keep staring at me? I was screaming my lungs out and when I saw one of them video-record me, I jumped at him with the intention of taking his phone away.

- You jerk, how dare you record me? What do you know about me and my life?

- You're nuts, woman!

- God, what a psychopath!

I could hear all sorts of people talking around me and I just couldn't understand why they wouldn't leave me alone.

- You should take a painkiller. Here you are, honey…

A woman was coming towards me, holding a white pill in her hand, and a bottle of water in the other. I struck her hand where she was holding the pill.

- How dare you call me honey? Who are you, woman? Are you my mother? My mother is here, upstairs, in this hospital. Do you know that? Leave! Leave my sight! All of you leave! Just leave me alone!!!

- Eve… Eve… Dana has showed up, too. She was rushing towards me. I saw her place her hands on her head and start crying. She jumped over me and put me down, hugging me. We were both crying.

- Eva, please… calm down! You're destroying yourself! What happened?

She was caressing my head while I had curled up in her arms. I didn't want to see anyone. I didn't want to speak to anyone. I wanted so much to disappear and not know anything about anyone.

I didn't know what hurt me most: the fact that my mother was in that condition, that I had to return to that damn foster home or seeing Dana and Johnny touching each other. I was happy to have found my mother, I knew where she was now and I could visit her whenever I wanted to. I could not however bear the thought of having to return to that room which I had to call home for the past years. I wanted to take my luggage and leave. It didn't matter where, I just knew that this horrible chapter had ended in my mind, while the ladies at the foster home would have been really thrilled to get rid of me.

I was still dreading the fact that I had to face Andrei and his parents. Dana didn't seem to care at all. She was listening to loud music and, once in a while, she would gently stroke Johnny's hair or touch him on the foot or elsewhere. Although I had told her that I would completely support her in this matter, I couldn't agree to what was happening. I was ashamed of her shame. Those people had helped me leave so I could find my mother. So, I couldn't really explain how you could erase everything that was beautiful and all the love that she had declared to Andrei just a few hours earlier. I didn't know the meaning of love, but I was feeding off Dana's stories and it felt like her and Andrei shared an innocent love. It seemed I was wrong. Or perhaps, that's what love was, it would appear in an instant and disappear as quickly as it appeared.

What is certain is that I had no confidence in Johnny. I saw him as a slick town boy and all he seemed to do was take advantage of my only true friend, clearly playing her. The age difference also seemed to be an issue, but who was I to judge their feelings? Perhaps, I wasn't thinking straight and my perspective was too bleak. We stopped at the petrol station. I wanted to take some cash out of my purse, but Johnny signaled me to relax. I think he wanted to show Dana what a man he was and, at the same time, he was perhaps thanking me as he managed to meet her through me. I don't know… and I didn't insist, either. I waited for him to step out of the car.

- Dana, what will you do when we get home? What will you tell Andrei?

- Well, Eva! I really don't know! I probably won't tell him anything for a while.

- What do you mean?

- Just like that! I'll go back like nothing happened and I'll decide what to do in the following days. I don't love Andrei anymore, but I still wouldn't want to be me to end it. It would be better to come from him, right? She smiled and took a long look at me.

- I don't understand what you're saying. How would it come from him? If he loves you, how could he give you up? You're crazy!

- I'm not crazy. You said you supported me.

- I do support you, but that doesn't mean I can't ask you anything or tell you whenever you cross the line a little!

- Cross the line? Why do you think I am crossing the line?

- That was not what I meant! "Diabolical was the word I was looking for", I thought, but I went on: or perhaps it was just an affair with Johnny and we can all forget about this, and you can go back to Andrei!

- No, no! That was no affair. I really love J. I want to be involved in a relationship with him. He seems like an amazing boy! And he is so attentive…

- An amazing boy? When exactly did you have time to figure that out? In these few hours?

- Eva, why are you so keen on ruining my joy? You should find yourself a man, too… perhaps you would then understand me!

- What do you mean I'm ruining your joy? I'm trying to open your eyes and make you become more cautious. Obviously, there's no point…

- My eyes are wide open, I don't understand why you think I'm not seeing it clearly. But, anyway…

- Exactly! Anyway! It's your business! I won't meddle, I'm here for you, but don't give me any chances to say "I told you so".

- Fine! I got it! Thanks for the advice. Oh, and thanks for being here for me! It wouldn't get more ironical than that.

- Leaving all this aside, Dana, I don't want to return to live at the foster home. I feel like I can't stay there for another second. How do you propose we proceed?

- You do realize that those imbecilic women there can't wait to get rid of us! We're an extra expense to them and I think they would love nothing more than to cast us out. We can leave, if you want to! I'll get a job and we'll rent a room somewhere. How about it?

- Yes, that's a great idea. But I don't want to quit school! Promise we finish high school? Just one year left to go. We'll work afternoons and nights, if we have to. Perhaps I could get you a job at the coffee shop… If not, I'm sure we'll find something. What do you say?

- Yes, let's do that! We return, fill in the papers saying that we want to leave and I'm pretty sure we'll find something in two-three days.

Johnny entered the car with a juice for each of us.

- Wow, you're so sweet! Thanks, babe! And she jumped all over him to lay a kiss on him.

I kept repeating "babe" in my head. It seemed amazingly pathetic, but I preferred to shut up.

- Thanks for the juice, Johnny, but you shouldn't have!, I said to him half-heartedly.

- Don't mention it! Where can I drop you off when we arrive?

- Johnny, perhaps you could help us! Eva and I don't want to stay in the foster home anymore…

- I hope you don't expect me to take you in!, he jumped, the only male in the car.

- No, no! Don't worry! I wouldn't stay at your house, anyway, but I wouldn't be so sure about Dana, though…

- I wouldn't either!, Dana said half-heartedly, visibly irritated by his reaction.

- So how could I help you, then?

- We would like to rent a room somewhere. We thought you might know someone who had a place to let. And it would be quite urgent! If not, I can visit the agencies when I finish my shift on Monday. We need to find a room!

- Right. Well, I will ask around. I have a few friends who have a few girls lodged in apartments downtown. But you would need to share, I don't know any details. If you want, I can ask!

- Please do!, I replied immediately, with the thought of ending this conversation as soon as possible. It seemed embarrassing for him to think that we would want to live at his house, after just a few hours spent together.

There was still around one hour of travel left and it seemed that the plain presence of this boy was irritating me. I was indeed helpful to him for giving me a hand in seeing my mother, but I did pay him, after all. I did not owe him anything. On the other hand, Dana seemed even more charmed by him and this was creating an even heavier discomfort.

I lay down on the backseat of the car and was looking at the lights on the road. I was trying to count them but I would quickly lose count, due to my thoughts.

Chapter 8

I was awaken by the clock's alarm. It was 5.45 AM. Half of me was pushing me to get out of bed, the other half was telling me to stay where I was and don't go anywhere. My classes began at 8.00 AM. I could have skipped the 30 minutes of jogging and get an extra shuteye. My conscience was twinging. Dana was sound asleep in her bed.

We had managed to move into an apartment in Bucharest, with other four girls. We had also changed schools, registering with a high school in the 5th District. There was no connection with the girls in the apartment, except for once in a while sharing the kitchen and the living room. I had worked all summer to raise money and I had managed to escape that "hell hole", as I liked to call it. I was in the 12th grade and I was pushing hard to earn my school graduation certificate. I wanted more than ever to go to university. I would finish classes at 1.00 PM, and at 2.00 PM I was heading to Lucas and Izabella, two children I was babysitting. I would quickly pick them up from nursery, take them home and mind them until around 8.00 PM, when Kate and Boris, their parents, would arrive. At 9.00 PM, I would start my shift at the restaurant next to my home, where I would work until 1.00 AM, sometimes even 2.00 AM. I would spend my Saturdays at the restaurant, from morning to evening, while every Sunday, I would go and visit my mother. That was the main reason I had come to the capital city, just so I could be closer to her.

Dana broke up with Andrei quite easily, but her relationship with Johnny lasted around a week. As I had predicted, to Johnny, she was nothing more than the usual girl, one or two nights of sex and that was it. Dana suffered her first heartbreak, when she figured out that all that glitters is not gold. She had abandoned school and was working in an underwear shop. She was sometimes doing videochat, similar to the other girls in the house, but that was not my kind of job and, no matter how tempting the money was, I hated selling my body online to all sorts of men. What I liked about her was that we stuck together, although she got to a point where she could afford more than I could. I was still a virgin and I hadn't encountered any man able to convince me to give that up.

I quickly put on some sports clothing and closed the door behind me, while turning my IPod on and trying to insert my earphones. Damn earphones, they would never stay still in my ears! Or perhaps my ears were crooked! The route I was going on was well-designated. I would run for about 5 km and I would always meet the same people. We were saying Hello to each other, although had never formally introduced ourselves. I didn't even know the names of these people, but I loved imagining what they were doing, what their jobs were and what kind of issues they were having. I would often see couples going to work, having a coffee at Starbucks or just walking next to each other. They were all in a rush and seldom was I given to see any gestures of affection between them. Most of the times, I would see angry wives shouting and men seeming absent or even bored. If I saw a kiss or a couple hugging, I liked to imagine they had been together for a while. However, their gestures suggested that they were on their first dates and still at the stage of discovering their partners.

My spare time was limited. After a good sweat, I would return to the house and jump straight into the shower. I had exactly 45 minutes to eat, get dressed and prepare my school bag. I would read quite a lot on the bus and would do my homework wherever I could. Sometimes, I would even go to the basement, in the restaurant's storage room and prepare whatever I could for the next day. On busy days, I barely had time to go to the bathroom and those were the days when I needed to study at night. Sometimes, I would just sleep one or two hours, but it didn't matter. I wanted too much to study and, willingly or not, I needed the money and had to work.

My high school colleagues were completely different from the ones I had had in primary school. The fact that I was no longer living in a dorm was probably a game-changer, but I could finally feel that I could compare with them, be at the same level. I loved exact sciences and was excelling in tests. Once, the mathematics teacher even proposed me to try and develop this path, but even if I wanted to, I had no time for it. My dream was to become a lawyer and I was hoping that the logic of the mind, focused on mathematics for all those years, would later on help me out, in Law. I liked history, too, but sometimes, it was difficult for me to remember all the years written in the books. Time in school was flying. I loved taking in the information and processing it at a later stage, when I was taking care of the two children. Sometimes, I would even recount to them some of the things I had learned in school on the day. Izabela was 3, and Lucas, 5. Whenever they saw me at the nursery door, they would run towards me as fast as they could. They would grab my leg and signaled me to go. I had a bicycle with a double carriage upfront, and I would always park my bike inside the nursery yard. In the evening, when I was leaving their house, I would come and leave it at the usual spot, in order to make it easier for me on the following day. After that, I would go to the restaurant. Once, a work mate even went on to ask me whether I wasn't afraid someone would steal it, but I wasn't. Who would take the trouble of stealing a yellow, rusty bike? I had improvised some belts for the young ones and I was pedaling in a hurry to get them home by 2.30 PM and put them to sleep. There were days when they would sleep like babies, but there were some other times when under no circumstance did they even want to lie in bed. Whenever I was lucky enough for them to sleep, I loved to read. Kate had a huge library where I would always find something new and interesting. She was working as architect, but she was also interested in literature. Sometimes, she would even recommend books for me to skim through. At 4.30 PM, I used to feed the children their snack and take them out to the park. I would let them do whatever they wanted and lower myself to their level. I was happy for them and I would appreciate how much some parents loved their children. Boris was a banker and would not spend too much time at home, but whenever he was home, he would play with them and show them all his affection. In a very awkward way, I hated him. Even though he was a wonderful father and a great man, I felt repulsed by him. And, later on, I would realize that I had this with all men. My childhood traumas had scarred me and I didn't know how I could control it. I hadn't seen my father in years and I didn't want to, either. Most the times, I imagined him being dead, but without actually having any feelings towards it. At 6.30 PM, I would return with the kids from the park and, if none of the parents was home, I would cook for them. Kate would always leave me whatever I was supposed to feed them. While they were eating, I would tell them all sorts of stories and promise to sing them a song at the end, if they ate everything in their plates. They were two nice and obedient children. They were sometimes crossing the line, but not much. At 7.15, I would bathe them and put them to bed. Most of the times, their mother would get home before 7.00 PM and would let me go early. If not, they knew I had to leave at 8.00 PM sharp in order to get to the restaurant in time. If she took care of the kids, I would tidy up the house a little bit and then leave. Kate and Boris liked me a lot and they would sometimes offer me bonuses or gifts. They wanted to make me feel like I was part of the family, but what they didn't know was that family was the last thing I was interested in. I've told them next to nothing about my childhood and I was avoiding any long conversations. We shared a relationship based on trust and I would not go anywhere beyond minding their children.

After leaving the bicycle, I would hop on the bus from a street near the nursery and would head to my second job. I was working as waitress, but I would also answer the phone and deal with bookings. The owner was an Italian lady, age around 55, who had spent her entire life in this restaurant. She was chubby and she loved sweets. Her name was Carla and she had no children or husband. Different men would come to visit her, but I couldn't say whether she had a solid relationship or not. She was behaving nicely towards us and wages were always paid on time. She would understand whenever I had an issue and she wasn't stiff at all. The manager was also Italian and his name was Dario. He was nice, but sometimes, he would really annoy me with his advances. He had the bad habit of always touching my behind when there was no one around, and I would always slap his hand. He seemed a macho, he was always speaking half Italian, half Romanian. I explained to him several times that I felt no attraction whatsoever towards him, but he just didn't seem able to understand! End of story! It was like I was speaking to him in a foreign language. He had screwed almost every girl working at the tavern, but it seemed as though we was playing them with his words and they didn't seem to mind it, not to mention that they would sometimes wonder which of them would Dario would end up at on the night. To me, it seemed funny.

- Eva, you haven't tried him yet?, a girl in the kitchen once asked me.

- No, and I don't plan to!, I replied with a smile on my face.

- You should! He's not bad at all and, believe me, the oral sex… it drives you crazy.

- Oh God! I don't want to know. Please, Sonia, keep these matters to yourself.

- Well, why do you feel so ashamed? It's quite normal. Don't tell me you don't like oral sex being performed on you, because I don't believe you!

I was all blushing and I couldn't believe the conversation I was having with a person who knew next to nothing about me.

- Come on, tell me! Stop pussyfooting!, she continued, displaying a low smile, as she was coming towards me, like she wanted to look me straight in the eye.

- I don't see anything funny in this and I don't see why you're laughing! I don't like talking about this.

- Come on, dear, you sound like you're not even a woman! Better yet, we should talk about princes and princesses! I haven't seen anything like it…

- I am indeed not yet a woman! I'm still a miss!

- A miss? No! I don't believe you! How old are you, Eva?

- I'm 18.

- My God, you're a treasure! She took me by the hand and started to spin me around, while analyzing me from head to toe. Are you really serious?

- Of course I am, what reason would I have to lie to you?

- Mind you, you have my appreciation! Still, time is flying and you don't know what an orgasm is. Mamma Mia! You haven't experienced ecstasy yet!

I was even more ashamed, so I went to do some dishes. She continued to chat.

- I heard the word "orgasm" and I knew that was my cue to be here!, Dario came in from the room next to us.

- Dario, you won't believe this! Eva is a virgin!

- Sonia, please, stop this nonsense of a conversation! It's my life and I don't like it when someone tries to analyze it!

- Come on, dear, no one analyzed your life! I just spoke a truth! Why do you get so worked up about it? I think I understand the issue now! You're missing… how should I put this nicely… some dick… Dario, what are you waiting for? Help her understand what absolute happiness is!

I could see her making fun of me and I felt a surge of anger. I blacked out. I jumped her and grabbed her by the neck, pushing her against the door frame.

- I told you to leave me alone. And not just once, but several times. Say my name one more time and you're dead! Is that clear?

She was grasping my hands and she went all red. Dario was a statue. He probably could not believe that I, the gentle and quiet girl, had just turned the poor cook lady into putty, with tears in her eyes.

- And you, I said to the Italian, if you touch my bum one more time, you're dead, too! Understood?

They were both staying still while I took my apron off, threw it on a table and went outside. I lit a cigarette and left for home. It had been a long day, and the last half an hour had been more intense than the rest. What made it so difficult for them to leave me alone when I was leaving everyone else alone?

Somehow, the heated discussion in the restaurant kitchen raised some questions in my mind. I sometimes felt the need to be touched and kissed, particularly when watching movies with erotic scenes. There were plenty of men hitting on me, older as well as younger, but none of them had been able to persuade me to even go out for dinner. I was similar to a robot with a very well-determined schedule. I wouldn't deviate from my route. Back in school, I had Robert, a classmate who was trying quite often to convince me to go on a date. My permanent excuse was that I was busy and had no time for dating. However, after asking me several times to just go out for a movie, I accepted to him coming to my house and watch a movie together. I didn't want to go to his house because there was a risk of giving him hopes higher than he would have expected, and I wasn't really in the mood to go out!

- We're on for Friday, right?, he asked for the tenth time just before exiting the school.

- Yes, Robert, we are. Tomorrow at 9.00 PM. I told you before!

- I know, I just wanted to make sure you haven't forgotten about it. Can I have the address?

- You can have it tomorrow, when we met each other at school again. I felt like bursting into laughter and couldn't believe how desperate he was.

- Don't forget to call in at the restaurant so they know you're not going, otherwise they might be upset with you!

- You do think of everything! I'll let them know today. You realize the effort I'm putting in this – I'm giving up a day of work just to watch a movie with you.

- Thank you! I'll make it up to you, one way or another!

I looked at my watch and realized it was time for me to hurry up, I was meant to pick the kids up from nursery and I was never late. I put my earphones in and called Dana, while walking rapidly.

- Lollipop, what are you up to? I loved to call her that.

- I'm fine, lollipop! Selling underwear to ugly crones.

- Ha, you're mean! That's us in a few years!

- No, no, we'll be beautiful crones! Are you done with school?

- Yes, I am, I'm heading for the nursery now. I wanted to ask you something.

- Shoot!

- I couldn't ditch Robert, a schoolmate, so I invited him at our place to watch a movie. And I was wondering if I could ask you to leave us alone for some time!

- Wow, my dear, this really makes me the happiest girl on the planet. It's time for you to join womanhood, I can prepare some candles, if you want! Anything, just to make you happy!

- Don't be mean! I just invited him for a movie!

- I'm not mean! Look, I'll sleep over at Claudio. It's tomorrow evening, right?

- Claudio? Who's that? Where did he come from? Yes, the date is tomorrow night.

- Did I not tell you? Let me share this with you quickly, just to get you a little horny and start you off for tomorrow evening.

- You're mean again! Tell me!

- Claudio is the manager of the underwear shops in the mall and I met him about two weeks ago, at the monthly meeting.

- You're nuts, Dana! You need a manager?

- Come on, Eva, you're getting too serious again! Just listen! The lad is amazing, well dressed, expensive clothes, the works!

- Is he not married?

- He is, but she's away for months. They also have a company in Italy, and she comes out here quite rarely. And slow down! I'm not marrying him, you know! We just rejoice our bodies. Well… more like me his body, and he's rejoicing my pocket!

- My God, Dana, you've gone completely insane!

- Eva, can you please stop with that? This is the reality, I fuck his brains out, he pays me well. Do you want me to lie to you? Still, he's almost 50, you don't really think I could be attracted by anything at that age! Anyway, he's good looking, he's working out at the gym quite a lot.

- You're crazy, but you know I'm here for you, no matter what! And if that's what you want, then… let this be it.

- Well, yes… for the time being, it's better than nothing. In two weeks, I'm going on holiday with him!

- Really??

- Yes, in Barcelona! He has some meetings and said he would take me with him. Shall I ask him to find someone for you, too, so you can come along with us? She was roaring with laughter when pronouncing this proposal.

- No, no, I'm fine! I don't want to go to Barcelona, for now!

- Wait! Just one more thing and I'm off, the shop is getting busy.

- Come on, be quick about it, I'm at the nursery in a few minutes, too!

- Do you know how I picked him up?

- How? You jumped him?

- Noooo! I went over, introduced myself and asked him to go to his office and talk about my employment contract.

- And?

- And… we did. I let him sit on his comfortable chair, then I approached his ear and asked him whether he wanted to fuck.

- You're out of your mind!

- I saw him reach for his pants, turned towards me and said: "Yes, I do! What do you want in exchange?" I said I didn't want anything for now, just some attention once in a while. I missed having sex and that was all there was to it.

- God, Dana, you can be so crazy sometimes! You're scaring me!

- One more thing, quickly! I let him give it to me from behind on the office. To tell you the truth, the old man was kind of slow, but he was pretty steady. It's big enough and at least I felt something! That's it! You can tell me tomorrow how big is Robert's.

- Forget it, you've really managed to put me in a state… I'm just here to pick up the kids… and you've been telling me about sex and everything else! Come on, I'm here, you mad woman!

- Kisses, Virgin Mary! She hung up bursting with laughter.

Dana was dealing with sex as if it was something usual, while to me, it was a taboo. She never avoided telling about it, at least not to me. Whenever she wanted a man, she would go over to him and tell him directly, or she would just make him come to her, and so on. Her issues in the foster home must have impacted her in this regard. She had tried so many times to persuade me to use a vibrator or teach me to masturbate, but I didn't even want to hear about it. I was dreaming of a first beautiful love night, with a gentle and calm man. Perhaps, like Robert? The thought was torturing me, but I had no feelings towards him! It was merely curiosity starting to hover around and I wanted to find out what sex was like. I would consider Robert more of a friend, but I can't deny I enjoyed the way he was looking at me.

- Eva!!! They were both running towards me.
- Lucas, Isa – I'm here to pick you up. Come on, get your bags and anything else you have up and get on the bike!

I took one by a hand, the other in my other hand and I started slightly biting them, alternatively. They were laughing happily and I, in turn, was glad to see this.

The route to their home was a route of festivity, singing and quarreling. They loved arguing with each other, but I would quickly reunite them and tell them how lucky they were to have each other. They couldn't understand what that meant, but when they loved each other, it was true love.

I made up their usual schedule and was happy to see Kate arrive home earlier. I loved talking to her and it seemed that I had a lot of things to learn from her. She was an extremely positive woman and would always encourage me to study, fight, never give up and end up a successful woman. She didn't know too much about me, I managed to tell her that every Sunday, I would visit my mother in hospital, and she had attempted to ask me why my mother was there, but I didn't have the heart to answer here. She immediately realized it was a topic I didn't want to discuss and understood the situation. She said I could ask for her help or advice, should I need it, and we stopped there. Before leaving, I stopped in the door.

- Kate, may I ask you something?
- Of course you may, Eva!
- What age were you when you lost your virginity? Barely had I uttered those words that I soon realized how stupid I could be. What got into me, asking such a question? God! I'm sorry, Kate, I don't know where that came from!
- Eva, don't worry. To be honest, you caught me by surprise with this question! She gently smiled and went on. But it's nothing uncommon.
- Forgive me, please! I asked because I think you are a great person and I wish to be like you, in a few years' time. Have a family, a career, a life similar to yours, and I'm really scared of making mistakes.
- Never say you want a life similar to someone else's, because you can never know what's underneath a person's mask. Sometimes, things seem nicer than they really are.
- What do you mean, Kate?
- Nothing, Eva. Now is not the time to chat, I need to go and bath the children. Someday, we'll sit down for a coffee. Alright?
- Alright. Thank you!
- Oh! She turned back, because she had already left for the children's room. Let me just answer that for you. I lost my virginity at 14. On a terribly cold weather, in an apartment building. It was horrible! I advise you to choose something nice for the first time, that's because from what I understand, this first time has not yet occurred. And you know why? Because you will remember it for your entire life. And if you're wondering whether you're at the right age, well… I don't know how many girls who are still virgins at 18. I'm off, it's getting late for the children.
- You're amazing, Kate! Thank you!
- Talk to you later!

I stood in the door for a while and heard her sing the bath song to the children. I loved this woman and wanted a lot to, one day, have children of my own and be a mother just like she was: dedicated, attentive and calm. Just like my mother had been, during my childhood.

The short conversation with Kate had given me food for thought. Their life seemed perfect and I could not imagine them having problems. Or perhaps it wasn't about problems between themselves, but just some other sort of things. Realistically speaking, I hadn't had too much time to analyze them. As Boris was away most of the time, I would only get to see them separately, with the children. Perhaps that was her problem, the fact that her husband was not spending enough time with the family. Be as it may, I still couldn't understand her. She had something not many women have: a family. And, in addition to that, she also had a great job.

In my attempt to find answers to the questions concerning Kate's life, I arrived at the restaurant. Carla was behind the counter, checking the money. She loved to do that a few times a day. She would remove them from the cash register and stick them in her bra. She was usually wearing long skirts without any pockets. In spite of that, it seemed funny enough and I would have wanted to ask her why she was doing that.

- Hello, Carla!, I said, in passing, while I was heading to the back to get changed.

- Eva, how are you?

I removed my earphones and gazed at her. She usually didn't talk to me unless she needed something or wanted to ask me a few things.

- I'm fine, I'm getting ready for work.

- Good for you, I wanted to ask you something! Just as I suspected earlier, I said to myself, she wanted something from me.

- Yes, go on!

- Do you think you could work a shift on Sunday? One of the girls asked me for a day off.

- Carla, I'm really sorry, you know I need my Sundays off. I would have definitely helped you on another day, but I can't.

- Can you not make an exception? You know I wouldn't be asking if it wasn't an emergency!

I suddenly remembered I was meant to ask her for tomorrow evening off. Be as it may, I was visiting my mother this Sunday and I didn't want to miss that. The moments I was spending with her were silent, but really important to me. I kept hoping that one time, I would go to her and she would recognize me. What if that moment would come this Sunday?

- Earth to Eva!, she interrupted me abruptly.

- I was just wondering how to work this out. I could come in this Sunday, and this Sunday only, but then, I would need tomorrow evening off. Is that OK?

- That sounds perfect! Have you got a date? Come on, tell me.

- No, no, I don't! I felt myself blushing. I just have some errands to run for school, that's all.

- Whatever you say, but just know that your eyes are glittering.

My eyes were glittering? What a crazy woman! Why would my eyes glitter? Because I'm seeing Robert? Especially since I don't have any feelings for him. Or was it just the hormones striking a clear reflection in my eyes? It was absurd, anyhow!

I was feeling guilty for not going to see my mother that week. I was having all sorts of thoughts. In a way, I knew it made no difference to her, but to me, it was the first time I was about to miss a visit. I called to let them know I wouldn't be able to come in that Sunday. The lady at the other end of the phone assured me that it was fine and that I could go and visit the following week. Even as it was, I still wasn't feeling well.

- Where is it that you can't go, dear?, Dario appeared behind me.

- Do you know it's rude to listen to other people's conversations?

- What would you have me do, then? Cover my ears up because Princess Eva is on the phone? Come on, don't be so serious, you sound like you were 50, not 17!

- I'm 18, but thanks anyway!

- Oh, even better! Do you want to come by my place tonight and have a glass of wine? Or for some pasta. My pasta is… finger-licious!

- No, but thanks for the invitation!

- You're so mean! There will come a time when you'll be begging me to come over and I won't be so willing then!

- Yes, definitely, I'm sure of that! Just wait for it! Come on, please, let me get changed, it's getting busy.

- Shall I come and give you a hand?

- God, you're unbelievable! NO!

I slammed the door in his face and heard him mumble something. He was truly annoying and irritating. I had no idea what the other girls could see in him, but to me, he was disgusting. Perhaps he was truly good between the sheets, otherwise I couldn't explain the girls' attitude in any way.

I finally managed to get changed and get down to work. I had plenty of thoughts: mother, Kate, Robert… I felt sorry I had accepted him coming over to my house, particularly because that meant I had to give up the Sunday spent with my mother. I felt no attraction towards him, so I was more certain than ever that nothing would happen. Sometimes, I failed to understand myself. My thoughts were heading in a direction, but my actions were heading the opposite way. My only consolation was that I could finally have a Friday off, at home. A movie never hurt anyone. I deserved to have some time off, once in a while.

- Eva, wake up! The order at table 15! The customer is screaming like mad!

- Yes, coming! I was on slow motion and was feeling quite disoriented.

I took the plates from the kitchen and brought them over to the restless gentleman.

- I'm terribly sorry for having made you wait. We're a little crowded. Pizza is here! Would you like some sauce, too?

- You're very beautiful!

- What? "I'm a man magnet now?", I said to myself.

- You're beautiful! It was merely a compliment!

- Thank you. That's really kind of you. Would you like anything else?

- Could I get your phone number?

- Sorry, but I don't think that's suitable!

- Please!

I wanted to leave when he grabbed me by the hand.

- Wait a minute! I don't bite, you know! He stood up and reached for his pocket. Here, take my card and call me. Or text me. Whichever suits you! I won't harm you!

- Sir…

- Call me Elan. Here, take my card. You won't be sorry, all I want is to talk! That's all!

He had such a calm voice that I couldn't believe he wasn't irritating, like all the other men hitting on me. I took a glance at his business card, which said "Lawyer Elan Dimitrias". I placed it in my back pocket and smiled politely.

- Enjoy your meal!

- Thanks! I'll be waiting, you know!

I went to the back and started looking at him from there. He was really attractive. He must have been around 25-27. Dark hair, black eyes. He would talk on the phone quite a lot and write emails. He was dressed in a navy tux, with his shirt unbuttoned at the top two buttons. What could such an elegant man be doing in that dump? I mean, the place was famous for the good food, but still! I looked at his business card again and I couldn't believe that everything around me was sexuality! Why? What was I doing wrong?

- Eva!! You seem pretty dazed up tonight! Dario scared the hell out of me, again.

- My God, I can't get rid of you today, can I? What's your problem with me today?

- I don't have any problems with you, just that we're really busy and you're into table flirting, from what I can see!

- What?!

- Come on! I saw you!

- You're a jerk! Honestly!

Quite so, I seemed to be a little bit dazed up and a butter-fingers that evening. All night, I avoided Mr. Elan's table and pretended not to see him. I noticed him trying to chat up two more waitresses and I soon realized that was his mode of operation, hitting on everyone. And, I wondered, the truth was that I could never see myself interested in such a man. I went to the back, took the business card out of my pocket and threw it straight in the bin. I was somewhat sad, but why? I was interested in a man at a table. And I was displaying signs of jealousy when I saw him talk to other girls. What a load of crap! "Eva, come off your high horse!", I said to myself. I looked in the mirror, slapped myself twice, and headed for the kitchen. When taking the food into the restaurant again, I took an unsuspecting look at his table. He had left. I was even sadder. I liked seeing him there. I took the food to the tables and tried to put on a smile for the poor customers. They had no fault whatsoever!

I prepared myself a coffee, took out a cigarette and signaled Carla that I was going for a smoke. She nodded positively. I had my own little spot, across the restaurant, on a small curb. I would always smoke 2 cigarettes at a time, while checking my Facebook, my Instagram… I would, at times, reply to a message or two, although there weren't too many people I had the habit of talking to. Robert had sent me 3 identical messages, 20 minutes apart.

Robert: "Did you give up the restaurant?"

Me: "No, unfortunately, we need to cancel."

Robert: "Please, don't do this! You promised!"

Me: "There's nothing I can do, they won't let me off tomorrow."

Robert: "I can come over and talk them. Would you like me to?"

Me: "And what exactly would you tell them? Could Eva please get some time off so we can spend Friday evening together? Calm down, it's sorted! I was just messing with you."

Robert: "Well, that's a relief! At one point, I thought you were serious. I'll see you in school tomorrow, anyway!

I dropped the phone when raising my eye sight and seeing before me a black car, with the window down, and driven by Elan.

- Not even on my way home can I get rid of you, can I?, he smiled shrewdly.

I didn't know what to answer, so I just had one long smoke.

- Why do you smoke? You're so beautiful, it's a shame about your skin!

Again, I failed to reply.

- Cat got your tongue, Eva?

- How do you know my name?

- Ah, well, so she speaks! You're phone's ringing!

My phone was on the ground. Robert was constantly writing to me, and now, Dana was calling me, as well.

- Do you want to get in the car, so we can chat a little? I won't try anything, I promise!

- I can't, I need to get back to work!

- Did you save my phone number?

- Yes, I did…

- Show me!

The feelings going through my body were unbelievable. I wanted to leave but, at the same time, I wanted to go, too. I wanted to tell him to leave me alone, but at the same time, I wanted him to insist. What a strange mix of feelings!

- How should I show you?

- Show me where you saved the number!

- Well, I have it on your business card.

- Show me the business card!

- It's in my purse.

- Alright, then, you give me your phone number and I'll write you my number down, so you don't have to bother looking for the card in your purse.

It was as though this man had seen me throw away his card. That was really strange!

- Could I please have it?

I gave it to him and waited for him to drive off, then I joyously left towards the restaurant. I was forcing myself to look serious, but I felt like dancing. I had no idea why, but that was exactly how I felt. Had I fallen in love? Were these the famous butterflies in the stomach? What strange and amazing feelings!

I still had two hours of my shift left. I was holding my phone in my pocket as though I was waiting for Elan to contact me. But every time the phone was vibrating, I would find that it was Robert again. What a bummer! I wasn't in the mood for him.

I quickly went over to the rubbish bin and stuck my hand inside to take the business card out. Why, oh why, had I tore it?

- Eva, have you begun looking for rubbish?

- Dario, leave me alone! I'm not in the mood.

I put the small pieces in my pocket with the intention of sticking them back together, at home.

I ran home from work. I couldn't wait to stick back together the business card. I was feeling really funny. My heart was pounding and I would check my phone every ten seconds.

Robert was driving me crazy with his texts and kept asking whether I was alright. I was fine, of course, but I just wasn't in the mood to reply. I could talk to him at school, in the morning. At one point, Dana called me to inquire about what time I would be getting home. I was really disappointed to find that it wasn't him. So now, there was a "he" in my mind and that was the reason why it all seemed so strange. If I closed my eyes, it seemed as though I couldn't even properly remember his face, but I was thinking about "him" like I was crazy. I could only remember the shirt unbuttoned at the top two buttons and that was enough to fuel the fantasies in my mind.

- Finally, you're home! Come on, I just barely managed to ditch Claudio! He is already starting to piss me off!

- Wow, you are nuts! A moment ago, you were telling me that you're about to elope together and go to Barcelona, and now he's pissing you off?

- I do want to see Barcelona, but I don't want to see him all the time. It's enough that I see him at work. Then again, how many times a day do you reckon we can bang? He really thinks he's charming. Ouch… you didn't take the washing out? She was struggling to remove the clothes from the washing machine, and texting with her other hand.

- Leave them, I'll do it now! I haven't had the time to. Who are you chatting with?

- An agent! I want us to move to an apartment, just by ourselves. I can't stand seeing these girls around.

- With what? I can't afford to pay a higher rent!

- I'll pay the difference, but at least it will just be the two of us. Look at this! You're coming here tomorrow with that boy, and what are you going to do? You won't even be able to scream! Lol… Come on, don't be ashamed, it will hurt the first time!

- Dana, what are you on about? We're just going to watch a movie and that's it.

- Eva, not even Lucas is going to believe that story. Let's be honest! It makes sense! Anyway, make him wear a condom. You never know…

- Please, stop it! Nothing is going to happen! You'll see!

- I really don't know what to believe. I think perhaps you might not be aware of it, or you just didn't realize it yet, but you may be a lesbian. Come on, tell me…

Dana and her bad jokes. She placed her arm around my neck and we both headed to the kitchen. She kept teasing me and saying all kind of silly things. I sat on the chair next to the window and lit a cigarette.

- All you do is smoke all day! You're annoying! You should quit!

That instantly reminded me of Elan. That was what he had told me. Where had he come from, all of a sudden, before me, in the street? Had he perhaps followed me? Was he just waiting for me to come out of the restaurant? What could he be doing now? Why wasn't he calling me?

- Eva!! I'm talking to you!! What's going on in your head?

- Sorry, I'm just tired.

- Tell me, what were you thinking about? Was it Robert? She giggled…

- You're mad! I wasn't thinking of Robert, no! I was thinking it would be awesome for the both of us to move into a flat. I wish I was earning more so that we could live in a large flat, just like in the movies.

- That's exactly where we'll be living! Just be patient, I think next week, probably on Monday or Tuesday, we're moving. I found something great downtown, I hope they accept our offer. This agent is really cool. I promised to invite him over to our new apartment, if we can move. Oh, and I told him we would both be here to protect him from the darkness! He then burst into laughter. I also told him you were a virgin and he looked so amazed. No one actually believes this!

- Dana, do you really need to talk to everyone about my sex life?

- Your non-existent sex life, you mean. Of course! I boast to everyone about having a virgin friend. What's the big deal? Your phone is ringing in your bag.

I hit the ceiling, I was certain Elan was calling me. In my crazy rush to reach the phone quicker, I managed to knock over the juice bottle. I shut my eyes before actually looking at the caller. I then glanced at the screen. It was a number I had not saved, it must have been him!

- Hello!, I answered poor-spiritedly, just as if waiting for him to say the first Hello.

- Eva?

- Yes, it's me! Who's this?

- It's Robert! I suddenly felt the overwhelming disappointment in my body.

- Hey, what number is this?

- I borrowed a friend's phone. My battery is dead and I thought I'd call and see if you got home safely.

- Yes, I'm home. Don't worry. I'll see you tomorrow, in school.

- Eva?

- Yes, Robert.

- I can't wait to come over tomorrow.

I went silent and gulped. All I wanted then was for him to not come over anymore. I didn't even want to speak to him on the phone anymore.

- Can you hear me?, he went on.

- Yes, I can! See you tomorrow. Kisses!

I hung up without allowing him to say anything else. I went back to the kitchen, while checking my phone. I still had no texts.

- Are you so desperate to talk to this boy? You stormed the room!

- Forgive me! You should have let me wipe the stove clean. Have you, by any chance, got a roll of tape in the house?

- Tape? Of course not! I'm not even going to school! If you haven't got any, how should I?

- Should I ask these girls? What do you think?

- What in God's name would they be using tape for? Stick their lips together while chatting online? Right!

- You're a lunatic! She made me laugh like crazy.

- What came into you, though? What do you need the tape for?

- I want to stick something back together. Nothing important. I'm off to take a shower.

I entered the bathroom and locked the door, then quickly took out the pieces of paper and started placing them on the toilet seat. I tried to place them together, like a puzzle, and eventually, I managed to re-create his business card.

Elan Dimitris – Lawyer – AEDUS & Associates – elan@aedus.com – and a phone number.

I had everything I needed. I saved his phone number in my phone and I reflected for a while on whether to call him or not. In the end, I promised not to call him if I had no sign from him, either. I had only seen him for a few minutes and already I was anxious to call him. It was all very strange. It had never happened to me before. I Googled the law firm. It seemed to be quite a large one. Was indeed my desire to become a lawyer pushing me towards him? It couldn't have been that because I felt butterflies in my stomach when he pulled up his car, in front of me, without knowing too much about him. It was something else. A part of me was warning me not to fall in love. I had often said to myself that all men are the same. All sorts of memories involving my father were going through my head. Bad memories. The beatings my mother had endured, the childhood screams were a true wake-up call for me. I had no need for a man in my life, that part of me was saying that I should remain alone for the rest of my life.

- Is someone in the bathroom? The knocks on the door gave me quite a scare.

- Yes, I'm fine! I'm just taking a shower and I'll be right out!

One of the two flat-mates woke me up from this nightmare where all women were battered and suffering for their entire lives, accompanied by a child. But suddenly, my thoughts took me to Kate. She has two wonderful children and Boris doesn't seem to beat her up. Perhaps there are still some good men left! Perhaps there is a chance for this Elan to turn out to be a wonderful man, whom I can fall in love with, get married, have children and be both lawyers. I started to dream at a distant future without realizing that I was in the bathroom of our quite small flat, still wearing my work clothes, and that there were three more people waiting outside, to take a shower. I stood up and watched myself in the mirror. I swiftly washed my face and told myself that I had to wake up to reality.

I had been waiting all night for Elan to get in touch. I had a few attempts to write to him myself, but I promised myself I would wait at least until Monday. I didn't want to seem desperate but, at the same time, I was truly frightened of these feelings. It was weird for me to feel like I did, particularly for a man whom I knew nothing about and whom I had seen for only a few minutes. I fell asleep holding my phone and I woke up for every notification I got. Robert was pestering me with his texts, and nothing else of interest.

I jumped in the shower and tried to get this whole story out of my head. I put my clothes on quite quickly and headed for the kitchen. I turned the coffee machine on while lighting a cigarette. I could see the morning rush as I gazed though the window. I loved having my coffee by the window and watch the people. Each of them would tell me their own story. I loved analyzing couples' behaviors and imagine just what everyone was thinking. Once in a while, I could see a lady past her 60s. People in this category were never in a rush. They would mind their own business, admire the trees, smile warmly and were looking for a place to chat with a neighbor or perhaps just with a simple passer-by. People at my age were really agitated. Phone in one hand, coffee in the other, earphones in, they would only cross the street along non-permitted routes and didn't seem to want to smile ever. They were most of the times sad, or should I say, very focused. I would most certainly look like one of them when stepping out of the apartment building.

Ever since Dana had told me we would be moving, I was displeased by everything in the house. The presence of the other girls was a torment, too. My early morning moment of serenity had been interrupted by the screams of one of them, in the next room. Who could be doing video-chat at 7.00 AM? Only someone desperate for money or someone sexually obsessed. I was sorry I hadn't gone out for my run, but it was too late already. I was meant to leave for school. It was that period of tests and I hadn't studied too much. I was sorry I had wasted all evening thinking about Mr. Elan, instead of just grabbing a book to read.

- Eva, how are you? I've been calling you!, Robert jumped me ever since I stepped in the school grounds.

- Pardon me, Robert, but you're suffocating me with all those phone calls and texts. Relax! It's like you've gone crazy. Honestly, now!

- Sorry, I was just thrilled and wanted to see how you were doing. I'll stop calling if it's bothering you.

- It's not that, it's more of the fact that you're acting like a child and seem so desperate!

- Right, then, should I still come by tonight? I need to know what to do!

His question gave some food for thought. Did I still want him to come over that evening or not? It took me a while to answer, during which time he was looking at me with a baffled expression.

- Yes, I'll be waiting!

I needed to spend time with someone in order to stop thinking about all the nonsense. After all, I had given up the Sunday with my mom just to see this boy. At the same time, I knew an evening along would have been nice, watching a movie on the couch.

- Ok, then, I'll be there around 09.30 PM! Which wine should I bring?

- I'll leave it to you to decide.

It really made no importance to me the kind of wine he would bring as I wasn't a connoisseur, nor did I enjoy drinking wine. I would have told him not to bring any wine, but that would have probably upset him even more. The poor boy was in no way guilty of my lunatic conditions – first, I wanted him to come over, the next second, I didn't! And so on.

In school, I tried to avoid Robert and sat at my desk, lonely. I made all sorts of notes and, during recess, I was trying to learn a little bit more for history or geography. I couldn't wait to go and see Lucas and Isa. I was hoping to catch Kate, even just for a bit. The conversation I had with her yesterday wasn't enough and it managed to leave a few unanswered questions. I think that finding out that she and Boris aren't fine would have been truly disappointing. Still, I refused to believe that.

At 2.00 PM, I finished classes and ran off to the nursery. Robert tried to have a conversation with me, but I told him I'd see him that evening and that I didn't have time on my hands just then. I didn't feel like talking to anybody else. I had gone into a bad mood and no one could understand me when I got into one of those. Dana would always say, whenever I was upset, only the stars would understand me. She couldn't grasp how I was able to shift from one state to another so rapidly. And, most of the times, the reasons I was giving her seemed childish.

I picked the kids up from nursery and got home with them. I changed their clothes and quickly put them to bed. Like never before, Lucas didn't want to sleep at all. He asked me to tell him all sorts of stories and play with his favorite train. When I thought I finally managed to trick him into playing with a toy and leave me alone, he would then appear right behind me and ask me to sit next to him. The poor boy needed attention and I was love-struck. I left my thoughts behind and started to play down to him. Eventually, it did me a lot of good. Children have the power to disconnect you from whatever is bad by taking you on a journey into their world. I let myself be drawn into his world, with toy cars and small trains. I noticed his moves and soon realized he was trying to copy his father. I hadn't seen it happen until then, but it was funny seeing him try and sit on the armchair, one foot above the other, and his hand on his forehead.

- How are you, Lucas?

- I'm fine! I'm thinking!, and he would rub his forehead, in a funny way.

- What are you thinking about?

- All these issues…

- Come on, Lucas, what issues are on your mind?

- Plenty, but I can't tell you about them!

- Come on, tell me! I'm here to listen, you know you can talk to me about anything.

- Promise not to tell anyone?

- I promise! And I showed him my hands so he wouldn't think I had my fingers crossed. It was one of our little secrets, whenever we would promise something, we would raise our hands and say: "I promise!"

- Alright, I'll tell you! And the lowered his childish voice and started whispering. I really like a girl at the nursery!

He came off the armchair and snugged up next to me, on the carpet. He had given up the idea of being like his father and he would soon return to being the small and cute boy he was.

- And she's always playing with another boy. And I don't know what to do. How should I draw her attention?

I couldn't believe that he had such issues, at his age. After all, attraction is something normal and it can happen, irrespective of the age, I said to myself. It's true, his question did confuse me somewhat, considering the situation I was in myself. My state of mind wasn't the most suitable for this conversation, but I tried to answer him nicely.

- You need to ignore her!

- What does "ignore" mean?

- It means not to mind her. Don't look at her at all and let her think that you completely forgot about her.

- Really? You think that's a good idea?

I couldn't believe the stupid things I was teaching this young boy. Instead of teaching him to love, show his feelings, let his actions unravel, I was teaching him to be prude from this young age. But, in the end, who could have told what the correct option was? I would rather I knew it myself.

- Yes, I do! But sometimes, it is also best to act on your feelings! I was confusing myself, let alone the little boy.

- Well, sometimes I feel like hugging her really hard and give her a kiss. But you're saying it would be best not to mind her. How should I proceed?

This time, he had really confused me and I didn't know what to tell him. Who was I to give him advice, though?

- Lucas, do you know what I think? I think you should ask your mother. She will know best what to do. OK?

- No! You promised you wouldn't tell anyone!

- Don't worry, I'm not telling if you don't want me to! I figured she could perhaps give you a more elaborate answer. But you know what? My opinion is that it would be best not to mind her! And she will come and play with you by herself. Try it out tomorrow and see how it goes. How about it?

- Yes, I'll do that! Give me five!

He held his hand out towards me and gave me a strong hi-five. It was like one of our little signals whenever we were feeling good or agreed to something.

- Let's wake Isa and go to the park!

- No-no! I've spoken to Isa and we agreed to watch Snow White today. I told her I would be the prince. And he grabbed a sword from next to the couch and started to imitate riding a horse and striking anything standing in his way with the sword.

- Are you sure? Still, be careful not to break something!

I barely finished talking and Lucas was already in Isa's room, trying to wake her up. The poor girl, dismayed after a long and sweet sleep, finally began to smile when hearing about cartoons. I quickly changed her into more practical clothes and I left both of them on the couch. They asked me to make them some popcorn and I didn't hesitate. I knew that would give me some peace and quiet, at least for about half an hour.

It was 5.30 PM when I heard a car park outside the house. It was probably Kate, the children's mother, who had come home earlier, which made me really happy because I would have been able to leave earlier and perhaps Kate would have even offered me a few minutes before leaving, just to have a quick chat. The discussion we had yesterday was troubling me.

- Good evening, children!, Boris said upon entering the house. Hi, Eva!

- Daddy, daddy! They both jumped him while he came in. Did you bring us any goodies?

- Well, let's have a look in the bag, shall we? Have you found any goodies in there?

Barely had he managed to put his bag down that both of them rushed to rummage it.

- You won't find anything in there, I tricked you! Come on, give daddy a kiss and I'll give you your presents! Come on, let's have that kiss!

A child's joy cannot be compared to anything else. They were so happy for getting a lollipop and so, they kissed Boris until he turned red. I let them enjoy themselves and went to the kitchen to grab my things. Holding both children in his arms, Boris followed me.

- Eva, please, would you be able to stick around until 6.30 PM – 7.00 PM, just to help me cook dinner, and then, you may go. Kate is going to be a little bit tonight!

- Yes, of course, no problem!

- Are you sure you won't be late for the restaurant? I wouldn't want you to get in trouble!

- Well… no, it's fine, don't worry!

- Thank you!

I wasn't going to the restaurant that night, but I wasn't going to tell Boris of my plans, either. Our relationship was quite cold and we would barely meet. He seemed quite communicative, but it seemed that there was a barrier in any discussions held with him, out of respect for Kate. That was how I imagined any of my relationship with the boyfriend or husband of any female person known to me should be. I didn't know whether it was right, but I tried to avoid him as much as possible.

I let him prepare dinner, while I was watching the children in the living room. We played all sorts of games, until eventually Boris finished cooking.

- Eva, would you like to have dinner with us?

- No, thank you, but I do need to go!

- I made some great pasta. Are you sure you don't want any?

- Well, perhaps some other time! I'm sure however that these two will eat all their pasta! Am I right, children?

- Yes, we will!, they both shouted in one voice.

I sat them at the table and said my goodbyes. I put my jacket on, earphones in and headed for the subway. I wanted to prepare something to eat, for when Robert would come by. The fridge was usually empty, so I had to stop at the shop at the corner of the street before going home.

I had already received two more messages from Robert, who wanted to make sure that I haven't forgotten about our date. I asked him what he wanted to have for dinner and he said that anything was fine. I insisted until we both reached the compromise of ordering some sushi. It was easier, I had no cooking to do, which gave me more time in the shower. I loved staying in the shower and the water pouring all over my body. The water had to be really hot and I would stay there until my skin was so reddish as if I was a crab.

The intercom bell made me put my cigarette out halfway through. Robert had arrived. In a strange way, I was happy to see him. I was starting to somewhat forget about Elan and I promised myself to relax a little, whilst I had the chance. Dana made good on her promise and didn't come home. She kept sending me all sorts of funny texts. She was certain that my first night of passionate love was to take place. I knew nothing was going to happen and didn't even bother replying to her.
- Eventually, I brought white wine – Pino Grigo. I thought it would go well with the Sushi!, Robert was standing in the doorway, all smiles. It's nice to see you!
- You, too! Come on in! We'll go to the kitchen and open the wine and, after that, we'll go to the bedroom. I have no idea when the other girls will be home.
- Oh, is it not just Dana living here with you?
- No, it's not, there are two more girls living here, as well, but next week, we're moving somewhere else, just the two of us.

I turned my back to him, just to open the bottle. I felt his eyes completely looking at my body and there was a storm of hormones crowding up the room. If it were up to him, I think he would have barely come in and go straight into the room, to bang me. For a man, it must be something natural. All this quiet and the fact that I knew my body shapes were being analyzed top to bottom was giving me a funny state: nice and annoying, at the same time.
- I can't open it. Will you help me?, I turned towards him, just to try and change the situation.
- Yes, of course! Pass me the bottle! How was your day?
- Same old. Just the usual things. You?
- Nothing much. Just waiting to come over. Cheers!
- Cheers! What shall we toast to?
- To love!
- Well, you're funny! To love it is, then!

This love is understood differently by a man and a woman. Or, at least, that's what every man around me was letting me think. They would only see it as sex, while I was seeing it as something unique.

- Shall we go to the bedroom? The Sushi order is coming soon and we'll eat there!
- Oh, yes, the bedroom! You inviting me to your bedroom sounds amazing!
- I would love to have other three rooms where to invite you, but unfortunately, the only room exclusively mine is this one.

I opened the door and welcomed him to my humble abode. Well, mine and Dana's, but even so, that was my private place. A double bed, two nightstands, a small wardrobe and a desk. I also had a small television set on the desk, but most of the times, I was using the laptop. The laptop was now connected to the TV set in order to make it easier to watch a movie.

- Your room is really nice. Well, both of yours. I see pictures of Dana here, too.
- Yes, it's both our room. Please stay on the right-hand side of the bed, this is my side. I would have also liked to have a sofa, but… perhaps in the next flat. I have the desk chair here, that is, if you're not comfortable sitting next to me in bed!
- I definitely want to sit next to you!
He literally jumped in bed next to me and approached my ear with his nose. I felt a shiver down my spine, but failed to say anything. He looked at me for a second, as if asking for permission, and then he started kissing me. He got completely on top of me and snuck his hand under my shirt. I didn't oppose. I kissed him back passionately and surrounded his body with my feet. I felt his hands reaching for my breasts. I was getting all sorts of feelings. It was the first time someone had touched my breasts. I was feeling all wet and my body was going crazy. My mind had flown far from reality and I didn't even realize that his hand was already in my pants. He gently passed his fingers close to the edge of my panties and suddenly, he stopped.
- What are you doing? Why did you stop?, I found myself speaking.
- I take it you like it! I just wanted to take my shirt off. You can touch me, too, you know. Let me take your shirt off, too. I want to see your breasts!
Barely had he finished the phrase and I was already on my knees, breasts showing, and leaned against the bed frame. He slowly leaned towards me and started gently caressing me, from the neck to the belly, while gently massaging my breasts.
- They're perfect! And he jumped to kiss them. I felt like I was losing my footing and I didn't know what else to do. I grabbed hold of him and I told him how much I loved him kissing my body.
While we were both chest-naked, and I was lying somewhere on the bed, screaming with pleasure, he took my pants off.
- Wait, wait, not now! I stood up, having only my panties on.
- I won't do anything, relax. I'm just going to kiss you top to bottom. I promise!
- Alright. And I laid back again, waiting to be scratched, just like a cat.
He started kissing me again, the ears, the neck, the nipples… He was already driving me crazy and I could no longer control myself. I closed my eyes and felt nothing but pleasure. He gently pulled my panties down and started to kiss me. Oral sex! He was performing oral sex on me! I couldn't really figure out how he was doing it and what exactly he was doing, but it was driving me mental! Eyes closed, I was clenching my teeth and I didn't want it to end. I wished he would just be down there forever.
- Robert, I can't take it any longer! My whole body is heating up. I feel like I'm floating!
- Relax! That was all he said and continued to kiss me all over.
He gave me a feeling which I didn't even think existed, I was on a different planet and I didn't know how to thank him for that. He climbed on top of me and was rubbing his pants against my naked body. I felt how horny he was and, for a few seconds, I lost contact with reality. Did I just have an orgasm or what exactly was that? Was it possible to have an orgasm without sexual intercourse?

- God, Robert, what was that?

- Well, I don't know… you tell me. Was it alright?

- Fantastic, I want more! How did you do that? I pushed him off me and climbed on top of him, instead. I was completely naked and I could feel his hands move on my bottom.

- You have a great body! It's just perfect! I can't wait to be inside you!

I played along and started doing the same thing. I kissed him on the ear, his chest muscles, then slowly down on the belly, around the bellybutton. I was moving my tongue up and down and from one side to another. I could see he was horny, with his eyes closed. That must have been how I looked when we was all over me.

He was slightly pushing me downwards, with one hand, towards his pants. With his other hand, he was taking his belt off and getting unbuttoned.

- Tell you what, I need a smoke!, I suddenly jumped up, next to the bed.

- What? Are you crazy? You want a smoke NOW?

- Yes, please! I left him with nothing else to say and started getting dressed. Come on, the Sushi should be here soon.

I went to the kitchen, holding my hand between my legs. It felt like it was hurting and I couldn't understand why. I lit up the cigarette and started looking out the window. None of the girls was home. At least, I was sure nobody had heard me scream.

Dana had written plenty of messages. She kept asking whether I managed to finally enter womanhood. I replied negatively, and she seemed pretty disappointed.

- I can't believe what you've done to me!, Robert came through the kitchen door, looking upset.

- What did I do to you? I gazed at him, surprised.

- You just left me like that! You stirred me up and then, you left.

- Well, I figured I wouldn't make it too easy for you, first time out! The doorbell rang. Look, food is here. I didn't want to leave you empty stomach, I figured you would have been hungry.

We unwrapped the Sushi in the kitchen, even though he insisted we went to eat in the bedroom. I didn't want to go there too soon. I was too scared to go to the bedroom again because I felt like I had no control over my body. And that was bothering me. At the same time, I had enjoyed it so much and I would have wanted to, but I said to myself that it was better not to! I brought glasses from the bedroom and we ate, while toasting several times. Most of the times, he would say that those toasts were for us. But I didn't really believe in "us" and would keep silent. I let him believe all sorts of things, but I knew that anything beyond one sex round would not happen. Robert wasn't attractive to me, as a man, but probably, in the absence of anything else, he had made me feel great in the bedroom.

- Come on, shall we go and lie down? It was the millionth time he was asking me the same question.

- Sure, but we're going to watch a movie! We haven't got too much time on our hands.

- What do you mean?

- Well, how long are we going to be here for? I need to wake up early in the morning, I'm going to the restaurant.

- Right, I get it! You're throwing me out!

- Come on, I'm not throwing you out! We'll just be an hour or two and then, each of us goes to sleep in their own bed, right?

- I thought I'd be sleeping with you!

- No! No way! Still, let's not overreact! I've invited you over for a movie, isn't it?

- I understand! That's fine, we'll just watch a movie and I'm going home after that. Don't worry! I won't do anything you don't want me to!

We went back to the room and it took a while to select a movie. It was quite dark in the room and the dim TV light was making me fall asleep. I placed my head on his arm and we started watching Sweet November. It was my favorite movie and I would watch it whenever I had the chance to. He would easily caress my hair and kiss my forehead. I felt like he was a good man and decided to cuddle up in his arms. I hadn't done that with anyone else before, except for mother and Dana. It felt strange, it was a pleasant feeling. I felt safe. It was peace and quiet.

We failed to see the movie as we had both fallen asleep. I woke up at 2.37 AM and I couldn't believe that Robert was still at my house. I hadn't even taken a shower, I only had a few hours to sleep and I didn't know how to wake him up sooner and show him out. I tried to make some noise around the room, but nothing. Eventually, I went close to him and slowly jotted him.

- Robert, you need to go!, I whispered in his ear.

- What? He was so dismayed that he must have forgotten where he was.

- Please! I'm off to the kitchen and have a smoke while you get ready. You can use the bathroom, it's down the hall, just to freshen up.

I kissed him on the cheek and headed towards the kitchen. I was looking for the cigarette pack and, to my surprise, it was empty. I was irritated and started looking through all the drawers. It wasn't too often that I ran out of cigarettes.

- What are you looking for?, Robert inquired from the doorstep, while buttoning his shirt.

- Cigarettes. Have you got any?

- No, I don't. You know I don't smoke. And you should…

- Yes, I know! I should quit, too. It's 3.00 AM, Robert, and I'm not in the mood for lectures, please! Come on, go, I'll see you at school!

- Perhaps we could see each other again this weekend, just let me know when you have time.

- Sure, we'll talk! Until then, go and get some sleep! I opened the front door and I realized the poor boy was feeling bad. All I had left to do was literally push him out of the house. I was really tired and, apart from that, I was also angry because I couldn't find any cigarettes. I looked through the pockets of my jeans, my jacket. Nothing still! Eventually, I reached in the pocket of a jacket on the rack, a jacket that was definitely not mine, and I found a pack of cigarettes. It belonged to the other girls. They would certainly not miss one cigarette and eventually, I would have paid for it. I sat on my favorite spot at the window and picked up my phone, which has been charging till then. Dana had sent me plenty of texts again, but my feet started shacking when I saw a text I had received from Elan.

11.52 PM: Hey, how are you? Are you alright? It's Elan. I've been meaning to call you one of these days, but I've been very busy. I just got home. I just wanted to see how you were! Breakfast tomorrow, 9.00 AM?

How had I forgotten my phone in the kitchen particularly then? I couldn't believe he had sent me a text. And why now? Couldn't he have done it earlier, so that I could have some time to reply?

I kept reading the text over and over again and I felt my heart pounding. There was no way I would be able to have breakfast with him tomorrow. I had to go to work and couldn't afford to ask for another day off. In a way, it was better to let him know that I couldn't. You know the saying: I'm not falling for it on the first date.

2.59 AM: Hi, Elan! Tomorrow…

I would write and delete. First, I was unsure whether or not to reply. Second, I didn't know what to write. Who could have helped me to figure out whether or not it was alright for me to reply to his text? It was already really late. But perhaps I would have seemed rude not to reply. Ouch, this is a hard one!

3.00 AM: Elan, I'm sorry! I didn't reply because…

And I stopped again. Why would I need to apologize to him for not replying to a text? After all, I was under no obligation to reply. I think it was the best choice. If he had wanted to see me, he would have insisted. He texted me close to midnight, just to invite me for breakfast on the following day. And what was I meant to do? Hit the ceiling? If he had truly wanted this, he would have called at least once by now. I made peace with myself and concluded that it was best not to reply to his text, then I went to bed. Around three hours of sleep would have sufficed, that is, if I managed to fall asleep straight away.

I took the phone with me, stuck it under my pillow and went to sleep in my home clothes. I was in no mood to have a shower then and I would have a shower in the morning, anyway, after the 30-minute run. Although there was a part of me hoping to receive another text, I was quite aware that he had nothing to write to me at 3.00 in the morning. I turned the ringtone even louder and activated the Vibrate mode, too. I wanted to make sure that I wouldn't miss any more of his signals.

Although I didn't think I was going to sleep, I did sleep like a log. I missed the first alarm at 6.30 AM, and snoozed the second one. I would usually jump straight out of bed as soon as the phone rang, but I could barely keep my eyes open then. My first thought was that I had no more time for running; my second thought went to Elan. I didn't receive any other texts from him. I also remembered Robert and what he had managed to make me feel. What was strange for me was that, even though I felt no attraction towards him as a man, he did manage to bring me in a state which I had never experienced till then. What was also strange was that he didn't text me, either. He must have grown tired of my behavior and he was trying to act indifferent. I jumped in the shower, played some music off YouTube and turned the tap on. The good thing about skipping the running part was that I had more time to spend under the hot water jet.

Without realizing the reason for it, I thought about mother. I was feeling significantly guilty for not being able to go and visit her on that coming Sunday. I had all kinds of scenarios in my head and thought of myself as a bad person. It was like I had a split personality. One was arguing that there was no way she would realize that I would be missing because she was completely absent towards anything happening around her, while the other part was making me feel horribly bad. I imagined my mother staring at the door all day and me, not showing up. I felt bad about not calling Maria and ask her to go. But since it was still early morning, I could have tried to ask her to go to the hospital. The thought of her going, instead of me, was somewhat comforting.

Eventually, I managed to leave the house, even though I had had a very lazy morning. It wasn't too often that I would be wasting time like I had, and it seemed that everything was playing back. I put my earphones in and selected an ABBA album. I don't know why, but I felt like listening to oldies.

- Good morning, Eva!, Mario smiled, standing in the doorway.
- Morning! Are you ready for work, then? Because I can barely pull myself together!
- Why, what happened? Did you hit the ceiling last night?
- Yes, I was hanging from the chandelier and we were playing Tarzan!
- Well, that really turns me on! Were you also wearing Tarzan's suit?
- No, I was wearing Eve's; that's my name, isn't it?
- That sounds even more interesting! I'd like to see your breasts one day! Even if just in passing…
- Are you truly a sexual maniac? Can we not have a conversation without you going there, seriously Dario…
- Come on, don't be so cranky! What do you want from me? I'm a man and you're attractive! And sometimes, I'm thinking out loud.

He held out the broom stick, but only after having smacked my bottom with it. Sometimes, his jokes were really funny, but other times, he was exaggerating and I felt like hitting him over the head with something. That morning, he had stayed within his normal boundaries, as opposed to what he could sometimes do.

I started the cleaning, but I felt the phone's vibrations in my pocket. It was Dana.

- Zuzis, why didn't you call me?, she chewed out.
- When was I supposed to call you? I thought you were asleep. I didn't think you were up so early! Or you still haven't managed to sleep yet?
- You reckon… we went to bed really early last night. I would have liked to go out somewhere, but guess what? He wanted to cook pasta for me. And we stayed in front of the TV and had pasta, as one would. And now, at 6.00 AM, he went to the gym and obviously, he woke me up, too! Let's move on, I've got nothing interesting. Tell me what happened with you. Is it done?
- Done what?
- Come on, Eva, you're not a child! Have you had sex?
- No… I went out of the restaurant because it seemed to me that everyone around heard the word "sex" and were staring at me.
- I can't believe it! What, in God's name? Have you been weaving? Or he wasn't even brave enough to touch you? The truth is I wanted to tell you, but it seemed to me that Robert is a wimp. But I said I wouldn't get involved…
- He wasn't a wimp at all. Indeed, he would have ripped the clothes of me, had I not stopped him!
- What do you mean? Why did you stop him?
- Right, can we talk tonight? I'm already at work.
- No, no. Tell me now. No one is going to mind us talking for two minutes. And anyway, I'm sure Carla didn't arrive yet.
- Where should I start? He came over. We kissed, we made out, but I stopped. I don't know why. That's how I felt then. He probably doesn't turn me on that much. Wait, there's someone calling on the other line!

"Elan calling"

I have no idea when exactly I hung up on Dana. I was looking at the screen and couldn't believe it. Why was he calling?

- Hello?

- Hey, how are you? It's Elan! I texted you last night.

- Hi, Elan! I'm fine. How are you? I was stuttering so hard that I could barely come up with two words. I was holding the phone with one hand, and looking for the lighter in my pockets, just to be able to light a cigarette, with the other hand. I felt I was blushing really badly and was jumping up and down for joy, while looking at the phone's screen over and over, just to be sure it was him I was talking to.

- Sorry, what was that? I was lighting a cigarette.

- I said I invited you for breakfast and it's already 8.30 AM, and I wasn't sure whether you wanted or not to come!

I glanced around the restaurant and we had already started to get busy. Even by magic, I still didn't have any chance of getting away. I started to bite my fists.

- I'm sorry, I can't make it… I'm working. Rain check, for sure!

- No problem, then, I'm right here! Look across the street!

I remember my feet having stuck to the ground and it was like time stood still. I had shown all sorts of manifestations, while he was just there, across the street, just looking at me. I was such an idiot. When I saw him cross the road and coming over, I wished my tongue was gone, and me with it. I was red as a lobster and couldn't even look at him. I was so ashamed!

- Come on, can I see some more of that joy? I loved seeing you smile.

I continued to keep my head down and I felt the tears pouring down my face. He kept talking and making jokes, but I could no longer hear him. I felt lost before him and the only reaction I had available to myself was to cry. I tried to walk away, without raising my head, but he pulled me by the hand and stopped me.

- Eva, what's wrong? He was truly shocked of seeing me cry. I figured you'd be happy to see me, instead you're crying! What happened? I just wanted to surprise, try and make up for not calling you the other days.

I raised my head and looked straight into his blue eyes. They seemed the most wonderful eyes in the world. It was like my mouth had been stitched up and I couldn't think about anything. All I could see was the awe on his face.

- Forgive me, please!, was all I could utter.

- What for? Have you done something wrong?

I didn't know what to answer. I didn't know if I had done something wrong or not. I didn't know whether my reaction was a reflection of my frustrations or whether it was just making me look like a spoiled child. The thought that a man had seen me happy was causing me pain.

- Right, I'm off, then. I truly apologize for having bothered you. He approached to give me a hug and say Goodbye.

- No, no! Wait! I don't want you to leave! I want us to have breakfast together! Let's go in.

- Eva, a few seconds ago, you were crying, now you want to have breakfast!

- Yes, it was the worst way to react, I know. I was wiping my tears away and, at the same time, pulling him to the restaurant. Carla was just coming in, too.

- Carla, I'll be staying with Elan for him to eat. I promised him. Please! I don't even know where all that courage came from, to tell Carla something like that.

- Alright, but not later than 9.15 AM. We need to start preparing the tables. We have an event today!

Elan seemed completely lost. He was staring at me and probably wondering what kind of weirdo I was. We sat at the table furthest to the back.

- What would you like to eat, so I can order it to the kitchen?

- An English breakfast, please.

- Alright, I'll be right back. Coffee or tea?

- Coffee, small, no milk, no sugar. Thank you!

I entered the kitchen and after having passed the doors separating it from the restaurant, I threw my eyes up and started asking myself how I could have been so stupid. I ordered two English breakfasts in the kitchen and was running around amongst pans, vegetables and dishes, like a mad woman. I looked up and saw the clock on the wall. It was 8.42 AM. I stopped thinking about the pathetic scenes I had caused, focusing instead on the little time I had left to spend with him. I rushed to the bar to make his coffee: small, no milk, no sugar. I kept repeating it in my head!

When I opened the doors, I felt my whole world crumbling. Elan was gone, he was no longer at the table. I looked left, right and couldn't believe how stupid I had been, reacting like I did. I changed color. I was desperately looking for my phone in my pocket. I called him while storming out of the restaurant.

- Why are you calling me? He was sat in one foot, with the other one leaned against the building. Cigarette in one hand, telephone in the other. His phone screen said: "Eva is calling".

- I thought you left! The muscles in my face were back to normal and I felt I had regained my breath. I had messed up again and was wondering what else I needed to do in order to completely ruin that morning. I thought I had done it all.

He threw the cigarette down on the pavement, not having smoked half. He was staring at me, while opening the door and nodding to enter. Everyone in the restaurant was looking at me like I was the maddest person on the planet. I have no idea how I ended up like that, but I wished I had a magical cape which would have helped me escape that place!

- Have you managed to calm down?, he inquired, while reaching out to touch my fingers.

- Yes, I have!

- Perfect! Could I please get my coffee, then?

I had forgotten about the coffee and about everything else. Our first date was a complete mess. I got up and headed for the bar, to prepare the coffee. I was trying to find a way out of that pathetic state, but nothing was coming to mind. I brought the coffee to the table about the same time as Dario brought the food. Dario was the only thing missing from the scene, everything else had been perfect.

- Oh, amore! Love is in the air, Dario was rumbling while laying our plates.

- Dario, please…

- Yes, of course, I know! I have to go! Enjoy! He took a pirouette and left.

- That's Dario, my workmate. I tried to change the subject and take the discussion to a different point.

- I understand! I know him! And now, if you managed to get over that funny part, can we eat peacefully?

- Yes, sure… I smiled and handed him some bread. Would you like some jam? I love strawberry jam! But we do have several other.

- Strawberry is just fine. So, what did you do last night?

- Last night… (imagine telling him that the previous night, I had rubbed myself against Robert, what would he have thought?)… I had dinner at home. And watched a movie.

- Well, yes, I know, I had dinner her last night with some friends and your mates said you asked for the day off. I asked Dario about you.

That was another blow to my head! Instead of coming to work last night, seeing this wonderful man, I had been getting horny with a man who I didn't consider attractive. The Lord works in mysterious ways. Or perhaps it was just me!

- Yes, I had some friends visiting and I said I would spend at least one night with them.

- Right! Are you working tomorrow?

- Yes, I am. From morning until after lunch. I have to catch up on the hours I missed yesterday.

- And what time do you finish?

- Around 4.00 PM, I think. I need to check and talk to Carla.

- Right, check it out and text me. Perhaps we can go see a movie!

- Perhaps?, I replied without giving it any thought, again.

- Yes, perhaps! Perhaps you don't want to, perhaps you don't like movies, perhaps you have something else to do! Perhaps!

- I want to, I really like movies and I have nothing else to do! I smiled with a full face and was trying to look as cool as a cucumber, but it wasn't working.

We continued to talk for a few minutes, after which I told him I really needed to get back to work. I would have gladly stayed with him for a few more hours. His unbuttoned shirt was driving me crazy. I was starting to have silly thoughts. When he left, he gave me a kiss on my right cheek. To make it a full house, I turned my other cheek, while he was pulling back. Another pathetic scene. There was no other end to this date!

After he left, I kept staring at the window for a few more seconds. I had no idea where this man had stampeded into my life, but I knew that he brought along some powerful ripples!

It was as if my life had changed in the blink of an eye. I felt butterflies in my stomach and had quite the thoughts, and I'm sure no one would have believed me to be the same Eva as I was a few hours back. I was completely dazzled. They were all making fun of me and were winking or jostling each other. It seemed strange for them to see me have breakfast with someone, at work. Let alone, such a handsome man!

- Well, Eva! Why didn't you tell me?, Dario pinched my bottom.

- Dario, next time, I'm slapping you! That's it! Please, stop that!

- Come on, dear, I was just kidding with you! Now, that you're hooked, you've got an even shorter fuse. You need to get on the horse as soon as possible! You'll feel a lot better afterwards, you'll see! You're too tight. Would you like me to give you a hand? I'll teach you, it's normal not to know!

- No, thanks! What a sweetheart you are, just as usual!, I couldn't have been more ironic than that.

- Right, come on, spill it out! Who is he? What does he do? And all the other questions which I haven't asked yet…

- Dario, let's do some work, as well! Shall we? You're so nice, but please… just leave me along, you've confused me! Have you got no one else to pick on? Please, don't ruin my joy!

- Are you in love?

- Yes! I'm in love!

He put on a long face and couldn't believe what I had just told him. I couldn't believe I had uttered those words, either. I felt the ice queen in me beginning to fade away. I was starting to feel the warmth in my heart, where love was also starting to settle in. This Elan had managed to put my hopes up and I knew that would only be the beginning!

I was somewhat troubled by the fact that I hadn't told Dana about Elan. First, I hadn't even had the chance to, and second, things did happen really fast. One night before, he had long gone from my thoughts, just to show up on that day and turn my life upside down. I planned to tell her in the evening, after work. She had promised to come and pick me up. The ultimate gift she had received from Claudio was a car and she was driving it around the city all evening. That was whenever she was not meant to be at his house, of course. It wasn't a fantastic car, a Ford Focus, but it was more than enough for us. She had it customized herself and there was always a nice smell inside, of cantaloupe.

On the other hand, Robert was also playing a part somewhere in my thoughts. He hadn't texted me at all. It was quite strange and I didn't understand why. He was always stressing me out with his excessive care and was asking me the same question over and over… where had he gone? I went out for a cigarette and tried to call him. His phone was off. He must have switched techniques. He must have noticed that I wasn't giving him too much attention when having acted like a gentleman, so he must have turned into a jerk. His loss! But I was somewhat worried.

Chapter 9

I didn't even realize when the day went by. I had made a lot of tips and that made me feel better than usual. I left around 8.00 PM, when my shift ended. Backpack on and cigarettes in one hand, I said Goodbye to my workmates. They were making all sorts of assumptions as to where I was headed that evening, but they had no grounds. I managed to take two smokes and Dana came along, in her mini-car.

- I'm taking the cigarette with me, mind you. I had no time to smoke today at all. Have you got anything to drink in here?

- Hi, Eva!

- Hi, Dana!, I replied smiling, while kissing her on the cheek. Come one, stop pretending to be mean! I'm quite tired!

- What in God's name are you up to? That restaurant is going to get you ill soon. Listen, we're moving out on Tuesday! I managed to rent an apartment on Decebal Boulevard, which is downtown!

- Wow, I can't believe it!!! How did you find it? How the hell are we going to afford the rent?

- We'll manage. At first, you can just pay what you pay here. But you need to let this joint of a restaurant go! It's quite far, as well, you know! Someone might rape you on the street one day, you know! But let's talk about Robert! I still can't believe you haven't acted on the moment! What happened? Is he that dumb?

- Wow, slow down there! He's not dumb at all, the poor boy! I just couldn't! I didn't feel ready!

- Yes, Eva, I know, you'll never be ready! There's always going to be a "what if", a "why not" or something else!

- You're nuts! Do I need to really bang the first fella that comes in my way?

- It's not about that. It's about the fact that you're preventing any man from coming closer to you. And I'm thinking it might have an impact on you in the future.

- You've gone haywire! Honestly, Dana! I'm not letting men come closer to me? What do you suggest I do? Wear a shirt that says "I'm a virgin" and just stick my boobs out? This is too much; you're started to annoy me!

- See? I can't talk to you because you get annoyed! I'm your friend and I'm just trying to tell you when something is wrong. I can't tell what, but we better find out together, and fast!

- And if we don't, what happens then? I'll just die a virgin! Cool! Maybe I can also have a child, as a virgin. Me and Virgin Mary, how about that?

- Yes, that would be a solution, too, wouldn't it? She glanced at me as if wanting to bang my head against the dashboard.

- Anyway, I have something to tell you!

- Right... what is it?

Bam! I heard a loud crashing sound and some other sounds, and when I came to later on, I had my hands on top of my head, all cuddled and the airbags popped out. By the time I began to realize what had happened, Dana was already on my side of the car, trying to pull me out as quickly as possible.

- Eva, are you alright?

- I'm fine!, I replied on a low tone. What the hell happened?? I managed to lie down on the grass next to the car and look at the sky. Dana ran onto the street and signaled a nurse to come over. I could hear a lot of sirens and, in the dark night, I could hear a lot of crying. We had had an accident. I slightly raised my head and saw smoke coming out from underneath the Ford's bonnet. I had a blurry vision, but I wouldn't have said that the car looked awful, but I couldn't understand who else was screaming their lungs out, on the other side of the road.

- What's your name?

- Eva.

- Age?

- 18. What happened?

- I'm Suri and I'll be examining you quickly, just to see if we need to send you to the hospital. Alright? Please, stay still!

- What happened?

- Give me your hand and follow this light with your eyes.

She was fully ignoring me while also asking me to do all sorts of things.

- Madam, please tell me what happened!

- How should I know, you lady? You've crashed into one another! I have no idea!

I realized she had finished her examination because she was already starting to collect her items. She seemed really upset, like I had bothered her.

- Right, so how am I? Am I alright?, I asked shamelessly. I was still lying down on the cold grass.

- You're just great! Come on now, stand up and perhaps next time, you'll stay away from trouble!

"Trouble"? She must be an idiot. What kind of trouble had we gotten ourselves into? Dana certainly must have been driving within the speed limit and it didn't seem to me like she had committed any offence. I first stood up using my elbows, then my bottom, and, with great difficulty, I eventually stood up. The sky was covered in red and blue. I could hear plenty of sirens and screams. I seemed to be quite far, but I could still her all of it. Where was Dana and why had she left me there by myself?

The police were everywhere and some gentleman in a funny-looking uniform were laying out some yellow tape. I couldn't see almost anything. Three cars were involved in the accident and there was a lot of commotion. I searched for Dana's car and went to get my backpack. I wanted a cigarette so badly. I was dizzy and still couldn't grasp what had just happened. While looking for my cigarettes in the backpack which I found further away from the car, I saw a woman banging her fists against an ambulance and screaming her lungs out. I realized something bad must have happened. I threw away the cigarette which I had just lit and rushed towards the woman. When I was just a few steps away, three men stopped me.

- Leave her! Leave her!, they kept saying, like a "Repeat" button had been activated.

- What the hell happened? What's wrong with this woman?? Where is Dana?

- Miss, are you alright?, one of the men asked.

- Yes, I'm fine! I was just seen by a stupid nurse. What happened? Do you know anything, gentlemen?

- Were you in one of the cars?

- In one of the cars? Yes! I was in that black Ford. And I pointed my finger to the car.

- Ok! I believe there's your friend! You should go there!

They didn't even get to finish why they had to say that I ran towards the crowd in front of me. I slipped as fast as I could and got in the first row. Dana was sitting on an improvised chair and was filling in some forms. In her other hand she had the phone she was talking to and crying. What the hell had happened?

- Dana! Dana! What are you doing?

- Eva! She jumped into my arms. I'm waiting for you here, Claudio! I found Eva! I'll call you after!

- Tell me, please, what happened?

- Are you ok?

- Yes, Dana, I'm fine! Just tell me already what happened here, I don't even know how many people I have already asked, a million times!

- I am not to blame. I was driving according to regulations, and two boys, with two different cars, were racing each other. One of them was going the other way. When I saw him in the distance ... and Dana started to cry and got down on her knees.

- Dana... tell me ... and calm down! Look, put your head here, on my chest.

- You know, one of them jumped a curb and drove over some people!

- Oh, my God! Has anyone died?

- I don't know really... I just know it was a family. Mother, father and child.

- And who did you see to be still alive?

- Just the child. It seems that the parents have died!

- No, no... I don't believe it! A woman was punching an ambulance. She was clearly his mother.

- No... she was the mother of one of the boys that were racing. He also died, the one with the car!

- Oh, my God... that is a tragedy, Dana! You have done nothing?

- No, no! The one with the car going the other way just scratched me a little. I tried to get as far away from the road as possible. I don't know how, but I did. We are alive and that's all that matters! She took me in her arms and knelt down beside me. I am sorry you had to go through this. Oh God! Oh, what a tragedy!

I couldn't hear her anymore. I couldn't believe I was living this nightmare! I was just thinking about that child. He was left alone! Because of a fool and the stupidity of some fools, a child would grow up without a mother and father. I was praying for the child to be older. Let it not be a kindergarten child. I did not want to imagine a small child, now carried through I don't know how many hospitals, to be handed over later to some women in a wretched orphanage. For a second I remembered the day when the doors of my orphanage opened and I walked out that infernal courtyard. I couldn't even imagine this child going through such an experience just because of a car race. No! No! It would have been too much!

I don't know how I got home. More likely Dana mostly dragged by. She didn't understand why this affected me so when she should have been the one to feel that way. She was asking me so many questions, to make sure I didn't lose my memory or I didn't have a seizure. I was perfectly aware, but my soul ached. Every piece of me was screaming. I do not know if the thought that that child would end up in an orphanage, whether the showmanship of some young people annoyed me even more or it was just nostalgia, the bad memories and my life that had passed made me feel bad. Many long-forgotten moments were going through my head. Some of them I thought had disappeared for good from my mind. I thought of my mother, my father, my former family. I had no family now. I had Dana, but I didn't have parents, or at least I didn't have them near me. I wouldn't have wanted my dad in my life, nor now, and maybe never. I don't remember a moment when I loved my dad. His gaze alone caused me pain and suffering. He never gave me a hug, a kiss, a sweet word. Just beatings, offenses and mean words. Words I have never forgotten! Sometimes at night I dream and scream as loud as I can, for the simple fact that I see this diabolical man in my dreams. Life can be really hard sometimes. And I don't know why we are given our destiny at birth, but mine was a terrible one. I couldn't imagine that anything could ever change. I was attracting evil and I was not allowed to enjoy anything. I don't know who decided this for me, but that was the truth. Whenever I felt a little joy and eagerness for life, another black cloud appeared in my life. I believed in fate and had read a lot about it. Everyone was talking about a "balance" of life, but, in my case, there was no balance issue. To me, everything was always bad and good things eluded me.

Even that day had been bad. After those feelings of joy, euphoria and ecstasy ... this tragedy happened. Some people have lost their lives, others have lost their parents or children, some had to live their entire lives with a trauma, and others have something happened to then they could never have imagined. It was yet another proof that life could change in a second.

Life doesn't prepare you for anything. Nor for better or worse. We are born without knowing if we will end up living good or bad. Most of the time we are born from the love between two people. But there are times when one appears in the world without being wanted. We grow a certain way. The way our grandparents, parents or someone else wants us to grow. We are like sponges in the first years of life. We gather everything the others give us. We don't know whether we are taking positive or negative things. For some, normality is the others' abnormality. And that's how we create personalities. Often true monsters. For a long time I had not seen a cheerful child, without any evil in him or her. Probably because of today's society one has to rear a child that way! One has to teach the child to be bad! Only he, that little human, how can he know when to stop and to want to be even worse? Will he ever know how to be better instead of worse? Will he succeed in choosing or discerning? Will he ever be able to give up the fight, to make peace, even with his head bowed?

Frustrated. We add our frustrations in our children, the little sponges next to us. And that's how we create little monsters. As my father created me, a child with a monster's soul.

It was a long night. I had almost any sleep. I could not get the images from the place of the accident of my mind and the idea that a child was left without parents made me feel extremely bad. I had also thought about my mother. I should have been by her today. I had given up my time with her for several hours of caresses and kissing. I wasn't even in the presence of any man I wanted.

While brushing my teeth, I looked in the mirror and marvelled at my red eyes. I was very tired, both emotionally and physically. I had to go to work and pretend that nothing had happened, that I was fine and that I was ready for work. Besides, the thought of having to smile in front of my customers made me feel even worse. I forced myself and managed to take a short shower. There was also no discussion to take the 30 minutes for jogging. I was beat.

While I was getting dressed, the phone rang twice. I had received two messages. I thought straight to Elan, which took me a little out of the state I was in.

Robert: 6:58: "Eva, I'm sorry I didn't call you! I'm not very well. My mother had a heart attack yesterday morning and I have been with her since, in the hospital. I do not know if there is still a chance for her to recover! I'm destroyed! I hope you are well!"

Robert: 6:59: "I'll see you tomorrow at school if I can get there. Kiss!"

I left the phone on the bed and crouched down, between the nightstand and the edge of the bed. Why was I just receiving bad news? Why was I attracting so much evil? I started crying. I put my head between my knees and I was trying to find something positive in my life. I only saw black and dark things. I gathered myself, picked up the phone and called Robert.

- Hello, Eva!, answered a voice seemly without any power left in it.

- How are you, Robert? I've read your texts and I am so sorry to hear you are going through this! You should have called me, to be there for you!

- Calm down, I didn't even came up to my senses yet! I'm still waiting to wake up from a nightmare! Anyway, they don't let me stay too long with her in the ward, but I'm staying here!

- What hospital are you at?

- At the Municipal.

- Ok, I'm coming there!

- Don't come now, because here will be visiting time soon, and then I want to go home! I haven't eaten anything since yesterday and I want to take a shower and change my clothes. I can see you later if you want!

- Yes... later? What did "later" mean? I had told Elan that I could go with him to the movies. What a bad person I was! Robert needed me and I was still thinking about ditching him.

- Can you still hear me?

- Yes, Robert! We'll talk on the phone, I have work late today ... I have to catch up on my hours. But if you need anything, please call me anytime. Go and eat something! Please send you mother many health wishes and I hope she'll get well, I'm sure she will!

I hung up and thought of my mother. I felt the need to see her. I quickly got out of the building and headed for the first cab.

- Speranța Hospital, please!

The driver didn't even look at me and started driving on the busy streets. The visiting hours started at 10 o'clock, but I had intended to ask a nurse to let me see her just for a short time. I already had a good relationship with them and I was sure I would succeed. I had to tell Carla that I would be late for one hour. Or maybe I shouldn't tell her anything, hoping she wouldn't notice. On the way to the hospital I thought of Dana. I didn't even say good morning to her. Maybe she was even more affected than I had been and I didn't even think about her. I saw her sleeping and I didn't want to disturb her.

- Dana, how are you? I called her from the emergency ward.

- I was asleep. What happened to you?

- Nothing, I'll go visiting my mum and then I'll go to work. But I haven't called you this morning to ask you how you were feeling. Are you ok?

- Yes, I'm fine! I haven't been sleeping very well, but I'll call you later, ok?

- Ok, sorry! I left in a hurry!

I could neither hear the roar from outside nor the commotion in the hospital. I managed to get 15 minutes with my mother before the visiting hours. I entered the room and saw her in the armchair, holding a handkerchief and a thread in her hand. She looked up at me and I quickly went to her feet, placing my head on her lap. I would have wanted her so much to take me in her arms, hold me at her chest, or at least acknowledge me. Tears ran down my cheeks and I clenched her legs with my hands. At one point I felt a warm hand on my face. I opened my eyes and felt my whole body soften. My mother was petting me! It was the first time after all these years when she touched me. I had not wondered anything, I just stood there, crying of joy and waiting to see what she would be doing. I didn't even want to move, I was so happy! I wanted to stay there forever. I was so happy that I chose to come and see her! Nothing else mattered anymore.

One of the mother's nurses was standing in the door. Even she admired that moment. Probably she was supposed to tell me to leave, but even she didn't want to break us up. But my mother, just like she knew, pulled her hand lightly from my head and looked out the window. Then I squeezed her even harder into my arms and I kissed her hand several times. We were happy as we had not been for a long time!

Life does not prepare you for the good or the evil to come. It does not tell you what suffering means, what joy is. It lets you get hit by them and gather them in your luggage called experiences. The years pass and all the time, looking back, you could say "I would have done it differently", but, unfortunately or fortunately, we do not know how this "otherwise" would have looked and where it would have taken us. A moment often brings more feelings and emotions than a full month. And we never know in advance when there comes a moment of great joy or dark times in our lives. We always wake up in the morning and wait to see what that day has to offer. Although, in principle, we know what we have to do, where we should go and what we should not do. But destiny is unique. Just like the human mind. Thoughts are permanent. The influences from childhood, teenage years and even the daily ones make us become certain people. Willingly or less willingly, we do most good and bad things under the influence of many moments that influenced us in a positive or negative way at one point.

I was on the bus, with my earphones in my ears and going to the restaurant. Tears ran down my cheek as I remembered, in my mind, my childhood, my past, but also the present. We were not happy! We had never been happy! I wondered if that was my fate, whether I had to live for another ten years just as unhappy. I realized that everyone had problems, but I did not understand why mine were always bigger and more complicated. Couldn't we be happy, full of joy? What was I doing wrong or what was wrong in my life? I escaped my beast of a father, I escaped from the hell from the orphanage, I was living an independent life and I could only decide for myself. And yet I was nowhere near fulfilled.

- Hello! I read on the lips of a gentleman sitting next to me on the bus. I quickly took my earphones out.
- Hello! Do I know you? He was a gentleman around 40, his hair was slightly grey.
- No, you don't know me! And I don't know you!
He took a business card out from the inside pocket of the chequered jacket and handed it to me as he looked into my eyes.

- What I am supposed to do with this? I don't understand! "Vogue" magazine... Alan Scrutz, photographer.

- Yes...

- I understand, you are probably a photographer at "Vogue" magazine. How can I help you?

- What is your name?

- Eva.

- Eva, why are you so grouchy? I don't want to do you any harm! I just introduced myself and I'm going to tell you what it is. I'm not here to kidnap you, rape you, or I know what's going on in your head.

- I haven't...

- Don't say anything anymore, just listen to me! I work for the "Vogue" magazine, as my business card shows. I take pictures and not only that. I was walking to the office and I saw you crying. In a very strange way I liked you, sad as you were. Your eyes conveyed an emotion I hadn't seen for a long time. I don't know why you're so upset, but you have something special. Were you told this before?

- No... I was shocked and didn't know whether to believe him. In a pretty big city, you had a good chance of getting to see all sorts of crazies.

- Good! Tell me, please, would you like us to stop talking a little. I'm not going to harm you, don't be scared! If I wanted to do something to you, I wouldn't approach you on the bus, in front of so many people. What do you say?

- I can't, I have to get to work! I'm already late! Maybe another time.

- Fine, I won't insist. I would like very much for you to come and do a shooting. I have several projects I'm working on now. You could come and give it a try and, if we are satisfied, and, of course, if you are satisfied with the money we offer you, we can try. What do you say?

- Me, having my picture taken for the "Vogue"? You must be kidding!

- I'm not kidding! I told you to take a test, this does not mean you'll be accepted. I'm giving you a chance you can take advantage of or you can totally ignore. I didn't say I would put you on the cover, I just told you have some talent, an emotion to convey and I liked that.

I had another stop up to the restaurant. This man was still talking about everything and nothing, but I was looking lost in his eyes. I didn't know whether this was for real. Maybe he was an organ trafficker who didn't know how to get me to get off the bus, so he could get me into a van and take me God knows where!

- Eva?

- Yes.

- What are you thinking about? Because you don't really listen to me!

- Nothing. I have one more stop and I have to get off.

- You work around here?

- Yes.

- Oh... that means you work for nothing. It would be such a shame not to give us a try!

- Well, what do you do on the bus in this area? Because I believe that you don't work for nothing!

- Ha-ha... you make me laugh! I'm going outside the city to look for places for some photo shoots. And, if you are asking what I took the bus, the answer is simple. I like getting to know new people and it is only me and the music in the car and that's about it. Is it enough for you?

- Well, yeah... This gentleman had stumped me and in my mind I was beginning to see myself in a make-up room, with the hair all made up and many photographers beside me. I would not be displeased!

- I must get off!

- Fine, Eva! I am waiting you call! Or, if you don't, I will understand that you're not interested.

- It was nice meeting you! Have a nice day!

- Good bye!

As I was trying to get off the bus, with my head turned towards him, so I could analyse him a little more, I stumbled and fell to my knees. I saw him start laughing as he looked out the window. Did I really have to trip? I was like a kindergarten kid whose mother bought bigger shoes, so that she could wear them next year too.

I looked at my watch and it was already 9:37. I should have been at work since 8:15 at the latest. I couldn't think of any excuse. I was just thinking about magazines and other stupid things.

- Eva... it seems the thing have gone to your head! Carla started on me even since I have entered.

- I'm sorry...

- I don't care if you are or not sorry! If you are too in love, you should go to your boyfriend and tell him to keep you at home!

- In love?

- Yes, yes, in love! I've told you to come by 8! Is that correct?

- Yes, I'm sorry! I'm late because…

- I haven't asked you why you were late! Because I don't care! It's what you all do! I give you a finger and you take the entire hand! I've had enough looking the other way!

- I don't understand! What other way?

- Meaning that you are late and you didn't event let me know!

- But I had never been late, it's the first time and I'm sorry!

- Do you know anything else than saying that you're sorry?

- Excuse me? I felt my blood starting to boil. I was standing in front of the restaurant and I was being held responsible by a woman for whom I had worked with all my heart. I had never done anything wrong and now, at the first offense, she was talking to me as if I was a slave, not an employee. She had clearly gone round the bend.

- You heard!

- I have heard what? Very well, Carla, here's the thing! I put my hand in my back pocket. Here, take the card, take the key and leave me the hell alone! If you didn't sleep well last night, don't take it out on me! I am neither your child to tell me off like this, neither your slave, nor anything! Find someone else for this crap and just leave me the hell alone!

- That means that you're leaving?

- Yes, I'm leaving! Right now! and I'll never come back, just so you know!

- Well, you won't be paid then for this month if you're leaving without any notice!

- Then please get yourself something nice from my money, something to make you happy! Good bye!

I turned around and quickly crossed the road to get to the bus stop. I couldn't believe I had just done this, but I didn't even look back. I was too proud and I wasn't going to allow Carla to talk to me like that, when she could ask me calmly and nicely what had happened. Then I could have explained it to her. But I didn't like being approached that way. Without thinking anymore, I took Alan's business card out the pocket and called him.

- It's Alan. How can I help you?
- Hi! It's Eva!
- Oh... you've been quick!
- Yes! Do you have time for a coffee?
- I do! You're not going to work?
- I quit. I'll wait for you at Juice cafe. It's opposite from the place I've got off the bus. A little down the street. Call me if you can't find it.
- Ok, I'll just get off and take the bus back.
- Fine. I'll wait for you!

I sat on the terrace and lit a cigarette. I asked for a short espresso and looked from time to time on the street to see if Alan had arrived. I didn't even think about Carla and her restaurant. I was taking the meeting with this gentleman from the bus as a sign and I told myself that it was time to do things that I liked and that could bring me happiness.

The meeting with the photographer had changed my life in a few days. I had quit my job at the restaurant and had agreed to go and talk about collaborating. I had taken a test and I had been accepted to take pictures for some flat irons and jewellery. They had offered 200 euros per week, irrespective of the number of pictures. They had also accepted the fact that I was in school and most of the time they scheduled me for photo shoots over the weekend. Alan had turned out to be a very nice guy, who had great confidence in me. I didn't understand why, but I wasn't too bothered. I was taking things as they were and trying not to ask so many questions.

I succeeded to move in with Dana in the new flat and everything was going very well. I had my room and bathroom. Not to say that I wouldn't have liked to stay with Dana in the same room, but now I had my privacy and it was super good. I was still going to take the children from school, but I told them that I might not be able to go anymore and that it would be better to find someone else. Sometimes I would call, when I had to go to the studio. Kate was very upset and tried to convince me any way she could not to give them up. Boris was also sad, but he always told me that he understood me, that I was young and it was normal to wish something else from my life. Lucas and Isa did not understand very well what was happening, but they sometimes asked me whether I would come back. I told them that, whatever happened, I would not give them up for good. I promised them and myself that had I not worked for them anymore, I would go there for my pleasure and take them to the park when I could.

Things were going pretty well at school, but my professors sometimes criticized me for losing my focus. They were probably right, but I began to think more about myself. I liked that I was making more money and I always wanted to discover more about myself.

My mother was the same. I was always going to see her on Sundays. Sometimes she petted me, other times she didn't. But I felt she recognized me. I didn't know how to explain it, but it was a nice feeling to be near her even without talking.

Oana Babagianu | **Eva**

I succeeded to get out with Elan to dinner a couple of times, but he proved to be a nutter. He always told me that I looked like his ex-girlfriend, Irina, and that is why he had taken me out. It was already boring to sit listening to him talking about a woman I didn't know. It all came down to how she was doing, what she was eating, what she was saying. I had tried to be a friend to him, but he was always rambling. I liked that he was a lawyer, especially if I managed to take him away from the "ex" subject and ask him about his cases. Sometimes I would spend hours talking with him on the phone. He would tell me what had happened in the courtroom or how much he missed Irina. He had been with her for 3 years and it seemed she turned his life upside down when she decided to leave him. She was Russian, had a strong character. He, a Jew, had fallen into her grasp and it seemed he had not yet come out, though she had long since left. At first I had hoped that there might be a connection between us, but it seemed that only my resemblance to Irina had drawn him to me. I couldn't accept being a man's girlfriend just because I reminded him of his ex. There may have been times when he would have wanted more than just a friendship between us, but he quickly realized that I was not "her" and returned to the friend-like relationship.

I sometimes talked to Dario, from my former job. No one besides him had even sent me a text asking why I hadn't come anymore. I didn't miss them either, so the feeling was mutual.

Dana was very happy about my new job. She was very supporting and always telling me that I deserved more. I didn't understand what "more" meant, but I let her talk. She had received a new car from the insurance company, and her relationship with Claudio seemed ok. She had a lot of free time and he didn't control her. She was working as much as she wanted and he was free to spend time with other men, because it seemed he didn't mind much. We were very happy in our new home and we tried to give it character as much as we could.

Chapter 10

Seven weeks had passed since I had stated to work for the magazine and I had received the first invitation to the staff party. We were allowed to bring up to three guests, but I only had Dana. I had made a few friends over there, but no one was too close. Alan was a professional and was doing his job very well. Sometimes it was hard, but it was understandable. Most of the girls were lazy. They did not come to the shooting when they were told, they were always stalling and ignored his advice. This way he quickly screened them and found new ones. There were about 4-5 girls who were there for a longer time and they already had their own group. They didn't care about anyone and just talked to each other. They had expensive bags, brand shoes and all kinds of jewellery. I was starting to learn some brands, but I still couldn't explain that they could spend so much money on a purse. But I also didn't bother too much.

I was a little worried because I didn't know what to wear to the party, but I went with Dana to the mall and bought myself a short, black dress with long sleeves. It wasn't a famous label, but I really liked it. It highlighted my well-worked body from morning jogging. It also showed a little cleavage. I had curled my hair and put on a set of fake pearls I had bought from an antique fair.

- Paint your lips red! Dana was shouting from the bathroom, while she was curling her hair in front of the mirror.

- Red? Is it not a little too much?

- Come on, don't start again! It's not too much! You have a black dress, black shoes... it would not look good. And I'd suggest you to take the black stiletto sandals. With these stilettos it seems you're going to the office! I still believed, Eva, that you have learned a thing or two from these people!

- So you say to wear mu sandals?

- Yeees! And take this lipstick... this shade of red looks very nice on you!

- How do you know?

- I just do!

I took the lipstick and went to the bathroom next to her. I had my own bathroom, but we liked to stay together when we were getting ready to go out. And her bathroom was bigger, which allowed us to do our thing better.

- Can't you put some music on YouTube? asked Dana, looking at me in the mirror.

- Put on some lipstick, change my shoes, put some music on! What else do you want, boss?

- Come on, don't be silly... You have no idea how to put on red lipstick! Ohhhh, Eva... when will you grow up? This is clearly something to do with the hormones! Maybe you'll find yourself a man tonight to bring you a little to earth, 'cause this cannot go on!

She took the lipstick and put it on me. I was moving and annoying her something fierce. But I was laughing and she was laughing too. It was real fun to get ready to go somewhere. I was the student and she was the teacher. We always left a disaster behind us. Clothes everywhere, shoes thrown on the floor, drawers pulled out and lots of smoke in the kitchen. I was always ready before her and I waited for a long time. I would smoke about two, three cigarettes and she wouldn't be ready yet!

- Dana!! We are still going somewhere today? You know I don't like to be late!

- Ohhh, Eva! You always do this! Call a taxi, I'll be ready in three minutes! Of course, ten minutes passed and the driver was almost out of patience. In the end, we succeeded to climb in the car.

- Snagov Palace, please!

The place where the party was held was sumptuously arranged. Lots of natural flowers, lots of bodyguards at the door and lots of sparkling stones on the ladies present. I was like from another movie. I hadn't realized that so many people would come.

We asked the taxi driver to leave us a hundred meters ahead, so that we had time to take the courage to enter. They were some tall stairs, with a very long red carpet. The doors were double and full of white flowers.

- Dana, where the hell are we?

- In good company, Eva! Come on, courage! Back straight, eyes ahead. You work for them, don't you? Or did you lie to me?

- But I can't see anyone I know, these people don't seem to work for the magazine...

- Well, probably they have invited other people. Otherwise you held your party there, at the magazine! Ohhh! Come on...

- Wait, let me look for the invitation on the mail, because they will surely ask for it. It seems we are in a different movie that those over there!

- You are such a sucker!

I took out the phone and quickly found Alan's invitation in the mail. Just as I had anticipated, a tall, good-looking gentleman with a headset in his ear asked me if we were on the list. He also seemed a little surprised, but I really was.

After taking a glass of champagne from a silver tray, I walked into a very large room, with a high ceiling and a huge golden chandelier. The whole room was painted in red, white, gold and a little green. It seemed to me that I was dreaming and I didn't quite understand how I had come to such a place. I could see balconies at the top of the room, where I could see noble ladies and gentlemen. Probably only VIPs were invited here. They were certainly some well-known people, but at first sight I did not recognize anyone.

- Eva, what are you doing? Alan took my hand, scaring me. You got here fine, right?

- Hey, Alan! Yes... Everything is... fine. This is Dana, my friend!

- Hello, Alan, nice to meet you! Dana extended her, smiling broadly and without any reservation. It's so nice here! Thank you for inviting us!

- I'm so glad you came. I hope you'll have a good time. The tables are somewhere in that direction, and Alan pointed his finger to the back of the room, I think you're at the table 27. Let me look on the list.

He took some papers from his pocket and confirmed, nodding his head.

- Yes, table 27. Ah, Eva, I'll introduce you to a gentlemen who manufactures some very exclusive creams. Maybe we'll get lucky, he'll like you and you'll get a good contract out of him. Ok?

- Ok... I had trouble finding my words. Alan, wait, don't go! I want to ask you something!

- Tell me please.

- Do you think we didn't dress very well?

He examined me from head to toe, took me by the hand, made me do a pirouette and told me that I looked great. He admired my red lipstick and sandals. His compliments were good to me and I managed to get over my internal frustrations. I felt too small and too insignificant to be there. I was lucky to have Alan, who always believed in me. He always told me that I have something special in my eyes and that I will certainly go far. He made me dream, but sometimes I would go down with my feet to the ground and reality hit.

- Eva, this is out table. Here are our numbers. Let's sit.

It was a round table, with a white tablecloth and a lot of cutlery and glasses. An arrangement of natural golden flowers with a few candles was placed in the middle. Everything looked perfect! No one had arrived yet at the table and it seemed a little strange to me for us to sit first.

- Come on, don't you want to go first to the bathroom? There's no one at the table! I whispered in Dana's ear.

- So what if there's nobody at the table? Look, I'll sit here first, where it says D-A-N-A. What an honour! Come on, girl, sit down, you seem like you swallowed something the wrong way. What the hell got into you? You are absurd with all your moods! This is a party, fell good and let your issues go. What the hell, you look like we are surrounded by princes and princesses and we are the servants. You work with some of these people, look around, maybe you'll find someone you know. But as I know how tongue-tied you are, no one will talk to you! What the hell!

- You are always scolding me. I'm just not used to this kind of people, what more do you want from me!?

- What kind of people, I don't understand? Do they have three legs, four eyes or something? These are normal people, Eva. Come to your senses! Look, let's see who we can talk with! We didn't come here to talk to each other! And tell me what you want to drink, because I want to call the waiter!

- I'm fine with a little champagne, thanks!

- Drink it up then! I've already finished my drink! A little champagne for us, please! Dana signalled to the waiter.

- Cheers!

- Cheers!

At Dana's insistence I drank three glasses. I was already laughing loudly and I hadn't even noticed that the world had already begun to sit at our table. There were three more girls and five boys. I knew two of the girls, Ella and Anastasia. They were also working at the magazine. I didn't know about the boys. We nodded slightly to each other, until one of the boys, a smaller one, got up from his chair and began to shake hands with everyone at the table. We introduced ourselves to the others and started to feel better. Dana was already in ecstasy and showed me many men in the room.

The music sang softly in the background until all the noise was interrupted by a "Good evening!" in the microphone. Two very nice looking ladies were on the stage. I didn't get to know a lot of people from the magazine, but I had never seen them before. I asked Ella softly if she knew who they were and she told me there were only two hosts.

After an elegant and fairly short speech, the start of the party was signalled! Various people climbed on the stage one by one, but I could hear them very well anymore. I was a little bit drunk and I wanted to dance. Dana was talking with some men and I couldn't explain how she could attract them so quickly. I would have wanted to talk to a person of the opposite sex, but nothing seemed to happen.

- Eva, as promised, let me introduce you to Mr Rwan Ruskwasi. The founder of the Amer and The Sea creams.

- No, this could happen to me. Alan came with that gentleman exactly when I could hardly see. But the champagne seemed to give me some courage!

- Good evening, mister R square! I jumped from my chair and kissed his cheek.

- Eva, what are you doing? Alan took my hand, as my reaction shocked him.

- It's ok, Alan! Mr R square took his aside, and he seemed to be amused, smiling under his moustache. I was still smiling and I didn't understand what I did wrong.

- I'm sorry for her, it seems she drank too much! And because she's not used to drink, this happened.

- What happened, Alan? What did I do? You introduced me to mister R...

- Rwan, Eva!

- Right, mister Rwan, and then I gave him a small kiss on the cheek, because he's very nice. I'm sorry if I did anything wrong! Let's shake hands, or Alan will scold me even more! I extended my hand to the gentleman and made him laugh out loud.

Alan was red in the face and did not know how to handle the situation. I don't know what that gentleman whispered in his ear, but Alan left and we remained just the two of us. When I looked down, I realized that I could barely see my sandals. I looked up and saw Mr R square looking at me. He was dressed in a suit and I could see only the two opened buttons of his shirt.

- Eva, do you want to take some air?

- I believe this is a good idea. I'll take my purse so I can go home after. But where could Dana be?

- Who's Dana?

- My friend... she was here somewhere.

- Leave her be, she'll come! Let's go!

We went in the gardens and the clean air made me feel better. I started to come back to my senses. When I saw a waiter with his tray full of glasses of champagne, I asked for another. Mr R seemed very attentive and elegant.

- Do you want to take a bottle?

- A bottle? Yes, why not!

- I like you! Let's drink it upstairs, what do you say?

- Upstairs where?

- Look, there, on the balcony. I took a room here for tonight. We'll stay outside and drink champagne. This way you'll be able to sit down. What do you say?

- Hmm... I don't know what to say! I started laughing and leaning slightly on his shoulder.

- Wait! Just wait a little! Just try and remain on your feet if you can! Come on, this way! I asked a waiter to bring a bottle of Dom Perignon up, on the balcony. Do you want some strawberries?

- I want strawberries too! I want everything!

I was in a very good mood and followed Mr R on a long hallway. We stopped in front of an elevator, he took out his card and pressed the button for the second floor, that is, if I saw correctly. As soon as the elevator's doors closed, the grabbed my back, put my leg around him and started kissing me. With the other hand he was trying to find my panties under the skirt.

I was feeling very good! He was kissing my neck while looking for my vagina with his hand. His beard burned me slightly, and that was making me feel even better.

- Do you like it, Eva? he asked me softly, while roughly kissing my ear.

- Yes, I like it! I like it a lot!

- He pushed me in a corner while desperately looking for the elevator's buttons.

- What are you doing?

I jumped on his back and started to kiss his neck. I put my hand down his trousers and felt his excited penis. He was so hard, my patience has already reached its limits, I felt like the entire body was engulfed by a pleasant warmth.

- R2, can you tell me what the hell are you doing?

- Oh, Eva!! He turned to me slightly nervous. Nervous and excited, a nice combination! I was trying to block the elevator. But it's not working, to hell with it!

Meanwhile we reached the second floor. When the elevator doors opened, I saw a waiter dressed in white with an empty tray in its hands. The poor man, he was wondering at the sate I was in. I looked in the mirror and started laughing. My hair was all over the place, the red lipstick smeared on the face and the dress was up to my midriff. It seemed to me that the waiter was lurching, but I believe that I, in fact, was lurching. So, as tipsy as I was, I saw Rwan taking out a 50-euro bill and stuffing it in the waiter's shirt pocket. Immediately after that he took my upside down on his shoulder. Was I really so light? I was thinking. I just saw the room door opening and closing and he dropped me on the bad, face up. I rose on my elbows and watched him trying to take off his jacket. A champagne bottle was on the table, in a bucket of ice, and a lot of strawberries next to it. This gentleman really kept his word!

- Do you want some more champagne? I can see your eyes sparkling from it. Or shall we get down to business?

- To business? What business do we have? Yes, give me some champagne, please! I want champagne!

- If you roll your eyes one more time at me I'll slap your butt and jump you right now!

- Ohh.. Well, first you could jump me! And we'll drink champagne later!

I put a hand between my thighs and played with my hair with the other. He was starting to lose his mind. He took off the belt and quickly took off his shoes. He started to take off his trousers, but he was in such a hurry that he threw himself over me like that, half dressed. The shirt off his trousers and the two opened buttons made me want to see more. I started to open the other buttons and I felt him ripping off my panties. He lifted up the dress up to my neck and started to kiss my nipples. I was feeling like I was in another world. I was so tipsy, but I also felt like that from his kisses that made me feel something I had never felt. He slowly kissed me lower and lower. My hands were lost in his hair, on his back, on his hands.

In just one movement he turned me around on my front, my back at him.

- Do you like doggie-style? he asked me while biting my back.

- I don't know! I was barely able to talk. But right now I think I would like anything!

- How come you don't now?

He turned me again so I was facing him. He already lost his trousers. I was watching in surprise to his penis and his legs sculpted at the gym. He started to bite my nipples even harder.

- Tell me! How come you don't know? Do you like mocking me? Tell me! How do you want me to fuck you?

- Fuck me as you like! Just fuck me already! I'm a virgin and I don't want to be one anymore!

I jumped with the hands around his neck and started kissing him. I saw him remaining as a stone for a few seconds and he seemed not to react anymore.

- What is going on? You don't want me anymore…

- How the hell are you a virgin?

- Ha-ha! Just like that! I'm a virgin! Have you not seen any virgins until now?

- At your age, in this world of glamour magazines? To be honest, no, I haven't! But it's an honour. I'm speechless! I'll take it slower then. But you didn't seem a virgin the way you moved.

- Oh, Mr R R you are talking too much! Really... I'll not be tipsy anymore and I'll go find Dana!

I tried to limb off that very high bed. I didn't know they made such high beds. Then, suddenly, he grabbed my legs and pulled me back to him.

- Get over here! You're not going anywhere!

He put me on my back, lied down beside me on his side and started to kiss me slowly all over my body. He petted me in on the pubis with his other hand and was driving me crazy. When he put his fingers in my vagina, I screamed and felt like all my body caught fire. After moving his hand several times, I was feeling to having reached another world, I felt he entered me. It hurt so much, but he kept exciting me, massaging my breasts and kissing my neck. So, the pain was mixing with pleasure and I couldn't tell what I liked more: the fact that I was hurting or that I was orgasming. I wanted those moments to never end. When I finally opened my eyes, I saw his perfect chest and his slight movements he was making. He seemed perfect to me! I saw the veins in his neck bulging and he let out a shout of pleasure and then he fell on me. After several long seconds, he got out of me and lied on the bed.

- I have never imagined having such a surprise tonight! he told me, staring at a point on the ceiling.

- What surprise? Having sex?

- Ha-ha! I have sex anytime I want! Just tell me... how come you remained a virgin until now? How old are you?

- Almost 20!

- Pppphhh... Incredible! What can I say? Congratulations! And welcome now to the world of ex-virgins!

- Well, yeah. It wasn't as bad as I had expected! However, I'd like some more champagne!

I went to the bathroom and put on one of the two white, very fluffy robes. I looked in the mirror and it was like I was another woman. But I was not sorry! I felt amazingly good! It was just that I didn't know anything about this man. I didn't even know his age. What a load of crap!

When I got out the bathroom, he was sitting naked in one of the armchairs and played with his phone. He poured champagne in both glasses and signalled me with his eyes to sit.

- Cheers! For your virginity that you have just lost!

- You're funny! Cheers!

- You know, if I hadn't seen any blood, I wouldn't have believed you when you told me you were a virgin!

- Why would I have lied to you? In any case... Where's my purse? Dana must be looking for me!

- You drove me crazy with Dana! Relax! We're both here, we're drinking champagne, we have strawberries.

He put his phone on the table and pulled me quickly on his lap. He stroked my face and he was looking at me like I was some kind of travesty.

- Well, yeah... I don't know anything about you. But I'm not sorry! This should happen sometimes. Can you at least tell me how old are you?

- Does it matter?

- Not much. But I'd like to know.

- 47.

- 47? Oh, my God!

- Old, right? Compared to your 20s. However, I don't look my age, do I?

I started to examine him more closely. His hair was black, with some grey in it. His eyes were brown and the features of his face were very fine. He had a slight beard and it made him look even sexier.

- Come on, tell me! Do I look that old? You're speechless!

- No, you don't. You really look much younger.

My state of drunkenness started to evaporate and I was looking desperate around to find my purse. I had to let Dana know that I'm ok. I got up, took my phone from the purse and, to my surprise, I didn't get any texts from her. I wrote one to her in which I let her know that I was ok and that we would talk later.

- Ok, are you happy now? Have you texted Dana?

- Yes. I'm very happy now. I'd like to get dressed and go home.

- As you wish. I can call you a taxi, if you want. But let's drink one more glass of champagne and then you'll leave. What do you say?

I didn't want to leave. I wanted to stay longer. I wanted to look at him and find out a bit more about the man who made me a woman. I was telling myself that I wasn't interested, but it seemed that I was more interested than I would have imagined. I felt alone. Even if my mind told me otherwise, I took off my robe and started to look for my panties. However, until I remembered that they were ripped, I felt his chest against my back, he let my head down a little and started to bite slightly my shoulders.

- You're not going anywhere! I want you one more time, two more times... many more times!

- Well...

Before I could say anything, he pushed me on the high bed and lifted my bottom in his hands. He slapped me twice and entered me powerfully and deep. That hurt a lot more, and I felt something very big in me. He kissed my back, he took all my hair in his right hand and he massaged my breasts and nipples with his other hand. He pulled in and out of me very powerfully. He hurt me, but I also liked it.

- Do you like it? he asked me, pulling my hair slightly when he saw I started to flag.

- Yes. I like it! I like it! And I feel like...

I couldn't say anything, as I felt my whole body on fire, trembling, and every cell in my body screamed in pleasure. I was orgasming and I literally couldn't tell in what world I was anymore.

We drunk all the champagne and had sex many times. I could barely stand. My vagina hurt and my muscles were sore, I felt them in my whole body. I had a shower around 3 a.m. and fell asleep still in my towel. I felt good, but very unlike myself. I wasn't used to being happy and feel the joy to the maximum. I didn't know a lot about this man, but I tried not to think too much about it.

The phone alarm woke me up suddenly. Rwan was sleeping naked next to me. His phone was ringing. I had no idea what time it was, but I looked on the nightstand and the electronic clock was showing 05:00. I had barely opened my eyes that I have heard him getting up from next to me. He sat down on the edge of the bed and rubbed his eyes.

- Come on, I have to go!

- It's 5 in the morning, where are we leaving so early in the morning? When I wanted to get out the bed, I realized how bad my head hurt.

- If you want, you can stay and sleep some more. The room is paid for until noon. But I have to go.

I couldn't event ask him where he was going, and he grabbed his phone and took it to his ear.

- Jo, I'll see you downstairs in front of the hotel in 10 minutes.

- Wait just a moment, mister mystery man! You wake me up at 5 in the morning, you talk to this Jo on the phone and leave... Who is Jo? If I can ask you that...

- My driver. He answered curtly, devoid of any interest for me. Tell me, should I call you a taxi or do you want to sleep some more here!

- Oh, thank you, you're very sweet! You don't have to call me a taxi, I can call one myself!

The anger and annoyance in my voice didn't count very much to him. He continued getting dressed and looking often to his watch. I was standing on my bottom on the bed wrapped in the duvet, not having any idea how to react.

- I understand! Do you have any money? I can leave you some lei if you don't have any.

While he was looking in the pockets of his jacket, I stood up as burned.

- No! You don't have to leave me any money! You are already a bit nasty!

He looked funny at me, a bit puzzled that I was calling him nasty. But what a jerk! Oh, my God, what a stupid thing I have done! What had I been thinking? What was I doing here with a man whose name I barely knew in a hotel room at 5 in the morning? And let's not forget that I had sex with him for the first time in my life. How stupid I could have been!

- Look, Eva, we had a good time! I promise we'll see each other again, but nobody must know! Not even Alan! Please, this must remain our secret. I'll get your number from Alan, or you can give it to me right now. You'll see, I'll give you a good contract with the creams we were supposed to talk about last night (he was smiling ironically), but I'll say this again: nobody must know what happened between us. It's better this way for both of us. You'll see I was right. Ok?

He got close to me, kissed me quickly, he took the phone from the table and left. Only after he closed the door behind him did I really realize what I had done. I went by the window and was looking lost at the lights around the hotel. I had dreamt of a first night of love with a man I would be in love with and feel that he loved me, too. I had dreamed of a marriage proposal made by the same man, then children, family ... but I was alone, in a hotel room, a room whose number I didn't even know. After a few good minutes of looking in the dark, hung-over after too much champagne, my virginity gone and disappointed, I gathered myself and started to look for my clothes. After putting on the dress, I realised that I didn't even have my panties. They were ripped, but I told myself to put them in my purse, to keep them as a souvenir for the rest of my life. I put on the sandals and started to look for my phone. I felt very strange without the panties on. Right when I found the phone under the robe on the armchair, Dana called.

- Hello…

- Eva, what the hell are you doing? I got drunk and woke up three times already. I am at the hotel desk, they threw us out the hall. I've met some nice people, because my partner, the girl I came with, left me. Whatever. Where are you?

- I'm coming right now! Wait for me there.

- But where are you, girl?

I didn't answer. I hung up on her. I didn't even know to answer her where I was. I suspected that I was staying at the hotel at whose desk she was. I didn't remember driving last night.

After closing the door behind me I learned the number of the room: 202. At least that! I was walking to the elevator and thought about all kinds of things.

What would I tell Dana? I couldn't lie to her!

What about Alan? Oh, God, I felt so ashamed!

Where did the mysterious Rwan disappear?

What was I thinking, that I have landed in this situation?

Would I see him again?

The elevator doors opened and I reached the lobby. I didn't see Dana, but there was a roaring noise from somewhere on the right. As I approached, I realized it was the hotel bar. Dana was reclining on a chair, with another 5-6 people. They all seemed very drunk. I approached Dana and gently whispered in her ear to go home. She immediately realized that something had happening. She got up, said goodbye to her new friends and we left for the hotel exit. We got in the first taxi to go home. Dana took my hand and told me:

- Come on, tell me everything...

It was already light outside when Dana entered the room and opened the curtains. It seemed I had slept very little and my entire body was trembling.

- Come on, lazybones! It's already noon, how much more do you want to sleep?

I opened my eyes a little, but the sunlight was too strong and it went directly into my eyes.

- Come on, Dana, let me sleep a bit longer!

I put the duvet over my face and tried to ignore her. Not a chance!

She took the duvet off me entirely. Besides being drunk, I was also cold.

- Come on, I don't want to drink my coffee alone! And Alan has already called 10 times!

- Alan? Oh, God, what do I do?

I jumped off the bed and went to the kitchen. He had really called me and left many texts.

- Dana, what do I do? Rwan told me he mustn't know a thing! What will I tell him?

- Eva, you're like a child! You don't have to explain to anyone anything about your life, especially about your sex life! If he asks you something, you'll tell him you talked and he told you that he would give you a contract for his creams. After all, you told me that this was about, wasn't it?

- Yeah... I'll call him! Come on, put the coffee on, that's why I woke you! I'm going to take the cigarettes from the purse.

I managed to get in the bathroom a bit and brush my teeth and wash my face. I had dark rings around my eyes, red eyes... horrible! I went back to the kitchen and, as I lit a cigarette, took mustered mu courage and called Alan.

- Eva, how are you? Are you ok?

- Hey, hi, Alan! Yes... sorry. I'm home. I overslept a bit today.

- Oh, it's good you're home! Honestly, I was a little worried. You weren't quite yourself last night. You don't have to drink, Eva! (Yeah... after last night I knew that too) And, my God, you got a bit crazy with Mr R.

- Yeah, I'm sorry! I know I don't have to drink!

- Anyway, I called him today...

- And? What did he say? (I didn't even let him finish what he had to say).

- Well, I was worried your attitude annoyed him. I told him you're not like that as a rule. But he told me that you were very fine and not to worry. And he told me that it was sure you would sign something with him next week. It's super good. He seemed pleased. This is good news, Eva!

- Oh, ok, got it...

- You're not happy? You can make a lot of money! You really do deserve this, Eva!

Yes, I surely do deserve a contract from R... Shit! At least that in exchange for my virginity!

- Eva, can you still hear me?

- Yes, yes! Sorry, Alan, but, you know, I was thinking this would be so cool...

- Yes!!! Come on, I'll hang up now, I'm glad you're ok and especially that you managed to impress him. We'll get there, you'll see!

I felt so bad to lie to him... He was a good man, who had helped me without any obligation, and as a hypocrite, I was hiding things from him. In fact, only one: that I had fucked the first man he had introduced to me on the evening of the gala, the same man who now offered us a contract. That was the real reason I had impressed him, not anything else. Or maybe Alan realized it, but he didn't want to tell me, so he wouldn't make me feel even worse?

I asked Dana about it, to see what she had to tell, because other opinions matter.

- I still believe you're such an innocent girl and, besides, a little stupid. The people I had seen last night... I believe they all have sex with anyone. And I also believe that Alan knew this better as anyone else there. It's just that he hadn't any suspicion that you had sex for the first time. And, no offence, but this man is making money from your contracts. So I don't believe he cares too much if have sex with one or other. On the contrary, I believe that it's good for him for you to keep them close. Wake up! This is the world we're living in.

- Off... what a situation...

- What situation? You must start get used to it! Don't think about him anymore and live your life, as this did not affect you. It really mustn't! Not all things in life are always pink.

- Well, when will I talk to him? What do you think?

- I believe he'll invite you to dinner, he'll send his driver to pick you up... He'll buy you a large bouquet of flowers and he'll ask you to marry him!

- Thanks! You're a big help!

- You can get mad all you want! I was trying to joke with you. You'd become a woman for nothing, you're still a child!

- Yeah...

- You're so tetchy! I cannot tell you when he'll call you, but I'm sure he will, sooner or later. If you see him at the magazine, you must behave as usual, just like you get to know each other at the party and that was all. You'll be polite, you'll not stare at him and get about your business. If he calls you to see you again, you'll obviously have only two options: you'll go or not!

- Well, and what should I do? Should I go or not?

- Well, he didn't even call you! You are thinking too far ahead! But you'll do whatever you want at that time. What would you want right now?

- I don't know! You're right, I got too far ahead. Maybe I'll never see him again!

I was lying to myself and I was lying to Dana. I knew exactly that I was looking forward to seeing him again. I was just thinking about the moment he would call me. I dreamed to be with him, to kiss me, to feel him again.

Chapter 11

Several days had passed, I was going to school, to work, everything was almost normal. I had not received any sign from him. Realistically speaking, I was always thinking about what had happened. Sometimes I had the feeling that it was all just a dream, but I immediately woke up and tried to accept the reality. Over time, I had made many scenarios for losing my virginity, but this situation had not been in any of my thoughts. My visit to my mother the week prior had been very reassuring. It was the place where I went full of sins, which I confessed to her and, although she never said anything, I went away a little reassured, with a cleaner soul and ready to sin again. It was my oasis of peace and the place where I can restart.

Dana was bugging me to ask Alan for Rwan's phone number, but I would never dare to do that. In fact, he saw that I changed a little when I went to the magazine, but I told him every day another lie. After all, it was nobody's business the things worrying me.

One evening, during the week, I felt the need to visit Kate and Boris. I wanted to see the little ones very much. I was missing my evenings with them. Their family reassured me and made me hope that one day I would have a kind and loving home, just like theirs. Of course, they also had problems, but I couldn't see the gestures and love between to another couple around me. Kate always told me that it was the respect they felt that held them together and bonded them.

And the healthiest thing is to always try to find solutions and to really want to fix things, because giving up is the easiest thing to do. She always told me about many of the difficult times they went through, that she often wanted to give up, to leave, but that something inside her kept her connected to the house. When I heard her tell about those difficult times, I wondered if I should have told her what I was going through. I was thinking that a second opinion would be helpful, along with Dana's, but I was ashamed of myself and didn't know how I could start, so I gave up.

- Eva, will you stay for dinner? Some friends will come to eat with us around 20:30. I've ordered some sushi, nothing special. I believe it would be good for you, you seem a little tired, you'll have the chance to relax a little!

- Kate, I don't know if i can stay. I have to go to school tomorrow morning, because I have neglected it sine I got this job.

- Do what you wish, but I still insist! In the end, nothing changes if you stay two-three hours for a dinner. You can sleep after that and, besides, you'll get to know new people!

Yes, well, last time I knew some new people I ended up in a hotel room, drunk and I lost my virginity. Well, what did I have to lose, nothing remained anyway, maybe just my soul, if I hadn't already lost that too.

- Oh, very well, I'll stay! I won't stay long, I'm craving some sushi! I smiled and took her lightly in my arms. I needed a hug and I would have stayed like that for a while, but I realized that the situation was already getting awkward. I withdrew slightly. Let me help you lay the table!

- Let's! we'll be six or seven at dinner. I'm not sure whether Gabi will bring their son. To be honest, he's very handsome, maybe you'll like him and something will come out of it. She laughed and raised her wine glass towards me to clink them.

- You're making me blush, Kate. I don't need a man right now. I have enough problems but thank you anyway!

- What problems do you have? And never say that you don't need a man! Every woman needs a man! What the hell! Tory really is super ok, I think you'll like him. And he comes from a good family, he is handsome and smart. He also studied architecture here and in Paris. Come on, I won't insist anymore, because I don't want to be like an old crone (she laughed) but maybe you can make a new friend. After all, the chemistry between two people cannot be arranged in any way, by anyone else.

I let her talk, but somehow it would have been nice for me to talk to a new, male person, maybe he could help me get the thing that happened last week out of my system.

Meanwhile, the sushi arrived, we arranged them on the table and Boris came with a new bottle of wine. He was very good at drinks and talked a lot about wine houses in France and Italy. They were making comparisons and discussing the years, taste and smell. It wasn't my thing, so I was looking on the phone, on Facebook, on Instagram, talking to Dana... I was getting bored. The little ones were already sleeping and I was really sorry that I hadn't stayed with them longer during the last few weeks

The animated discussion they had about wines was interrupted by the door bell and I was very happy, that I could apologize faster and leave. Dana was going to coffee with some friends and it would have been nice to be there with them, but now I couldn't go back on my word, I had to stay just for a little while.

- Hey, darlings! Welcome, oh, you shouldn't, we already have some good wines, but, if you want, we'll start with yours. Kate could be heard talking in the hallway, seeming very happy. But where is Tory? We have a nice girl for him here and I was thinking to introduce them.

Well... that Tory hadn't come, my good mood all but vanished and I wanted to be with Dana and the girls. As my morale was low, I didn't want to get bored with other older people. I stood up, looking for my jacket and what I had left there, when Kate entered the living room with their guests. I felt my blood freeze in my veins, my heart stopped beating and I couldn't move anymore.

- Eva, they are Gabi and Rwan, our old friends, well, in fact they were first Boris's friends and then mine. This is Eva, she was out nanny...

Kate was smiling widely, making introductions, but I couldn't look away from Rwan. I couldn't hear anything anymore, my ears were ringing loudly. The greatest shock was when he shook my hand, as he hadn't known me. Not a muscle moved on his face, on the contrary, it seemed we have never seen each other before. He kissed my cheek and told me it was nice meeting me. I actually didn't know what to believe anymore. How could he be so hypocrite and false? Or maybe he didn't remember me? Come on... one can't find virgins everywhere, at any street corner.

- Eva, are you feeling fine? Boris asked me, squeezing my hand, because I remained there standing, while everyone had sat at the table.

- Yes, yes, I'm fine! I gathered my wits, turned towards them and avoided to look at Rwan. I got a little sick and I remembered I had something to do at home! Please, don't be mad, but I'll go!

- But, Eva, why go? Are you ok? What happened? You're very pale. Let me bring you some lemon water. Sit down for a bit, to calm down, Kate came quickly and very worried beside me.

I gathered every scrap of strength and pride I had left, I reassured her that I was just fine and it had been just a moment I had felt a bit dizzy.

- Let me call you a taxi! I'm sorry I kept you for so long, I really didn't realize how tired you were, Kate continued to excuse herself.

- No, no, it's nothing, Kate, I'm really fine! I started a fake laugh, but I think everybody knew for what it was. I'll manage by myself!

- Please, Eva, don't be stubborn! You're not looking very well, do you want to go to the hospital?

- No, Kate! What hospital? I just had to get home quickly. Please...

- You know, R2 started, and I felt an even stronger wave of nausea, out driver is already downstairs and he won't have anything to do until we'll eat dinner. He can drive her without any troubles and then he can come back for us.

- Yes-yes! It's a very good idea, completed his wife, Gabi, while standing from the chair and coming next to me. She was such a nice lady, with perfect features! She wore a yellow suit, skirt and jacket, and a string of wonderful pearls around her neck. She smelt of a sweet perfume from head to toes and, when she took my hand, I felt an extraordinary warmth. She had a fine skin and seemed to be an exceptional lady.

While I was examining Gabi, Rwan had already got dressed and was standing at the door, ready to walk me downstairs to his driver. I felt like I had some drugs, and I couldn't talk at all. They all seemed worried about me, but I was more worried about this situation.

When the elevator doors closed and I found myself alone with him in such a tight place, I thought I was going to kill him. I simply hated him! He was like a ghost that had disappeared and now appeared totally by chance, to throw everything spinning.

- How are you? he asked me laughing, coming closer to me and caressing my face.

- What? How am I? Take your hands off me, you insensitive prick! I got in the opposite corner and threw his hand off my face.

- You are so aggressive! What happened? I hope you didn't tell anything to Kate or Boris.

- Excuse me? Yes, I told them everything! That's why they invited you in their home. You really couldn't tell?

- What did you say? Are you nuts? How could you do such a thing?

- Just like that... Well I didn't think that the family I used to work for knew you, so I started to tell them and when I said your name, they told me they knew you and then they felt sorry for me and invited you to dinner so I can see you one more time.

- You're talking nonsense…

- Why would you think that? Very strange, but, in the state I was in, I felt a strange excitement.

- Boris wouldn't do such a thing, he would have told me!

There were two more floors to the ground floor. Without thinking anymore, I jumped him and kissed him. He didn't respond. He grabbed my bottom hand and tried to get his hand under my shirt. I was all wet and I couldn't believe we had reached the ground floor. I wanted to block the elevator, the time, everything. When the doors opened, I arranged my clothes, looked in the mirror, and saw that he was completely at sea.

- I still want you, you know! I whispered in his ear and left. I didn't look back, but I didn't hear footsteps. He was still standing in the door of the elevator and I was trying to keep myself on my feet until I left the building, so he couldn't see me. I knew he was looking at me and I didn't want to turn my head at all.

After I exited the building, I pulled out my pack of cigarettes and leaned on the first wall. I couldn't understand anything in my life anymore. What the hell was this man doing in the home of the family I loved the most? How could I have jumped him in the elevator? Where did all this courage and boldness come from? What would I tell Kate? Pretend I don't know him? And him? What was he going to do next?

After I finished the cigarette, I kept asking myself a million things. I felt sad, but at the same time, I was excited, I felt like a liar, but also excited. How could I manage this mix of feelings in me? What lesson did I have to learn from this? Why had God arranged things so that I could meet him right in Kate's house? And what an amazing woman Gabi was! The hypocrisy within me spoke and a feeling of something more began to emerge. She had had inspired luxury, beauty, calmness and I was starting to analyse myself, wishing I could be like that. If, at the house, I had started to feel bad for her, now I felt bad because I wasn't something more! That I didn't try to look better and be more elegant. It was time to change something!

I got in the taxi and left for Dana. I told her on WhatsApp what I had had to go through and she couldn't believe it. She kept asking me where his driver was and he did not understand that we could not meet the driver in the state we were when we reached the ground floor. I didn't understand why had he come with me to the elevator? Did he expect that too? He could have just sat quietly at the table and write me a text asking if I had told anything to the two of them. Or maybe he needed my verbal confirmation.

I was so excited that I wished I was a man, went to a brothel, relaxed and went home. But unfortunately for this situation, I was a woman.

The next day of school was an ordeal. I couldn't focus and I kept watching the phone every two minutes. I was expecting something from Rwan. I didn't understand why he wasn't calling. I wanted to know more, I wanted to see him and understand what the hell was going on. What was this whole story about? If it had been a simple night of sex with a stranger for him, then I deserved for him to come and tell me to my face, or at least in a text. Fate had made us meet again. I felt that our story was not over and that there were things to settle.

Kate had written me a few texts asking whether I was fine. The poor woman didn't understand what had happened to me. She wouldn't have thought it in a million attempts. I felt guilty when I thought of her, but in a weird way I no longer felt guilty when I thought of Gabi, a feeling I had had when I had met her. I was thinking how it would have all gone down if Rwan's son, Tory, had come too, and Kate had tried to introduce us. It was already becoming too awkward in my head and I thought I was playing in a melodrama. In a very strange way, it occurred to me at one point to write to Kate to introduce me to Gabi's son, however, but I told myself that I should wait a little longer. I had a crazy desire to see his father staring at me sitting on the couch in the living room with Tory, knowing he couldn't tell her that we fucked like crazy a few nights ago. It passed quickly and I returned with my feet to the ground. One way or another, I had to find Mr R.

When I got to the magazine, Alan was very happy and excited. He was talking about projects and contracts, and he kept repeating that I would make a lot of money. There were a lot of people there and I was shuffling around, not finding my place.

- Eva, are you ok? You seem very nervous! Sonia, one of the ladies in newsroom asked me.

- Yes, I'm a little stressed, but it will pass soon!

- Can I help you with something? I don't like seeing you like this! You are usually so calm. You seem a different person now.

- You know... I think you could help me! I felt immense courage all of a sudden, real crazy. Mr Rwan R, the one with the creams, told me he would offer me a contract, but I've never heard from him again. And I thought so much about it, that I need some money and it could be really good for us to sign something as soon as possible. I'd still like to contact him myself, at least I'll try my luck. Do you think it would be wrong?

I had become a diabolical and foolish woman. I was lying to the poor woman with no shame and I couldn't believe that I, Eva, was the one talking.

- Oh, wait a moment, I don't think I know now what this all about! What did you say his name was?

- Mr Ruskwasi. He has the Amer and The Sea creams. He approached me at the party and he promised me he would contact me, but he never did.

I was like a wheedling cat to Sonia and I was pretending so well that the dear woman sat at the desk and started looking through the emails.

- Did you ask Alan? He should have it! She was very focused at the computer.

- I didn't want to bother Alan. Relax, I don't want to make a fuss! It's ok if I won't have it, in the end maybe this is just fate. It's just that I thought I could have a bigger contract! I started laughing, but it was just not mu laugh.

- I have found his email and his secretary's phone. Do you want them?

- Well.. Whatever you say! I was trying not to show how hard I wished I could get in touch with him in any way possible. Maybe, though, I shouldn't bother them? Wait for him to contact me, what do you think?

- I really do not know. You know, it's possible he had already forgotten everything about it, as important as they are! But can you write them an email, after all, what do you have to lose? Be polite and ask if they are still interested. Ah, yes! I know Dora – his assistant. She's a very nice old lady. Of course you have seen here around here, she comes quite often since they have projects with us. Do you want me to call her?

- Oh, no, no! Let's just not bother them! Maybe I'd better write an email, or even wait.

- Come on, I'll write an email to Dora. She'll surely help us, she's very nice!

I couldn't believe what I was doing. What had gotten into me? This woman, Dora, didn't even know me. How stupid! I kept trying to explain to Sonia that she didn't have to contact them, but she thought she was doing me some good. Finally I was left without any contact information for Rwan, but also with the email sent by Sonia. What a mess!
I just left and got about my business. I kept thinking how stupid I was and in what a mess I had landed. I was in no mood for anything. I gathered my things, ordered a taxi and left for home. I just wanted to take a hot bath and get lost in a movie. I needed to be with me for a while.

Chapter 12

Several days passed and I was beginning to try forgetting about seeing him again, but at the same time I felt that things were not yet ended between us. It was a Sunday afternoon. I had come back from my mother and was staying home alone, waiting for Dana. I poured myself a glass of wine and lit a cigarette. I was reading some jokes on the phone and I was trying to amuse myself, but I couldn't manage. I scrolled to see the news, because it seemed important to me to stay in touch and to know what was happening in the world when I heard the doorbell. I got up, with the glass in one hand and the phone in the other. Dana had probably forgotten her keys.

With my eyes on the phone, I opened the door and when I looked up I saw a very tall man, dressed in a black suit and a headpiece on.

- Eva? he asked, seeming a little lost.

- Yeah... I looked down and I realised I was wearing only my panties and a t-shirt. I hid behind the door and only let my head out. Who are you?

- My name is Jo. I think you'd better put something on and let me in to talk.

- Well, how could I let you in if I don't even know who you are?

 - I'm Mr R.'s driver.

I felt my knees going weak and I was just staying there, staring at him.

- So, may I come in or not? he insisted.

- Yes, please, go in the kitchen. I'm going to put a robe.

While I was showing him to sit on a chair, I asked myself a thousand questions. I quickly went to the bathroom and closed the door behind me. What was that man doing here? How the hell did he find out my address? What a stupid thing to do! What a crazy man!

What a strange story! I didn't know whether to go back to the kitchen or stay in the bathroom. I was so glad that his driver was here, but I didn't understand why wasn't he? Had he sent him to take me with him? Tell me never to think about him again? What the hell did he want from me?

- Would you like a glass of wine? I asked him, trying to change the subject a little and postpone the talk about Rwan.

- No, thanks! I don't drink. He had a warm and welcoming voice. He was blond, with brown eyes, this skin was a bit olive. I couldn't figure out his origin. From his accent he seemed Russian. So... he wanted to continue, but I didn't let him.

- So, what are you doing here, in my home?

- I've come to see you in your panties. You're hot!

- Excuse me? What the hell is wrong with you? I just didn't understand anything. Did Rwan tell him that we had a good fuck and he came here to try his luck?

- I was joking! You're too serious. Mr R. sent me.

- Soooo... He couldn't call me? He'd rather send you?

- You know, maybe it would have better to call you, I wouldn't have to come here! I'm just joking. Don't look at me like that, I'm not here to hurt you!

- Well then, why are you here? I couldn't wait to find out why he sent his driver to my house. I would have wanted to find out more, where he had the address from, why did he behave like a ghost, but I was glad and I have even this sign from him.

- Tonight Mr R. will leave for a golf tournament in Madrid for three days and asked me to invite you, to go with him...

- Do you mean to go with him to play golf?

- You and him, and some friends with other girls.

- I don't understand! What about his wife?

- It's not your business what his wife does! He started to raise his voice and seemed a bit irritated that I asked about Gabi. Maybe he didn't know I had met her.

- I just asked, you don't have to get upset!

- Are you coming? We don't have much time!

- Come where?

- To drive you to the airport. The plane takes off at 20:55.

- What?

I looked at my watch and it was 17:12. My heart was beating hard and I wanted to get up immediately, get dressed and pack my bags. I longed to go to see him, to touch him, to feel him. I wanted to be with him! At the same time, I didn't want to show Jo that I'm so desperate, but I think it was easy enough to realise that hormones went crazy in my body.

- Just like that! I could tell you more in the car. You must tell me first if you want to come or not.

- Well, I don't know... I have to go to school...

- You have to go to school?

- Yes, and to work, too.

- It's not a problem with the magazine. He'll let them know!

- How come he'll let them know? All my thoughts suddenly stared to spin around in my head, and I didn't understand anything. So all the people at the magazine knew about this thing that happened between me and this gentleman?

- I'll say it again. I'll tell you more in the car! But right know you have to tell me if you want to go or not, so I can let him know.

- Rwan?

- Yes! He's waiting for my text. And it would be easier if we could go past that you'll tell me you don't want to go and I'd try to convince you and you'd accept and so on and so forth.

This man was getting more and more strange. His voice did not seem warm anymore, it seemed to me like I was talking to a police officer.

- Look, Jo, I bent towards him, you know you don't impress me if you try to look so tough!

- I'm not even trying to impress you. He came in my face as well, and it seemed we were nose to nose over my small kitchen table. If I wanted to impress you, I would have tried to jump on you when you opened the door in just your panties.

- Excuse me? You probably think you've come to a whore's flat! I think you're confusing me, boy! I pulled back and lit another cigarette.

- Not at all! He took the cigarette from my hand, put it out in the ashtray and asked me once more: So, are you going?

- Yes, I'll go! I put my hand on the cigarette pack. But after I'll smoke another one.

- I lit my cigarette and put my feet on the table. I drank the wine and inhaled greedily the smoke. He took out his phone and started texting.

- Yeah, you really have nice legs! You have 30 minutes to go out the door. I'll wait down in the car.

He got to his feet, pulled the door after him, and I stood with my feet up, cigarette in hand, and eyes pointed to the door. I put out the cigarette, put my hand on the phone and called Dana. When I told her what I was going to do, she laughed and said that she envied me. She started to tell me that I am a Cinderella and she laughed at me for going among the rich. While she was chatting, I also started packing. I didn't even know what the weather was like in Madrid. I had a small bag, but enough for how many clothes I would take with me. I didn't know what to think first. I just wanted to get in the shower quickly and shave my legs. I couldn't go there with hair on my legs. I had to look and smell flawless. I didn't have elegant clothes, just something I had worn in a few photo shoots, but I didn't even want to look like a bimbo. Who would be there? What were we to do there? What would Rwan tell when he'll see me at the airport?

I managed to get ready in 15 minutes, with the shower, shaving my legs and luggage ready. I was standing by the door all dressed up and waiting for another 15 minutes to pass. I couldn't get down there that fast. And so it was bad enough that my face betrayed my eagerness to accept to go there, to go down to Jo, to the car, so fast, it would have been too much.

I wrote an email to the school to say that I would not go for the next few days, because I felt bad. I was already missing a lot and I started to think whether I was going to finish this school anymore and whether I would sit my baccalaureate exams. But I quickly changed my mind, because I was going to spend the next three days with the first and only man in my life. I was happy, eager and full of good feelings in my mind, but also in my body. I took a deep breath, checked my passport and closed the door behind me. I got in the elevator and started to say a prayer. I remembered my mother, how she always prayed and how I went to church when I was little, every Sunday. That brought tears in my eyes and I began to get sad. I missed my mom harder than ever. Probably because of the guilt that was struggling with the happiness in me. I would have liked to be the mother the one who closed the door behind me and told me whether I was doing was good or bad. But, unfortunately, she wasn't there.

I exited the building and saw Jo in a black Porsche Cayenne, with tinted windows. He opened the window and told me to get in the back.

Before I opened the car door, my heart clenched a little, thinking that Rwan would be on the back seat. The tinted windows misled me, he wasn't there. I had a small blue bag, which I put next to me on the backseat. I sat down diagonally to Jo to see him. The leather with which the inside of the car was upholstered was black and, suddenly, music was heard from a radio. Nobody said anything for several minutes. Jo was playing with the phone and was focused on the traffic. He glanced at me from time to time, as if wanting to make sure I wouldn't jump out of the car.

- And what did you say you'd tell me when we'd leave? I stared so as to break the ice.

- I should understand that you have never been there?

- Been where?

- On a trip with Mr R!

- No... it's the first time! What the hell? I thought to myself. How many women go to the airport daily with him? The question was a little awkward. I was scheduled for another trip and I didn't know?

He smiled to me perversely in the mirror.

- I have no idea! This is not my job. I have to take you to the airport and train you.

- What to train me? How to have sex? Or he's calling me to read the papers together in the morning?

My irony irritated him a little and he didn't seem to find the right answer. He put his hand in his jacket pocket and pulled out an envelope that he held out to me, while his gaze was in front of him, on the road.

- You have everything you need there. Until I was able to open the envelope, he continued. The return ticket, the company card...

- What company card?

- Ha-ha... he laughed, looking in the mirror and realizing that I was totally on another planet. You have a card for these days. You have 500 euros for every 24 hours. In the end...

- What? Where are you taking me, boy? You probably believe that I am some whore and I need 500 euros a day to let my body be used by other men! Stop the hell this car!

I wanted to open the door, but it was blocked.

- Wait! Don't jump off when the car is still moving! I'll take you back, no problem. Just let me finish. And no, I'm not taking you there to prostitute yourself. I'm not taking you there to be Mr Rwan's partner for three days. After he told me that I calmed down a little.

- Ok, so... why do I need money?

- Oh, if you want to go for free, there's no problem! You can give me the money when you'll get back! He started to laugh and stopped the car.

- So, you understand me! You'll go to a golf tournament in Madrid, where 10 men will go, including Mr R. each of them will be accompanied, but not by their wives. Yes, you'll go there to fuck, but only with Mr Rwan, not with anybody else.

- I don't understand, we'll go together as a group and each man left his wife at home, each took a girl/mistress/prostitute or whatever and left for Madrid!

- Exactly.

- Well, had I not gone, who'll go with Rwan?

- He probably goes alone and suffers a lot because you're not there! He was ironic and annoyed me.

The strange thing was that I didn't want to get out the car, I wanted to be at the airport already, to see and talk to him. I had so many questions for him. And, of course, I wanted him to touch me, kiss me, and, and the same time, I was telling myself that I was not a prostitute.

- Jo, look, here's the thing. Maybe you think I'm some kind of whore of your boss. I don't know how many details you know, but Rwan was the first and only man in my life!

- Ha-ha! You fell so hard for him? He was looking out the window, with a cod demeanour.

- No, I don't think I fell for him! Even so, probably you won't believe me, but I had been a virgin and I hadn't been with any men since then.

He turned to me and examined me from head to toe. He seemed very surprised at what I was telling him and he was not inclined to believe me.

- I'll say that again. I'm not a prostitute! I started to cry and put my hands over my eyes.

- Please, Eva, let's not get dramatic here! He also seemed a little surprised by my reaction, but he didn't want to show it too much. Do you want me to take you back home?

- No, you'll not take me home! I want to see him, I want to talk to him and I want to clear some things!

- You'll see him and clear out whatever you want. Let's go, ok?

- Yes! I looked out the window and didn't know what to think about myself. I didn't know if I had made the right choice. Right for me, that is. Because it wasn't at all ok to go golfing and having sex with a married man. But this married man had been my first man, without me knowing that a wife was waiting for him at home, that he had a child my age and many other things.

- I'll get going, but please, please, no more drama. You'll listen and ask me if you don't understand. Ok?

I nodded.

- You can use the card whenever you want. The name of the company is on it, but you have the passcode on the first page in the envelope. Besides the money for every 24 hours, you'll get a bonus in the end, depending on what Mr R will tell Dora – his personal assistant.

My thoughts screeched to a halt when I heard about Dora, the one to whom Sonia sent the email about me. What had that woman possibly said when she had read that I was asking about Mr R, and she had known all along I was going to go with him for three days to Madrid. So awkward!

- Sorry, I didn't hear you, I told Jo, without telling him what direction my thoughts went in.

- From the thing with his secretary.

- I got it! The card is always with you and you can spend the money as you like. However, my opinion is that you should invest a little in some lingerie, hair, make-up... this sort of things. Anyway, it's your choice, I'm only giving you some advice!

- Meaning what, I don't look good or what?

- It's not me who has to like you, I'm only saying what I think. You do whatever you want! Good! The other nine girls you'll meet at the airport. My advice is not to get too close with any of them. Some are old and may take control very easily.

- Old at what?

- At the job (he laughed). They are old mistresses, you silly girl! Wake up!

- Oh! I was so lost, but I still tried to process the information and not forget something important. So I'll meet the girls at the airport. What about Rwan?

- Mr Rwan will fly business class with the other gentlemen. You'll fly coach and a minibus will wait for you in Madrid. It'll take you to the hotel, you'll check in and you'll find out the programme.

- How will I find it out?

- One of the girls will tell you.

- And when I'll see him?

- Whenever you'll get at the hotel. In fact it's like a villa, only you will be there. Come on, don't be sad, you'll really have fun! No girl ever came back from there sad, some even smiling from ear to ear.

I didn't understand if he was talking about one of the girls or one who was especially with Rwan. I didn't ask anything anymore. I would find more there.

- The secret is that when he is with any other person outside the group, do not behave like his mistress. And, Eva, she raised her finger, as if wanting to make me pay attention, don't forget she has a wife! You are there for a short time and maybe, if you behave properly, you'll go again. But, I repeat, he is a married man, with an ok situation, don't ever try to do something crazy, because you will regret it!

- So what will you do to me? Will you kill me, like the Russian mob? At least tell me everything now, so I'll know what I should wait.

- I believe that it would be best not to wait anything!

We got closer to the airport and it seemed I didn't know anything and I was slower than ever. I wanted to call Dana, to tell her everything, but I didn't have the courage to tell her the mess I was in.

- Before you get out of the car, save my phone number. Any questions you have the other girls can't answer to, text me. You shouldn't talk to anyone else, but it's your choice.

- Good, now what do I do?

- You get off, take your luggage and to the gate 58. You'll see a group of girls...

- Well, what if there are many groups, what should I tell them? Will I ask them all, to see what the mistresses group is?

- Come on, you're not stupid, you'll get it immediately, you'll see it in their eyes. There's one always wearing a hat, if she's here today.

- Is it possible for one of them not to come?

- Of course! They may get bored, others may fall in love, others may run away with some other man, and so on. It's not that simple here either. Come on, go, I must leave!

I opened the car door more frightened than ever. The airport lights seemed to blind me. I had no idea who I was going to meet, how I was going to meet the mistresses group, and I really didn't know if I was going to Madrid, where I would get to see Rwan. I was starting to ask myself a lot of questions, and, for a second, I stopped in place and looked back. There was no one there, no Jo, no car. I was forced to make a decision as soon as possible: to go ahead and take a risk, or to get, take a taxi and to go home, back in my kitchen?

It hadn't been easy, but I decided to go. I wanted to see him so much, but I was a little scared for my life. I didn't know this Jo and I never thought I would go through this in my life. I was starting to imagine all kinds of scenarios: maybe he was sending me to a criminal group trafficking girls, or I might end up carrying drugs and other thousands and thousands of scenarios.

- You must be Eva!

A girl about 30, tall, dark, with straightened hair and a little barely-there make-up, surprised me. She was wearing black leather trousers, a black turtleneck and trainers. I was wondering how come she knew I was Eva?

- Yeah... I didn't know what else to say.

- I'm Rosie! Come here, with us! You're probably a little scared, as it's the first time you're coming. Have you known Rwan long?

- Not really. I didn't even know what to say, because they wouldn't have believed me that I only saw him once in my life, actually twice.

- These are the other girls. Girls, this is Eva!

I saw eight girls, some beautiful, some horrible. They all looked at me and examined me from head to toe. I was worried that I was going to look ugly, but some of them looked a lot worse than me. I just nodded and tried not to stare at them. I didn't know what I could tell them, nor did I care much for their name. They introduced themselves, but I didn't remember any other names.

- Come on, let's get you a coffee! Rosie invited me. Do you smoke?

- Yes, I do!

- Me too, let's have a smoke, because after passing the check-in point, we don't have anywhere to smoke.

I trailed her like a dog on the leash. I kept thinking that none of the girls wore a hat. And I didn't know where she knew my name from? I had so many questions, but my mouth was clenched. She bought two coffees and I went out the airport doors.

- Are you nervous? Rosie asked while taking out her cigarettes from her pocket.

- Nervous? I don't think so.

- You seem very nervous. Relax! There's nothing bad, you'll like it! Everything will be fun. We'll eat, drink, ah... and the most important thing... we'll have sex. After all, I believe you like to be with Rwan, that's why you're here, right?

- When will I get to see him? The words got out my mouth involuntarily.

- You're so eager! You'll see him directly at the villa. They're on the same flight, but they fly business, we fly coach. We sometimes even leave on different flights. I should understand that you don't know anything about it?

- Not really. I had only 30 minutes to decide whether to come.

- I see. Well, what would you like to know?

- I really don't know what I want to know. I just want to get there already!

- You'll have to wait several hours. The time will pass very quickly, you'll see!

- And... each girl here... I didn't even know how to ask.

- Yes....

- Each of them is with a man, I suppose?

- Yes. Some are old at this, some new, just like you. I have been doing this for about 4 years already. I could say I see Boris as my husband.

I was a little shocked, thinking about Kate's Boris, but it couldn't be him.

- How do you mean, your husband?

- When we are going on holidays, when he comes to my house. I know he has a family and two children, but I don't care. I am his oasis of peace!

There were too many things in common with the Boris I knew. It couldn't be him! The one I knew had a happy marriage with Kate. He couldn't do that to the kids! And if it was him, how would I face him? How could I not tell him anything? Pretend I don't know him? I would have liked to ask her his last name, but I stopped. What could I have told her? That I worked as a nanny for his children? This situation seemed embarrassing to me, but I still hoped it wasn't the Boris I knew. But if it was him, everyone would have thought he had recruited me for Rwan, from his own home, while I was taking care of his children. Of, God, what a situation! What the hell was I doing there? How did I get like this? For several seconds I thought to leave. I wanted to see Rwan so much, but I couldn't see Boris with some woman, other than Kate.

- Eva, do you feel fine? Rosie asked while putting off her cigarette.

- Yeah. A little tired.

- Drink your coffee and let's go.

She took off before me and started to play with her phone. I stayed there and examined her from top to bottom. Indeed, she had an admirable body and her long, brown hair was perfectly straight on her back. But even so, the image with Kate with the children and Boris in the living room, still appeared in my mind. I couldn't believe that Boris, the one having two children, was also Rosie's Boris!

I quickly drank the coffee, took a deep breath, and went after her. Besides the fact that I was destroyed, with all my thoughts, this thing with Boris had also jumped out. I had started the holiday in Madrid well. What surprised me the most was my desire to see R2. Regardless of all the danger I could throw myself in, there was a voice inside my head urging me to go. Although he had a family, a wife and a child, the surprise was that I didn't feel guilty at all. I wasn't interested in them and I was dreaming with my eyes open when I was able to touch him.

I remained very quiet until we boarded the plane. They all knew each other, they joked and told stories from other trips. I was asking myself another question: if I didn't come, who would be in my place? I had a moment when I wanted to ask Rosie, but I refrained. I didn't want to be the subject of the gossip mill and hopefully I would be able to ask him when I saw him.

I sat next to Rosie and Maggie on the plane. Maggie she was a blonde girl with long hair and very long nails. My attention was drawn to them whenever I wanted to look out the window. She was smiling a lot and had perfect teeth. I don't think she was much older than me, but I didn't ask her. Unlike Rosie, she wasn't talking about her lover. Or no, it wasn't her lover, she was his mistress. He had to be the boyfriend. We had seats on the last rows of the plane. The business class was in front of us and only a curtain separated us. I was sitting in the middle and couldn't look down the aisle. I wish I could have seen him get on the plane. I was still scared and I was still wondering if I had been crazy when I had decided to get on the plane, without even having a confirmation from him.

After a time, Maggie saw that I was stressed, she put her hand on my leg and squeezed a little, telling me to relax because everything would be fine. They did not understand that I had not seen this man many times, that he had been the first man in my life and that I was not a prostitute like them. I wouldn't even dare try to explain them, because they most certainly wouldn't understand what I was talking about.

I closed my eyes and tried to sleep. But now the empty feeling in my stomach made me want to move almost all the time.

When the flight attendant announced that all boarded the plane and we can take off, I sat up and tried to look in front of the plane. I had no chance to see anything, the curtain that separated the business from the coach was drawn.

- Hey, what are you doing? Sit down! Rosie pulled me down lightly.

- I'm not doing anything! I just wanted to see if he boarded the plane!

- Eva, it seems you didn't understand the rules very well or they weren't explained to you! You don't have to draw attention to you! That's if you want to come again! Now you know what you want. Just be patient, we'll get there and you will get tired of him, believe me!

- Will I?

- Ha-ha! Or maybe you're some nymphomaniac, I wouldn't know! You just don't get to make mistakes, many good girls were in your place, but some of them were sent home...

- How come, sent home?

- Just like that! They didn't understand that all of them are married and we cannot wreck their families. Some of them got jealous of the wives, others wanted more or they didn't respected that we must pretend we don't know them when we are in public. Do you understand?

- I'm trying to understand. I still don't understand what I'm doing here!

- How come, you don't know what you're doing here? You're not going to the library to read of camping with the friends from college.

- I've never said that. But what if I hadn't come? What would have happened?

- Well, I don't know! The last few times, Rwan was mostly alone, or he found some girl there, were we went, for a night or two.

- Why was he alone? Didn't he have anyone to bring along?

- Indeed! You're so naive, Eva! Of course he could find instantly someone. But something unpleasant happened with his last mistress, and I believe he was affected by it.

The discussion became more and more interesting and I didn't want to miss anything he said. I was all ears and I focused as hard as I could. I let her talk and I would say anything only when she stopped talking.

- Well, what happened? That is, if you can tell me, of course.

- Hm... It's not a secret, but I'd rather you wouldn't tell that you know about it from me.

- Of course, this will remain between us.

- She got pregnant and she didn't want to get abortion. They had been together for some time and she started to believe that he would leave his family and live with her and the baby, had it been born.

- Oh, I get it...

- That's why I'm telling you this! We don't have to forget our place, it's very important!

- So, what did they do?

- We don't know any details. Just that, in the end, she had that abortion. Rwan gave her some money and forbid her to ever come close to him again.

- And was the deal respected? By her, I mean...

- I don't have the slightest idea! But I've never seen her since. And after her, I told you, he never came with any other girl. He told us that you'll be coming, and, to be honest, I was a little surprised, because we used to see almost always alone.

- How long ago was this thing?

- What thing?

- This scandal with his former mistress.

- I think some six months ago. I don't know exactly. Probably after he met you. Isn't it?

- Yeah.

- So, Eva, be discreet and do not try to stand out, because you won't solve anything!

- Listen, may I ask you something?

- Yes.

- Was there any girl to be a mistress in the beginning and then the relationship became official?

- Ha-ha! Of course not! Once you know this part of their life, could you be the wife of one of them? Of course not! There were some so good that they made them get a divorce, but they still remained lovers. But I don't think they solved anything. I never thought of that. I know my place and I won't think of anything more. I wouldn't like to stay home, raise children and he would go on business trips with another woman. I'd rather be the other woman. Do you understand?

- I'm trying.

And, in the end, you'll get no headaches. You don't fight, you don't get jealous, you don't ask for explanations. As a mistress you are exactly what a wife is not. Or, rather, you are what a wife forgot to be. At least, that's what I think.

I kept listening to her and I was thinking of Gabi. I hadn't seen any fault with her that night, at Kate and Boris's house. She was a stylish lady, past, of course, her prime. She probably wasn't satisfying Rwan sexually anymore and so he needed a mistress. And now, I was the mistress. I couldn't think I had attracted him too sexually since I was a beginner. But now, after finding out about his former girlfriend, I was probably his only option. And the fact that I had not spoken about him, neither at the magazine, nor with Alan, had made him choose me as an escort in this mini-vacation. What I was looking forward to most was when I was going to have a conversation with him and get some answers at least some to the questions I had. I kept on imagining, close my eyes and remember our first and only night together.

Finally, we arrived in Madrid. It was a trip full of strange moods and discussions with Rosie. I succeeded to close my eyes for a short time, but I couldn't get any sleep. I expected to see Rwan at the luggage carousel, but it didn't happen. We took three taxis when we exited the airport. I was in same car with Rosie, Maggie and another girl, Amy. They each took out their make-up kits from their bags and started to adjust their make-up. I didn't have much to do with it, but I took a lipstick out of my bag and moistened my lips a little.

- How long will it take to the villa? I asked Maggie softly.

- About 40 minutes. Not very long.

Each of them played with their phones. I took mine out and started writing to Dana. She kept asking how I was and what I was doing. She couldn't believe that I had not yet met Mr R. She encouraged me and told me to enjoy myself and not to worry about stupid things. I thought about texting Alan that I wouldn't get the magazine next week. But I decided to write to him only the next day, in the morning. The fact that I was neglecting school more and more made me think, but that didn't grab my interest at the moment.

- Eva, Rosie turned towards me, from the front seat, look, you're not allowed to take pictures at the villa nor from the places we'll go to. I don't know if they told you, but I'd better warn you so there's no fuss for nothing!

- Ok, thanks.

It was like I was in a mob movie, in which I was not allowed to divulge information. It seemed exciting and interesting, but at the same time, a little out there. There may have been some crazy girls who took pictures of the men, and then they threatened to show them to their wives.

After going on a forest road, we reached a high black gate made of wrought iron. On a cream plate was written "Casa Rio". For a few seconds I saw the doors of the orphanage and the moment when they first opened in front of me came to mind. My stomach clenched and I was hardly able to stop my tears.

A smallish house sat on the top of the hill, on the right, that was lit up from all sides. It was dark and I could hardly see anything. Indeed, there was a golf course, somewhere, on the left, and that calmed me. There was a lot of gravel and the taxi wheels could be heard in the quiet of the night. I initially thought of a large and luxurious hotel. But, really, we had to have privacy. The gentlemen could not risk anything. Were all men like that?

When we got out of the taxi, my heart started beating hard. I knew it wasn't long before I could see him. I kept following Rosie and entered the door of the house immediately after her. The girls began to greet the lady at the desk. She was a petite lady, very tanned, with lots of Botox in her lips and a lot of bracelets on her arms. She was smiling all the time and kept complimenting my guild partners. After they kissed and hugged, they each started left or right, seeming to know where to go. I had no idea about anything. Maggie saw me looking a little lost and asked the lady at the desk to tell me where to go.

- What's your name? the lady at the desk came and took my hand.

- Eva.

- I see. And you're here with Mr Ruskwasi, aren't you?

- Yes…

- Suite 11. On the first floor, the first door on the left.

- Thank you!

I did not know what to do. Should I ask for the key or to climb up the stairs and go to the room? I kept looking to the left and right, seeing no one. I was alone in the lobby of a villa whose name I could barely remember.

- You can go upstairs! the lady's voice, with an unmistakable accent, interrupted my thoughts.

- Key? I gathered my courage and asked.

- It's open, don't worry!

I slowly climbed up the stairs and looked at the paintings on the walls. They seemed to be kings and queens from the Spanish history. But as I had little idea of history, I was just looking, lost, at their faces. When the stairs were ended and I reached the first floor, my blood froze in my veins. I was trembling all over and feeling completely lost and disoriented. I didn't know if I would find Rwan in the room or not. I didn't know what to do, to stay in the room and wait until he fancied seeing me, change me and to go downstairs, I had no idea. Eventually I decided to press the door handle and go inside. I had come too far, and I couldn't go back even if wanted to.

And, to be honest, I didn't even want to change anything. I felt glad I was there and I couldn't wait to see him again!

When I got in, I saw a large living room, with a table for six on the left, and an electric fireplace in front of me. Next to it was a couch with a small table, on which a bottle of champagne was kept cold, with two glasses set beside it. I dropped my bag down next to the door and approached the window with creamy, luxurious curtains. It was dark outside and I could only see a forest and a gazebo next to a barbecue. The light was dim and I couldn't realise where the bedroom was. As I turned my gaze back to the front door, I noticed a small niche near the table. I went there slowly and saw a wardrobe on the right and a door on the left – there was probably the bedroom. I opened the door and entered the room. I closed the door behind me and leaned back on it. A pair of trousers and a shirt was laid on the big bed in the middle of the room. So he was there. Or he had been there. When I looked at the bedside table, I saw a watch and a wallet. In the complete silence of the room, I could hear the water running in the bathroom. I was beginning to shake and I wanted to go and open the bathroom door, but I hesitated. I wanted to get the phone out of my pocket and text Dana. I had no idea what to do. No one told me how to behave, if I could go in the room when he was there, if we would sleep in the same bed. I just started writing Dana when I heard that the water stopped running. I froze. I was waiting the door to open at any moment. I wanted to sit down, but I couldn't peel myself off the doorframe. I closed my eyes and tried to listen and imagine he moves he made in the bathroom. When I heard the door handle, I opened my eyes. He appeared in front of me with his hair wet, chest-bared and wearing only a white towel covering his bottom half.

- Oh, you're already here? he asked, a small smile paying in the corner of his mouth.
I couldn't make a sound. I was watching him and couldn't believe that I was there. When I saw him coming closer, I thought I would fall right there on the floor.

I was looking at him, but not in his eyes. He slowly got closer and gently lifted my head, his hand on my chin. He was wrapped in a white towel, he had drops of water on him and some drops on the lips. He examined me from head to toes, and I was boiling inside. I wished to kiss him, embrace him but I felt like I was glued on the door I leaning on.

- Did you miss me? He asked me softly, while getting his lips close to my ear.

I felt that I couldn't control any part of my body. I closed my eyes and let him kiss my neck. With a short movement he put his arm around me and threw me on the bed. I stayed there, laid on the bed, turned on and very eager. He stretched next to me on the bed and, smiling dirty to me, put his hand down my jeans. I felt him entering me with two fingers and I leaned my head back and started to moan softly. I loved what he was doing to me and made me wanting more. My hands crumpled the sheet on the bed. He was moving his hand slowly but rhythmic. I was very wet and my whole body was hot. I tried to resist, but I was moaning louder and louder. I opened my eyes slightly and saw him looking at me. I tried to open my mouth, to say something, but I was too turned on to say anything, and very close to orgasm. I couldn't understand how I could feel like this only because he had his fingers in me. His smell and his presence drove me even crazier. But he still wouldn't stop. I could hear him breathing heavily in my ear and continued with the same rhythmic movement. I felt like I broke off this reality and a thrill went thought my body, from toes to the top of the head. I shuddered, caught in pleasure and let my body enjoy what I felt. I had sensations I had never imagined.

I opened my eyes when he took his hand from my jeans. He was in the same position, watching me closely.

- Did you enjoy it?

- Yes, a lot! I was watching him and I didn't know what to do, jump him, kiss him, get off the bed... I had no idea.

- Come on, go and take a shower! It's late!

- Where will we sleep? the words came out my mouth without thinking too much about it.

- Here.

- Together?

- Yes, together! Or maybe you don't want to sleep with me?

- Yes, I do! I tried to hide my enthusiasm, but I don't think I really succeeded.

He got off the bed and went to check his phone. I didn't know what to do, but I thought I should take a shower. I got off the bed and closed the bathroom door behind me. There were mirrors everywhere, and I was very disturbed. I leaned again on the door. It was like I was living in a movie. I have never imagined anything like that! I heard Rwan talking on the phone, in the room. I tried to listen, but I couldn't puck out what he was saying. He probably called Gabi, his wife, to let her know he was well and that he missed her, all that while being naked in the room with me.

I took off my clothes and started the shower. I put my hair up in a bun and carefully entered the stall, letting the water running down my back. It was a huge bathroom, with a shower but also with a tub. Everything was white and the fittings were golden. The floor was made of marble. While examining my surroundings, I heard the bathroom door opening.

- May I come in? he asked me standing in the door. I looked at him between the drops and I saw him naked in front of me. He didn't wear the towel and was staying naked there, smiling.

- Yes! I'm in the shower! I told him, staring at his penis.

He opened the door of the shower and got in next to me. He caressed my face and let my hair down. He was giving me a feeling of happiness, excitement and desire. I wanted so much to see him and now I was standing with him in a shower, in a villa in Madrid. He was watching me and wasn't saying anything. He was examining my body, but he wasn't doing anything. When my eyes met his, I couldn't restrain myself anymore. I jumped with my hands around his neck and started kissing him. The water rained on us, but I felt his hands all over my body. He was pulling me towards him and moved his fingers everywhere. He got down with his lips from my ear to my neck and then on my breasts. I leaned my head backwards and I felt like losing control over my body. He lifted me up and put my legs around his waist, continuing to kiss my nipples. When he entered me, I cried out and closed my eyes. I was transported in another world. He was lifting me up and down quickly and everything became more and more intense. Everything was quick and very pleasant. I didn't want it to end; I felt so good and I had one orgasm after another. The wet hair covered my face, but I reached his ear and started to kiss him hotly. I saw him closing his eyes and let his hands dropping from under my bottom. I pushed him to the shower wall and started to kiss and caress him. It was my turn to take over. I gripped his chin with my fingers, I bit slightly his lip and I lifted his arms. I started to kiss him and rubbed slightly on his body. I loved hearing him moaning. The thought that I was the one making him feel pleasure turned me on. I got slowly to my knees and started sucking him. That's when I saw him like I've never seen him before, powerless and very excited. Now he was the one wishing it would never end.

It was 7 in the morning when I heard the alarm going off on Rwan's phone. I had barely slept. I wanted to talk to him some more, but, after the shower, we went to bed and he fell asleep immediately. I deserved a discussion. I had understood that I was his mistress in this trip in Madrid, but I had a million questions and the answers were all different in my head. I had to hear them from him, and the fact that I didn't know a thing made me nervous.

- How did you sleep? he asked me, getting suddenly off the bed, to pull the curtains off.

- So and so.

He sat on the edge of the bed and starting working on his phone. I sat on the bed, naked, covered only by a sheet. I didn't know how to start the discussion with him.

- Rwan...

- Yes. He answered me without turning to me, keeping writing on the phone. When he noticed that I wasn't saying anything anymore, he turned. What is it?

- I don't know, I wished we talked a little. I haven't seen you since our first night, I knew nothing about you. After that, I saw you with your wife at Kate's and Boris's. It was shocking. And then you sent some driver to take me to the airport, without having any confirmation that you were the one who sent him.

He smiled, put the phone down on the nightstand and sit in the armchair.

- Why do women ask so many questions?

- Do you think my questions don't have any sense?

- I didn't say that! You're right, I should have called you and told you that Jo would pick you up. But I had no time.

- And what would have happened hadn't I come?

- Well, I couldn't force you! You wouldn't have come and that would have been that!

- What about Kate and Boris? Did you know that worked for them before working at the magazine?

- I found out.

- What would I do if they would ever find out I am their friend's mistress?

- They won't, at least not Kate!

- What about Boris?

- Boris knows! He's also here!

I couldn't believe that all I suspected was indeed true. He was also here, in another room, with Rosie. He was the man she was talking about.

- Oh, my God, what a situation!

- I'll ask you, Eva, to behave normal. I talked to him about it and he asked me to assure him that you'd never do something stupid. His family is his family, this is another part of his life that Kate doesn't know about. And I hope she'll never find out!

- Just like Gabi, right? I blurted.

- Exactly. That's why I considered this long and hard before I called you here. My wife has never met any of the girls I was seeing. Now this is a more special situation and I hope I did not do anything stupid!

- Well, then why did you call me here? Why didn't you bring another girl, one who didn't know your wife?

- I don't know what you expect me to say. Don't think I fell in love with you and, like that, I would risk everything! I liked you and Boris assured me you're a quiet and tactful person, and you'd never to something foolish.

That made me imagine the conversation between the two of them, taking about me at a glass of drink, talking about the famous Eva.

\- Ok.

\- And what else do you want to know?

\- I don't know what I want to know! And now what will we do? After returning from Madrid?

\- Eva, I don't know what to say! If you want, we'll see each other again. If you want! If not, not problem!

\- I see.

In fact, I didn't see a thing. I was even more lost than before.

\- You know, I think we should see where this is going without forcing things. Don't think so much and don't get so many ideas. I will never force you to do anything you did not want. If you want to accompany me on certain trips, or to see each other every now and then, in the city, I would be pleased. If not, I understand! I'll delete your number and that would be that. Ok?

\- Ok.

\- Let's get dressed and go downstairs to have breakfast. Please, behave as usual with Boris, it would be preferable you pretend you've never met him before. It would be better for your relationship with Rosie.

\- Well, what about him?

\- He'll do the same. I talked to him about this. Relax, there will be not more talk on this subject.

He went to take a shower and I kept looking out the window, thinking about all kinds of things, but nothing concrete. Eventually I had to get over the questions in my mind and enjoy my time there, because, in the end, I had chosen to do it. I was with him for a few days and it wasn't worth sitting and thinking about what it would happen next. I promised myself that I would leave my worries for later and act as a perfect mistress.

He got down to have breakfast before me. I had to take a shower. I would have liked to call Dana, but it was not the right time. I wrote a few messages on WhatsApp. I took a quick shower, pun on a little foundation and pulled on a pair of jeans and a white t-shirt. I took a sweater over my shoulders and arranged my hair a little. I was worried whether I was dressed properly, but I didn't have many clothes with me anyway. And, after all, I was there for the first time, it was understandable if I would make mistakes. I put on a little lipstick, took my phone and pulled the door behind me. One of the girls I had met the day before was in front of me in the hallway, holding hands with a man. From the back he looked older, but she was couldn't take her eyes off him. I was wondering if she was acting or she was so in love. Who knew…

Many golf bags were stored downstairs next to the desk. I could hear a lot noise from the right side. That's how I figured that there was the breakfast room. I didn't know what to do, whether I should go there or wait for Rosie or Rwan. I was leafing through the brochures on the desk when Amy appeared.

\- Good morning, Eva! How are you?

\- Hi, Amy! I'm fine, I'm just staying around. I don't know where to go…

\- Come with me! How did you sleep? You never came down last night.

\- I slept well.

She took my hand and I followed her to the dining room. Almost all the girls were there, together with their lovers. I couldn't see Rwan, but I saw Rosie sitting in Boris's lap. Boris was with his back to me. Rosie made a sign with her hand, and then Boris also turned around. He smiled slightly to me and winked.

- This is Eva, Amy introduced me, and all the girls turned towards me, greeting me warmly.

I felt like everyone knew me already and they didn't seem impressed of me. Amy disappeared to take some food and I remained a little lost in the door. That's when I suddenly felt a hand on my back. It was Rwan, who invited me to sit next to him at the table. He told me to go and get something I wanted to eat. I tried to avoid looking at Boris, because I didn't know how to react. They were all talking and joking, I felt like I fell right from the sky above.

- You don't want to eat anything? Rwan asked me again.

- Yes, I'll eat something! What are we doing after breakfast?

- We, the boys, we'll go to play some golf. You can go shopping with the girls, or you can stay here. You can do whatever you want! We'll come in the afternoon make a barbecue or something. Relax a little! I don't like that you're so nervous. You didn't look nervous at all last night in the shower!

I smiled.

- I understand! I don't know if I want to go shopping. What could I buy?

- I don't know. Whatever you want! Jo did give you the card, didn't he?

- Yes, he gave it to me.

- Well then, go buy some nice things for tonight.

- What nice things should I buy?

- I don't know... I'll let you surprise me! That is, if you want that, if you don't, talk to Mery, the lady at the desk, and she'll show you around. But I don't think anyone will remain here, at the villa. It's your decision. Your schedule is open until I get back, because I'll put you to work, you know!

He pulled my hair slightly and bit my ear. When I saw he wasn't bothered by the presence of all the other people, I kissed him lightly and, under the table, I put my hand on the zipper of his trousers and caressed him softly. I saw his eye rolling and he gripped my neck hard.

- Do you want to go upstairs? he whispered softly.

- Anytime! Shall we?

- Oh, Eva, the things you do to me! Unfortunately, we don't have time! And you have to eat something, to keep up your strength!

- Don't you worry about that!

- Come one, go and take something to eat.

- Will you turn this from lovers into parental affection? I won't remain hungry, don't you worry!

I got up to take something to eat from the all-you-can-eat buffet. Boris got beside me.

- Eva, how are you?

- Hi, Boris... I'm fine... I didn't know what to say and how to behave.

- Relax, I know how strange this is for you to be in this situation. But this is also strange for me! But hey, this is life! You know very well I love Kate, but this is my way to relax from time to time. You'll understand in time.

- That's the man! We are here to have a good time, let's do it right!

I felt my soul hurting for the things that happened to Kate, without her knowledge, but I wasn't thinking at all about Gabi. I told myself I won't think about anything, I would care about my relationship with Rwan and make the best of these days I would spend with him, because I couldn't know whether there would be a second time. So put some food on my plate and sat back down at the table next to him. He was caught in a discussion with one of the gentlemen and, from time to time, he would caress my leg, he would turn to me to smile.

His gaze drove me crazy. I could barely eat. The way his hand travelled on my leg turned me on.

Rosie came to ask me whether I would go with her in town shopping. I told her I would. While I was talking, Rwan got up and exited the dining room. I put down cutlery and I got up to follow him. I wanted to stay with him until he went golfing. I saw him entering the men's room next to the front desk. I didn't even stay to thing, and I entered after him. His zipper was already down. I pushed him in one of the stalls and I locked the door.

- Eva...

- You turned me on too much at the table. Fuck me quickly and you can go in peace after that!

- You're driving me crazy!

The place was so narrow! I pushed his pants down, he sat on the toilet seat and I sat in his arms, my back turned from him and my hands on the door. The noises he made tuned me on even more. I felt him deep in me, he caught my hair in one hand and he pulled it hard. He caressed my breasts with his other hand.

- Pull my hair harder! I love it!

I felt how he bit my back and it felt like he pulled my hair off my head, while I was transported in another world. It didn't take long until he also orgasmed. Only after that he let my hair go and the squeezed bot my breasts hard.

- You're extraordinary! It's the first time I had sex in a public toilet. Oh, but this was so good! I love your insanity!

I turned to him and kissed him.

- Let's go out of here! I could see he was about to lose again his control. All the others had heard us for sure!

- Yeah, like they're not all here for the same reasons: sex and golf!

- You're right.

We got quickly out the men's room. There was nobody there, but I couldn't know whether there was someone there before. I hadn't heard anything, I only felt. I let him standing there and got directly to the room. I threw myself on the bed and I watched the ceiling. I felt marvellous. Was it normal to want to have sex with him all the time? Was there something wrong with him?

I went with the girls to town. I wasn't at ease. I didn't understand why. Probably this life was so new to me! I was wondering what these girls were doing when they were not holidaying with their lovers. Did they work? Or were they just waiting for the phone to ring and show up at the airport? Have they ever thought of leaving everything behind and rebuilding their lives, with a man only of their own, to have children, to have a normal life? But in the end, what was a normal life? Who could have defined the general state of normal for all mankind? No one.

I was in the taxi with Maggie and Rosie. It seemed that they knew a smattering of Spanish and they explained to the driver where to drive us. They were in a very good mood and happy. I was still a bit out there and I resolved to come back to my senses quicker. After all, I chose to be there and, besides, I was enjoying myself. I felt wonderfully with Rwan. In fact, I was feeling very well having sex with Rwan, as we hadn't done much else together.

- Eva, well go to El Corte Ingles, and, after that, we'll go to a small Spanish restaurant to eat. What do you say?

- Yes... I don't even know what El Corte whatever you said was! But I'll come with you, you're responsible for the programme!

- It's a mall, with all the shops, continued Rosie, maybe you want to get something special?

- No... I answered a bit unsure.

- Come on, you must get something! We'll go there and look. Ok?

- Maybe we'll also visit the sex shop, laughed Maggie out loud.

- Yes, yes, we'll go! What will you dress like tonight, Eva? Rosie asked.

- Dress like what?

- Well, if you don't dress up now, in the beginning, when will you do it? In fact, even I, after all these years, I surprise Boris every now and then. You know, men like these things, especially when they don't get it at home.

So that was the surprise Rwan talked about.

- Well, what should I dress up like, Rosie?

- Come on, we'll see there! We'll help you get something nice.

While I was trailing them from shop to shop, my mind was only to the sex shop we would get to visit. I didn't believe those girls could imagine that Rwan was the first man in my life and one could count on the fingers the sex sessions I had until then. I would have liked to ask some more questions, to tell me what I should do. I wanted to remain Rwan's mistress forever and I was willing to take some lessons from the more experienced mistresses. Maybe, if I didn't do my job right, he would bring another, more experienced, girl instead of me. I started to imagine Rosie in many scenarios with Boris and I started to laugh quietly.

- Why are you laughing? Maggie asked. What are you thinking about, you crazy girl? I couldn't tell that I had just imagined Boris with his arms and legs tied and Rosie on top.

- Nothing interesting, I was amusing myself. Are you done here?

- Let's go to the third floor, the lingerie section, then we'll go. You don't want anything?

- I don't think so...

- Oh, yes, I know! In the beginning, we all saved money. Until you realise you don't have to save it. If you're ok, he'll get you a car, pay your rent... So you should enjoy this money!

- Well, Maggie, what if I don't do my job right? Or what does it mean to do your job right?

- Eva, you should know that not only the sex is important. It is very important, but these men could have sex with three different women every day, they can afford it. This is why you have to give him peace. Not to ask questions, not to annoy him, to smile to him, to relax him. They all come pretty stressed from home, full of problems, remonstrations and worries. You must be his oasis of calmness, his joy and his sex toy. Even there are just a few days, they're enough to charge their batteries.

- I understood! Thank you for your advice! May I ask you something, Maggie?

- Of course, anything.

- How often do you get to see...? I'm sorry, I don't know his name!

- Benny.

- Benny, sorry.

- Well, I have been with him for two and a half years already. Maybe one a month we go on a trip, sometimes just me and him, sometimes with the golf group.

- So, you see each other once a month.

- Oh, no! there are weeks when he comes to see me every day. Or maybe I don't get to see him for two weeks and then he comes and sleeps at my place for two nights. It's not a rule. It's just that I am always there for him. He knows that I am always available and we don't have a fixed schedule. Everything depends mostly on his schedule. And, of course, on his wife.

- Oh, I see! So you don't work anymore?

- No, I haven't worked for about two years. I believe that I gave up my job a month or two after we met, I don't even remember. It's not easy to be a mistress either, Eva! You must be very aware that it won't ever become anything more. You must never disturb him, never call, never make scenes. They have been married for 20, 25, 30 years. Most of them. And you must be really stupid to believe that they would leave their wives for us. This is why you must understand from the start your place, it's very important!

I really wanted to ask her if she loved Benny, but I told myself not to ask too many questions right from the first discussion.

Meanwhile, we climbed to the third floor, where we found Rosie trying on some bras. At their urging, I bought a white silk pyjama and a short robe. It seemed too much to spend 230 euros on the set, but I was ashamed to say anything at the cashier's. It seemed more interesting to sleep naked instead in a 230-euro silk set, but I didn't say anything. I left with a small bag, but they barely could carry all their things with them.

We exited the mall, we walked for about four-five minutes on foot and we sat down at a terrace. It was a beautiful day, with a lot of sun. The girls ordered food and a bottle of white wine. We toasted to ourselves and we didn't even realise when we had already finished a second bottle. I was dizzy, but I felt good. I was laughing with them and felt more relaxed. When we sat up to leave, I told them that I didn't believe I could walk straight and they stared to laugh at me. But it was true, I was walking and leaning to a side, then to the other. We took a taxi and went to the sex shop. The driver was also laughing with us. We were singing and humming all kinds of songs. When he saw that the place we wanted to go was a sex shop, I saw him passing his hand through his hair and then on his trousers. He also became turned on seeing all three of us all dressed up. He was a bit sorry to see us get out of the taxi, h would have liked to ask him to join us, but Rosie told him, before closing the door, that shed wished him a night full of naughty sex with his wife at home. Poor man, it seemed she said that just to spite him more. Do all men go crazy when they think about having sex with another woman?

We returned to the villa after each of us bought something from the sex shop. In out drunken state, we had a lot of fun and laughed a lot. Everyone looked at us like we were crazy, but it was really fun. I didn't dare tell the girls that it was the first time when I had went to such a shop. There were many strange things in the shop, but I didn't ask any questions. I really hadn't wanted to know anything about those things. I bought a mesh suit. It was made of single piece, with long sleeves and matching trousers. I got quickly to our room and put it in a drawer. The gentlemen hadn't returned yet. I got advantage of the opportunity and called Dana to tell her what we had done. She had a lot of fun and then started to give me advice. I laughed with her on the phone and told her I wished she were with me.

After I ended the call, I started to think. I didn't understand my purpose in Rwan's life. Yes, the sexual purpose, but still, why did these men who were there maintain their relationship with one mistress for so long? Just like Maggie said about Bonny, she was already like a second wife, who really didn't ask questions, didn't bother him, had sex, cooked for him and so on. Why do they need this? Wouldn't it be better to go to a luxury brothel, to choose a model each time they were in the mood for sex? In his case, he had stability at home with his wife, and he had stability with Maggie. How strange. I was beginning to wonder if this was what Rwan was looking for. Did he want to have a long-term secret relationship, or did he just want to enjoy my body for a while? Especially since he knew that I had been only his until now. As cold and distant a man he seemed, I could not imagine a different relationship with him except for sex. We had spent very little time together, but he clearly wasn't a talkative man and he didn't seem to let you approach him easily. Or maybe I was wrong. I didn't really know much about him and I wasn't sure if I wanted to find out.

- Eva, what are you doing? I heard Rwan behind me. I hadn't heard when he opened the door.

- Hey, fine. Here, I'm in the room. What about you? How was golfing?

- As usual, relaxing. You? How was your day?

- I've been with the girls to see Madrid.

- Good! How did you like the city?

How did I like the city? I had seen a mall, a restaurant and a sex shop. What could I have answered to such a question?

- Interesting.

- Aha...

After this short answer, he undressed completely in front of me, without any inhibition and went to the bathroom. I remained there, in the same place. I didn't know what to do. Should I go to him? Should I leave alone? Was he waiting for me? When I heard the water running in the shower, I undressed quickly and dressed in the suit I had bought. I made a high ponytail, I put on quickly some red lipstick and put on my stiletto shoes. I looked in the mirror and realised I liked how I looked in this costume. I took a chair from the table in the middle of the room and sat with my legs crossed looking to bathroom door.

- Eva, can you please bring my a robe? It must be in the wardrobe, he cried from the bathroom, without opening the door. I didn't answer. I wanted him to get out to see me.

- Eva? he cried again.

When he saw I wasn't answering, he opened the door and stuck his head out. He has water drops on his face and his hair was wet. He stared at me when he saw me and got out of the bathroom, standing in the door, naked and wet from head to toes. He became hard immediately and got closer to me with several quick steps.

- Wait! I told him.

- How come, wait? and he jumped me. I loved it in the extreme, but I wanted to keep him waiting a little. Maggie's words were echoing inside my head. I had to do my job right. I wriggled from underneath him and stood. I just then realised how turned on I was that my legs were trembling.

- You stay on the chair! I want to play a game!

- What game? I don't like games! Come here!

He sat on the chair and beckoned me to sit there in his arms.

- Why do you hurry? I prepared all this for you, so you'll have to play with me a little, that is, if you want to fuck me. Or maybe you don't!

- What do you think? Do I want to or don't I?

I went behind the chair and started kissing him on this ear, while my hands played with his nipples. I loved the way he threw his head back and clenched his hands on the armrests.

- Eva, I won't last long! I'll rape you!

- Hmmm... I didn't say anything and licked his ear, while looking at his penis.
- Please, Eve…
- What are you asking me?
 - I want to fuck you!
- This is too banal! How turned on are you, from 1 to 10?
- 10!
- I don't believe you!

I went in front of him and got on my knees. I was looking him in the eyes while playing my fingers all over his crotch.

- Now I want you to look at me, take my ponytail in your hand and answer five questions. All this time I'll kiss you all and touch you all over.
- I'll answer any number of questions you want, but only after!

He tried to get off the chair, but I pushed him back and started leaving red lipstick marks all over his abdomen.

- Do you like having sex with me?
- Yes, a lot!

He answered without thinking too much and kept pulling my hair.

- What am I doing here?
- Sex!
- Why me?
- Because you've been a virgin and because I like you.
- What if I hadn't been a virgin?
- You'd probably still be here. Come on, you have one more left!

I got closer to his penis with my lips and, even if I wanted to go down on him, I sat up and climbed in his lap and put him in me. He put his hands on my bottom and started to pull me towards him, as if he wanted to get in me completely.

- I had one more question.

He was extraordinarily turned on. He didn't even hear me.

- Rwan...
- Eva...

I couldn't resist for long, I was close to orgasm. I wanted to sit up before he came, but I liked it too much.

The sex lasted a long time. We fucked on the bed, on the carpet and on the table. Only our moans could be heard. I had many orgasms and I wished it never ended. When I tried to say something, he out his hand over my mouth and told me not to speak, to enjoy what I felt. It was the best sex I had had until then. When he finally came, we were back on the chair. He squeezed me hard in his arms and bit me softly on my shoulder.

- That was so good!

He got up and went towards the bathroom when, instead opening the door, turned back to me.

- Eva, you're on the pill, right?
- Pill? I didn't even know what he was trying to ask.
- Birth control...
- Of course not!
- What did you say? he turned annoyed to me.

- How could I be? I haven't have sex until I met you, and I've never been to a gynaecologist.

- This is a problem!

He took the robe from the wardrobe and sat on another chair next to me.

- I think you realise I don't want to have children with you or anyone else!

His words sounded harsh, but it made sense.

- I think I don't want to have children with you either. Maybe I don't want to come with you on any more trips!

I was upset and didn't process what I was saying.

- No problem, you won't! But tomorrow, when we'll leave, you'll take the morning-after pill. Just to be sure!

- What's that, the morning-after pill?

- A pill to make sure you're not pregnant.

- I see.

- I'll text the front desks to send someone to buy it.

- Really? Is this really necessary?

- Very!

He got up and took his phone out.

What was so urgent about taking this pill now? Did he really think I would keep the baby, even if I was pregnant? I realised, once again, that I was merely a sex toy and that he was not interested in me at all. I felt my soul break. Maybe I should have asked myself first what I was going to do if I was pregnant. I had tears in my eyes and I just wanted to get out of there and go to my flat. What the hell was I doing with this man on a trip meant just for fucking? I hadn't seen anything like that in movies, much less believed that it could happen to me.

He never spoke a word to me again. He went to the shower, got dressed, and looked as if he didn't see me there. I was in the same position, just pulled a towel over me. I avoided his eyes. I didn't want to look in his eyes, because I didn't want him to see that I had been crying. He didn't even look at me. It made me feel that he wanted to get rid of me and that he didn't know how to make me feel this and just disappear.

He closed the door after him and went downstairs to dinner. He didn't ask me anything. How could I have gone downstairs now, with all the others, when the man I had come with on the trip didn't even look at me anymore. And the reason was that I was not on the pill! Maybe I should have dreamt I must have protected myself and known that he would be very upset if I didn't do this!

I cried a lot. I remembered my mother and how much I missed her. I was sorry that I agreed to go on the trip with him. I wanted to slap myself and I couldn't understand how I could have sold my body to a man I didn't really know anything about!

I heard someone knocking at the door.

- Eva?

- Who's there? It was a woman's voice.

- It's Luna, from the front desk.

What the hell did this woman want now? I just didn't want to see her or anyone! I got up, put the robe and opened the door slightly.

- May I come in?

- What happened? I really didn't want her to come in and see me in my mesh costume and the robe over it.

- I have to give you something.

I couldn't refuse her, she seemed very persistent.

- Please, do come in.

I signalled her to enter the room. I saw her looking at my legs as she saw the mesh.

- I've brought you a pill. Mr Rwan asked me to give it to you.

- Of course. He couldn't get up here and give it to me?

- I don't know... I just did what he asked me to do.

- Yes, but honestly, do you have a reserve of these pills at the front desk? Do you also sell condoms and...

I stopped myself because I realised that I was becoming very rude. And the poor woman didn't really have anything to do it. She was looking strangely at me, she couldn't believe what came out of my mouth.

- I'm sorry, it's not your fault! I'm just a little annoyed.

- It's fine! You just have to take one today and one tomorrow at the same time.

I didn't think anymore, I opened the minibar, took out a bottle of water and swallowed the pill.

- Look, I opened my mouth in her face, just to make sure I swallowed it. You go now and tell Mr Rwan. And tell him that I don't want having children with him.

Surprised and a little stunned, Luna didn't tell anything anymore. She put the other pill on the table and closed the door behind her.

I didn't go down to dinner. I didn't feel I could. I called the front desk and asked for some sandwiches. I could hear laughter and music. They were enjoying themselves. Maybe they were dancing and having fun. I talked to Dana a little on the phone and told her what had happened. She was shocked too. I was even more shocked when I looked at the clock, it was already 01:42 and Rwan hadn't come up to the room. He hadn't event texted me. I wondered what he had said to the others. Or maybe no one had noticed my absence. After all, I was new there and maybe it was the first and only time I went. More than sure. The strange feeling that I had was that although I had wanted to leave earlier, now I wanted him to come up to the room and talk to me. I could explain to him the fact that really I didn't want to have a child with him, that I didn't know that I had to take pills and that, worst case scenario, if I was pregnant, I would certainly have an abortion. Although this was going through my head most of the time, I still had moments when I told myself that I was a fool, that I left myself be humiliated enough and that it would be appropriate to leave there as soon as possible.

I kept thinking about the discussions I had with my colleagues at school or work about mistresses. They always found a negative explanation. Maybe they did it for the money, for sex, for gifts, or just because they extremely looked and could have almost any man. I have never heard a woman give any positive arguments for a mistress. And I hadn't heard much from the men. Either because they were in the same situation, or because they wanted to benefit of such a situation. Or, in an extraordinarily happy case, they were totally devoted to their wives or girlfriends. I was asking myself if the men who cheated with another woman still loved their wives! Had Rwan still loved Gabi? Had they still had sex? How was it? Did she put on costumes for him to look as good as she could? But the most important question was: did she know he was cheating on her? I knew I could never find out these things. At least not from Rwan. If he had a nervous breakdown about me not taking birth control pills, how would he react to something much worse? I didn't want to think about beating or violence.

Lost in my thoughts, I noticed it was already 3. And he hadn't come to the room. I could still hear noise from downstairs, but not as loud as a few hours ago. Maybe he wasn't going to come up at all. Maybe he had another room with another girl. Or maybe he was just having fun downstairs and he didn't even think about me and I had spent so many hours trying to find explanations and excuses. I didn't know anything about this man, absolutely anything. And yet I wanted to find out so much. It was just like having an angel on my shoulder, telling me to get about my business and forget he existed, and a devil on the other shoulder telling me not to give up.

It was almost 4 when the door of the room opened. He entered, but he didn't turn on the lights. He looked for his clothes in the dark and came to bed quietly, lying next to me, without touching me. I was pretending I was sleeping. He turned his back to me and didn't say a word. I smelled whiskey on him. I would have liked to take me in his arms. Or maybe not to come up at all. I couldn't sleep anymore. I wondered if he had fallen asleep.

The sun started to rise. I hadn't closed an eye all night. This situation I had found myself in seemed so strange. And really, for what? For a foolish thing. I got up quietly and went to have a shower. I felt the need to stay there a little, all by myself. I let the water run down my body for several minutes. I was thinking of something and at the same time of anything. Would that be my life? I was the only one responsible and I blamed myself for that. This was not how my mother had raised me, this was not the thing for which she had struggled her entire life with my jerk of a father. And yet, I wasn't completely sure I didn't want what was happening to me. I couldn't understand why I was so undecided, why I wasn't able to make a decision. Was this situation what I wanted or not? I had many regrets and had to get out of this situation as quickly as possible. I put on my robe and started to dry my hair. When I looked up in the mirror, I saw Rwan behind me. He smiled at me in the mirror.

- How did you sleep?

- Either he was dumb, or he was pretending. How could I sleep? Probably this man had some mental issues.

- Not very well. What about you?

- I got a bit drunk last night. Why haven't you come downstairs?

- Really, Rwan? Really?

I cut off the hair dryer and turned to him. I was really annoyed and I believe he noticed that, too.

- Are you really asking why I hadn't come down? When you made such a scene that I wasn't on the pill, like I should have known about all this stuff. Then you sent that woman with that pill. Why haven't you come with it?

- I thought you'd feel more comfortable with her than with me.

He was sitting on the toilet seat and I was leaning on the heater next to the window.

- Feel better with a stranger, who comes to my room and tells me to take quickly the morning-after pill, because the gentleman had not felt like coming himself! Oh, and something more, Rwan! I would not have wanted children with you! I do not know what you went through and with whom, but believe me, I am not here to reel you in with a child, to bind you to me for the rest of my life and ask you for child support. But it's normal not to know anything about all of this, because you don't know anything about me, as I don't know anything about you either. Is that how you are with everyone? I mean, in fact, with the women you take with you on trips? I do not understand you! Actually, I don't understand how I got into this situation!

I started to cry, and he was just staying there looking at me. He wasn't saying anything.

- Do you think I came here for the money I received daily? Or to run to the mall and shopping? No! I have no idea what this life means! You didn't tell me anything. You sent a driver over to pick me, you threw me on a plane together with some women I didn't know and you're expecting that I knew I had to be on the pill... what else do I need to know, Rwan? I have already leaned to have sex! With you, because I didn't even know that! Tell me, Rwan, what else should I anticipate?

- Eva, you're taking all too seriously!

- Really? Is that what you think? That I took everything seriously? No, I didn't take anything seriously! I would have wanted you to talk to me for at least five minutes. Tell me exactly what this secret world of yours is. I came because I wanted to be with you and to see you. And please don't understand that I fell in love with you. Because it's not true! However, you were the first man in my life and I barely know your last name.

- Ok, today we're going home and you'll calm down a little.

- Really?

He didn't answer my questions anymore and went out of the bathroom. He left me there and I couldn't believe what was happening to me. This man wasn't really right in the head! I went out after him.

- Damn it! Rwan, can't you really give me two minutes to tell me something?

- What do you want me to say, Eva? What do you expect me to say? I don't understand!

- I don't know! I really don't know, but just tell me something, anything.

- I think we have to go back and relax a little. I think it was too much for you and we must take it slower.

- Is that what you believe?

- Yes, I do.

- Maybe if you explained things to me, I would have understood them faster and easier!

- You know, I really don't need problems, I didn't come here to get even more stressed. I came to relax, to feel good and charge my batteries. I think that is enough and we don't have to continue this discussion any longer.

- I see! So, I have to understand that it's all over between us?

- I didn't say that.

- I'm asking you that.

- What are you asking?

- Is it over?

- What is over, Eva? The only thing that is over is this trip. Let's pack the luggage and go downstairs for breakfast. A car will pick us up at 10 to get us to the airport.

How difficult the communication between us could be. I was simply overwhelmed by a feeling of frustration. I got dressed, quickly packed my bag and went down before him for breakfast. The time I had spent in that room and tried to understand this man who could not be understood had been enough.

Of course, all the people downstairs were happy and everyone was just smiles. It could be read on my face that something was not fine, but nobody came to ask me anything. I had a coffee and went outside to smoke. I called Dana and talked to her as I smoked two cigarettes. She had promised me she would wait for me at the airport. I wanted to get home as soon as possible.

All the way from the airport to my home, Dana had criticized me for not going about things in the right way. That I should have been sweet and gentle, that I should not have asked for explanations, and that I had reacted like a crazy, jealous lover. I thought she was just talking stupid things and I didn't want to contradict her anymore. I had only seen Rwan for a few seconds at the villa and that had been that. I was confused too. It had all happened very fast and very strange. I was wondering if I would ever see him again or this was the end of a crazy, unexpected story. Probably he was already looking for another girl for his new trip. I set myself many times not to think about it anymore and resume my life, to finish school, to go to the magazine, to go see my mother, whom I had neglected lately and to try to find a boy my age, with the head on his shoulders and without any other complications. I was wondering what to do with the wonderful card I had received as a reward before I left for Madrid. I wasn't going to spend any money on it, so I threw it in a drawer when I got home. I was tired and I just wanted to sleep. I undressed, turned my phone on silent and went to bed. I had to rest my mind and body.

When I got up in the morning, I was more confused than before I went to sleep. I was upset, disappointed, frustrated and it was as if I wanted the time to fly and go for this time of my life to pass already. It seemed to me that I had been complicating my life I was and wondering if I would still be in the same situation if I had a whole family, a loving father, a mother less tormented by her life and a normal childhood. The idea that I should talk to a psychologist began to take shape in my mind. Probably the childhood traumas were following me and I always got in such sad situations without knowing how to get out of them.

I got dressed and left the house. I was slowly going to school, and with my eyes on the phone, I was trying to move my mind to something else. The weird thing was that I didn't like boys my age. None of my colleagues were appealing to me, and they all seemed wimps to me. Was it normal? I think the problem was with me again. I could not concentrate in classes, I was looking forward to the break and I thought I had a little more and I too the baccalaureate exam.

I went to the magazine in the afternoon. Alan was very happy to see me. I was wondering whether he knew anything about my escapade in Madrid. I wished he wouldn't find out anything.

- Eva, I missed you! He was standing with a coffee from Starbucks in his hand and leaning on the door frame.

- I missed you too, Alan! I came back. How are you? What's new? Do we have something interesting?

- Yes, we do! I scheduled some photo shoots for you. And it seems we have already got the cream contract!

- What cream?

- Amer and The Sea! Have you forgotten?

- Of ...

- Yes, yes! Mr Ruskwasi's.

This man was really crazy. Or maybe he sent over the contract before we went to Madrid.

- I see! This is so great! Do you happen to know when he had sent the contract?

- Just this morning.

- Today?!

- Yes, today. Dora emailed us the latest details and probably we'll have to have the photo shoot by the end of the week. We haven't decided exactly on the decor yet, but these things are being discussed now. And your share will be very generous. I hope you will be satisfied! We'll show you your figures after we know more details.

- I see...

- You seem a little confused! What's the problem? If you don't like it, just tell me and I'll find someone else!

I thought about it for a while. Maybe it was better to choose another girl instead. But, as always, the mad part of me didn't let me give up this chapter of my life.

- No, it's really fine! I'm sorry, I had a difficult weekend! I'm really glad, thank you, Alan! I jumped and kissed his cheek. You'll let me know the details and when we'll have the photo shoot, won't you?

- Will you be in town next weekend?

- Yes, I won't go anywhere! Just keep me posted!

I left the office and I just couldn't believe it. This man was either crazy, or he didn't actually care what happened in Madrid and wanted to continue the business part of our relationship. In the end, I think it was possible for us to not even cross paths during this entire business. And then I just had to see everything as a business and forget that I had ever known this Mr Rwan.

On Thursday I received all the details for the Saturday morning shooting. We had all the details, the place, the time, the price and the names of those in the team. The only thing I was looking for in those lines was whether Rwan would be there. Dora's name was mentioned and the contact details of other individuals in the company, but nothing else. Dana advised me to contact Rwan and talk to him about that, but it didn't seem like a good idea. As long as he never contacted me by phone, I was not going to initiate the communication this time. And, finally, I had to do my job and focus on making money and advance in my professional life, not dreaming of crazy things and trips with married men and mistresses.

I met with Alan on Friday to get a coffee and actually sign the contract.

- Maybe it would be better to read it before signing!

- Alan, I really won't read all these pages! What could they take from me? I don't have anything!

- It is not about this, it is that in the future much bigger contracts can come your way and you have to be careful! Not all people are reliable and they can cheat you on your commission, payments and so on!

- As long as you're with me, I won't worry about what I sign! Have you read it?

- I have. You haven't.

- Well, if you have read it, that's enough! Do we get rich?

- Ha-ha, that would be the day! We will split a small commission from the sales due to your ads and appearances. You should be thankful to your parents for this wonderful face!

I instantly got sad. Poor Alan! He didn't know anything about my parents, but this was a delicate subject and it didn't do me any good to open this memory box. I imagined my father in a bar, drunk, with many empty bottles beside him. I wondered if he was still alive or had alcohol been fatal to him. I was just hoping that he had not started another family. Not because I was jealous, but because I didn't want other people to suffer. What he had done to me and my mother was enough. My childhood had been a nightmare. And, despite this, I would have preferred to grow up with his beatings and have my mother healthy beside me, rather than being thrown into that orphanage, where not even an animal deserved to live, let alone a child who just lost their parents.

- Eva! I'm talking to you! What happened? You're pale as a ghost! Are you ill?

- I'm sorry, Alan, I'm fine!

- So, everything is set for Saturday. You should get a good sleep tomorrow night, please! You must be rested and without any dark circles under your eyes!

- Ay-ay, sir!

I liked Alan a lot. Although we were not very close, I saw him like someone I could trust and could rely on at any time. I knew he cared about me too and was trying to make a living for me. He probably wanted to be like some kind of father or uncle to me, and I really liked the idea. Sometimes I wondered if he knew anything about me and Rwan. My instincts told me that he did and that he wanted to keep it quiet and not ask questions, he was too well bred for that. I felt an impulse in my mind to talk to him about this whole story one day, but not now.

Chapter 13

I arrived at the headquarters of the magazine on Friday. Studio 5 was booked for us. The photo shoot had allotted a fixed period of time. The plate next to the door read "Amer and The Sea 10-18". We had to observe the team's schedule. Although the photos looked spectacular in the magazine or in the advertising videos, the work to be done was considerable. The planning and observing the schedule were fundamental. I started the make-up at 7:45 am and my hairstylists started combing my hair at the same time. It was all a well-oiled machine for them. It was the first time for me being part of something that complex. Probably everyone out there knew about it and they were behaving like I was a little child. They explained to me every step very patiently. They all seemed to have known each other for a long time. They were making jokes, helping each other and telling all kinds of things about their families, children or holidays.

Behind the place reserved for beautifying me, a table full of food and soft drinks was set. From what those present were saying, it was very important to eat, drink as much liquids as possible and smile. The truth is that an empty stomach leads to nerves, stress and discomfort. They also put some food on a small plate for me and they told me to eat now, as I can, through brushes and hair brushes, because later it would be impossible. I couldn't swallow anything, I had managed to drink a coffee before I left home and it was enough for me.

Although it was about creativity on the part of each team, fun was the key. Everyone was smiling, they were making jokes and they were having a good time. It seemed that this work was a pleasure for them and that made me feel more at ease. My heart was beating hard in my chest and I was very nervous. There were not too many familiar faces and, although a feeling of fear gripped my soul, I tried to radiate peace and calmness.

- Are you ready, Eva? Alan whispered in my ear.

- Oh, it's so good that you're here! I thought you wouldn't come!

My soul felt a little more at ease and the tremors in my body started to subside.

- How could I let you alone, and especially today? I've just been caught in traffic. But here you are, so beautiful! The girls really know how to do an extraordinary make up, and let's not forget the stylists. Well, to be honest, we all must admit how beautiful Eva is, isn't it?

- Yees! several people answered at the same time.

- Alan, you're making me blush! Please, stop it! You know I don't like it!

- Come on, you have to relax a little! The pictures would be better if you do. Believe me, I know! You must be as natural as possible.

- I'll try!

- Come on, you can do it, you were not chosen for nothing to be the face of these creams!

- Do you really think that?

- I don't think, I know it!

It was then that I realised Alan knew about me and Rwan. His expression was telling me that and no other word was needed. We have both understood that it was a secret and we must pretend, I believing that he hadn't found out, and he believing that I didn't know that he had found out about it.

I started to like the idea to have my picture taken. I liked the attention I was getting. I felt a little embarrassed when I had to keep changing clothes with so many people present, and especially when I had to pose with the top of my body naked. My breasts were not visible in the pictures, but all the men there saw them. It seemed very natural to them and although I was worried that they would sit and stare at my nipples, they didn't do that. Time was flying and I became more and more relaxed. Alan was all smiles and it made me happy seeing him satisfied. I would be grateful to him for the rest of life for the day he approached me.

I woke up on Sunday morning and went straight to my mother. I needed to see her and hold her in my arms. She was my oasis of tranquillity and my soul became cleaner there. Although it was hard for me every time I got to the hospital and tears kept running down my face, as long as I was with her, I was the calmest person in the world.

When I opened the door to her room and saw her in her chair, with her eyes on the door, I felt she was waiting for me. She also needed to see me. Alone between the walls of the room, day by day, even though the doctors and nurses said she wasn't aware of what was happening to her, I knew her soul was there and, with it, all her love for me. I felt her closer than ever and when I looked into her eyes, it was the first time in a long time that I knew she really missed me.

Even though my mother could not always be near me, and sometimes absent in my presence, I knew that her thoughts were with me! There, in the darkness of her mind, she found light and prayed for me. I also knew that if she could change my fate, she would have given up her life trying.

I sat down to her feet and held her in my arms. I put my head in her lap and started crying. I started telling her what I had been experiencing and what I went through lately. I was crying in hiccups and asking her for forgiveness. I would have wanted to be a better child, to come and tell her more beautiful things, but, unfortunately that was it and I couldn't change anything now. Maybe if someone looked at me from the outside, they would have said that I was talking to no one, but I knew she would hear me and understand me. Her eyes were now drawn to the window. When I raised my head I saw tears running down his cheeks. I knew my mother was there, with me, and that she was suffering for me. I wiped her tears and kissed her sweetly on the forehead. I squeezed her hands and told her how much I loved her and that I knew she heard and understood me. And immediately, as if by a miracle, her eyes turned to my eyes. It was the first time my mother looked me in the eye. I hadn't felt so much joy for so long, almost never. I needed her and she needed me. Now I knew there was a chance and my mother could recover. Although no doctor gave her any hope, I knew and felt that. And I was going to go up to the end of the world for her!

I got up reluctantly from sitting next to her armchair, but I left that place more confident than ever. Although I was always coming out of the hospital doors sad and full of pain in my soul, this time everything was different. The word MOTHER has no other synonyms, because a mother is unique, for each of us. And now I had a new mission, I wanted to bring my mother home with me.

After the photo shoot, I never thought how much my life would change. I hadn't realized that for even a second. Everything had turned on its head. There were posters with me in the bus stops, I appeared in magazines with all kinds of promotions and even in pharmacies or supermarkets. The phone was always ringing for new contracts and I was approached by many people on social networks. And it all happened very quickly. In two weeks, the "just Eva" that I knew was no longer, I was Eva, the face of the Amer and the Sea creams.

I received invitations to all kinds of events and I didn't feel prepared for what was happening now in my life. Alan supported me and managed the situation for me. I was totally lost and I didn't understand how everything could change so quickly.

- Eva, we'll have an important gala next week and you have to be there! I have already made your schedule for the following weeks! Alan told me while we were both drinking our coffees on the terrace next to the magazine's studios.

- I see! But, Alan, what will I do with the school? I haven't been to school for two weeks!

- Unfortunately, you'll have to find another solution to finish it, maybe distance learning! It would be pity losing all these opportunities!

- I know, but this year I was supposed to sit the baccalaureate exam!

- We'll find a way. Right now you're on demand, Eva, and you never know if this time will return again. You should take advantage of it and, who knows, you'll be a famous model. That's if you're not one already!

- Eh, I'm not...

- Yes, you really are! I can't cope anymore with all the demands for contracts for you! You don't even realise what you got into! Oh, here's Tony!

I saw Alan getting up and greeting a tall, well-dressed and very handsome boy.

- Tony, this is Eva! Eva, this is Tony!

We shook hands and we both smiled to each other.

- You're the famous Eva?

- Famous Eva? Is that what they are calling me now?

- It's what I call you. You're prettier in flesh that you are in the pictures!

- Thank you, you're very nice!

- Eva, this is the son of Mr Rwan, the owner of the creams!

I felt the ground slipping under me. I stood in front of him and I couldn't believe I had go to through this awkward moment.

- Does she know my father? Tony asked Alan.

- Sort of.

- I hope you didn't get to know him too well, Tony laughed towards me.

- What does this mean? he saw the expression on my face changing.

- I'm just joking! My father is a man very interested in young girls and it was just a joke.

- No, Tony! Alan said. This is not the case! Eva is a good girl and she wouldn't do something like this. Even so, you shouldn't damage your father's reputation!

- Come on, Alan, everybody knows my father! And, Eva, if you haven't heard already, you'll hear it for sure!

I couldn't imagine something like that. My heart was beating fast and I didn't know how to react. I had initially thought that Tony knew the entire story about what happened between me and Rwan, but it seemed he didn't. It was just the way in which he saw his father. However, I had been his mistress for a few days and, even more important, his father had been the first and only man in my life.

- Come on, I have frightened you badly! Relax, now that I've met you, nobody will try anything with you!

- What does it mean?

- Come on, Eva, are always do uptight? You tell her, Alan, I won't bite. Shall we have a coffee?

- Please! Alan invited him to sit down and joint us.

I looked in Alan's eyes and I didn't understand what was happening. Tony couldn't take his eyes off me and asked me a lot of questions, but I could barely open my mouth. I didn't understand whether it was a game or it was just fate chose to turn everything again upside down.

- I assume you come to the gala on Thursday too, Eva! Don't you?

- I suppose I am! Alan knows what I have to do and what I don't!

- Yes, we'll go together. Will you come, too?

- Yes, I'll come too! I'm in town for a few days and I said to myself that I had to go there. Maybe I would meet a beautiful girl, but now that I've met Eva, there's no need for that. Will you go with me?

- Go where?

- To the gala! Would you like to go with me?

- I?

- Yes, you!

I didn't know what to answer. I lost my head. I wanted to go with him for two reasons, because I thought he was a nice boy and because I wanted to see Rwan's face when I showed up hand in hand with his boy at such an event.

- Yes, I will!

Alan changed his expression. He couldn't believe either the game I played.

- Perfect, give me your number and we'll talk.

He wrote my number, he got up, kissed me on the cheek and left. He was a tall, dark, back-eyed boy. He wore some low bottom jeans, a slightly low-cut t-shirt letting his gym-sculpted chest to be seen and a leather jacket. I followed him with my eyes until he got too far. He had something of this father in him, but I couldn't tell what.

It was 18:30. I was with Dana at home, all dressed up, made up and hair arranged. We were waiting for Tony to come and pick us up. We had talked a lot on the phone and through texts during the last several days.

- You are so beautiful, Eva! Tony won't know what hit him!

- Oh, Dana, it would have been so good if all these things with his father hadn't happencd!

- Come on, enough already! He can't find out.

- He doesn't, but I do! And so does Rwan! Half of me can't wait to see Rwan's face, but the other half hurts because I would have liked to meet Tony before everything that had happened.

- Unfortunately, life does not give us the easiest path. It was meant to be! What did Tony say, will he introduce me to a young boy? Maybe I'll also get rid of my sugar daddy!

- You're so crazy! Yes, he said he'll bring a friend along.

- I can't wait! Let's go down.

When we exited the building, we saw Tony leaning against his car. He opened the door for me and kissed me on the cheek. He was very smartly dressed and his perfume permeated the car. His friend opened the door for Dana. We were introduced and we learned that his name was Eduard. He asked us to call him Eddie. Dana signalled me that he was very nice and she was delighted.

- Well, famous Eva, how are you? Are you ready for us to appear before the media?

- Media? What media?

- Well, a lot of media representatives will be there! And they are all very eager to find out who is your lover!

- Then it's good I don't have any! Isn't it?

- Well, then, what am I?

- You're Tony, the owner of the cream I advertise. The owner and the model. It won't be anything strange.

- That's what you think, Eddie said. Tony does not usually come with girls at events. It'll be an exception!

- In the end, we can enter separately, I said while looking in the mirror to see whether I still had lipstick on my lips.

- Eva, you're starting again with your stupid ideas, Dana jumped as if burned, then talking to Tony. You must get used to her, only after you'll know her a little better you'll be able to understand a small part of Eva.

- Are you so hard to decode? Tony asked me while looking at me in the mirror. I quickly answered to him.

- It doesn't seem to me like that, but I don't know what to say.

- You're a little quiet, you had more courage on the phone and when we were texting. What happened? Did my physical presence impress you?

- Really, Tony? How old are you?

- 27.

- Thanks, but that was not the purpose of the question.

- Are we there yet? Dana interrupted the discussion between me and the arrogant gentleman.

- Yes! I'll leave the car to the parking attendant and we'll be good to go. Are you ready?

We all opened the doors and got off the car. The boys wanted to open us the doors by themselves, but they didn't realise in time that we are not two well-bred girls, with some exceptional education.

- You should have left me open you the door, Tony said smiling to me.

- I'm sorry, I'm not used to such a treatment.

- Well, you should get used to.

He pushed my hair aside and kissed me again on the cheek. He took my hand, surprising me, and pulled me after him. I was looking at him and he seemed more and more nice. How much I wish I hadn't known his father, or at least that nothing had happened between us. Or maybe I wouldn't be now hand in hand with his son if he hadn't offered me the contract. And I didn't even know if he had given me this chance to get revenge on me, or maybe he had no involvement in this whole thing. However, it was certain that, because of him or at least his company, I was now where and who I was. I wondered whether he would be present in the restaurant. And if so, what should I do, how should I behave? Did he know that his son would accompany me to this event?

- Eva, I'm talking to you!

- I'm sorry, Tony, I wasn't paying attention!

- Where did your mind go?

- Far away.

- How far?

- Tell me, what haven't I heard?

- Are you nervous?

- I ream really not.

- Good! Well then, get ready!

The last word did not even get out of his mouth, as we saw all the cameras and camcorders turning to us. I didn't realize whether they were surprised that Tony was with me or that I was with Tony. Two reporters tried to ask us a few questions, but I was shocked and Tony was distracted. He winked at me and squeezed my hand. After we managed to get past them, he stopped in the middle of the stairs, pulled me hard from my waist and started kissing me. I had no reaction. I was completely shocked. I was only seeing flashes and I decided then to close my eyes, to hold him in my arms and to kiss him.

- Come on, love birds! Dana and Eddie shouted to us.

I saw happiness on Tony's face. He smiled to me, caressed my face and took my hand again.

- Did you like it?

- Yes, but what was that?

- I just felt like it. I wanted to kiss you.

- But like that, in front of everyone? Especially those journalists, I haven't got used yet to this world.

- Yet.

- I really haven't yet!

- You'll be! You're already famous, Eva!

- Stop this nonsense!

We entered the room and a beautiful lady led us to our table. There were four of us and two more couples. Tony and Eddie knew them, so they introduced us. A lot of people were coming to our table to talk to Tony. Most of them exclaimed, "Oh, so you are Eva!" as if they were talking in the presence of a poster. I could feel them looking at me and thinking how much sex I had to have with Tony to be the face of the creams. But they didn't know that it was the first time I got out with this boy and that the back story was actually much more complicated.

My thoughts turned to Rwan. I was wondering whether he was there too. Whether I were going to see him and especially under these circumstances, in the presence of his son. I didn't know if it would be right for Tony to tell him I had met his father, even his mother, or it was better to keep my mouth shut and leave this discussion for another time. I asked Dana and she advised me not to ruin the evening and that the right time will come. So I put all my thoughts aside and when Tony invited me to dance, I accepted without thinking of anything else.

We went to the dance floor and out bodies got close together. We danced on the song "A star is born" and I felt like we were creating a connection that became tighter and tighter. He looked me in the eye and held his hands on my waist. I put my hands lightly on his face and started kissing him. What strange and pleasant feelings passed through my body. I had butterflies in my stomach and I didn't want that moment to end.

We had partied until 5 in the morning. Dana seemed to get along very well with Eddie and I was getting along extraordinarily well with Tony. They asked us to go to Tony's apartment, but we vehemently refused. Dana seemed to want to, but I wasn't going to make the same mistakes all over again, especially with this son. I explained to Dana that I didn't feel good about doing this and asked her to understand me.

- You're very stubborn, both of you, but especially you, Eva! Tony said visibly annoyed, while we were leaving the restaurant.

- Let's take it slow, Tony, really! I'm also very tired.

- How low do you want to go?

- Let's let time bring everything together, what do you say?

- Well, I can't really say anything, can I? I can't! I'll leave anyway tomorrow with Eddie for Paris.

- Really?

- Really, really. We'll stay there for three days.

- Come with us, Eddie shouted in front of us.

- Yes, it's really a wonderful idea! Tony said.

- Really?

- Can you say anything else than "really"? Will you come to Paris with me or not?

- Come on, Eva, let's go! Dana jumped to try and convince me.

- Really?!

- Really! they all shouted together and started laughing.

- Come on, this way I won't get upset with you that you don't want to come at my place tonight! We'll leave you at home, you'll pack up you bags and we'll come tomorrow at 12 to pick you up and go to the airport.

Oh, my God, this was all just crazy!

I wanted to go, but I didn't know how to react again. It seemed to me all over again the story with Rwan and I was scared. I was also thinking of the unavoidable moment when his father would find out about us, if he had not already found out.

- Eva, stop thinking a thousand thoughts and ask yourself a thousand questions just once in your life! Let's go!

- Dana, you really don't know what you're talking about!

- Now, answer me truthfully, do you want to go?

- Yes, I do!

It came out of my mouth involuntarily and without realising I thought aloud.

- Then we'll go! Guys, it had been decided, we'll come with you tomorrow! We'll wait for you to pick us up.

- We got lucky with Dana, because, were it up to you, Eva, we should take everything slow! But it's all right, we'll slowly take the plane to Paris!

I got home and saw Dana happier than ever. Honestly, in my heart, I was just like her, but I didn't want to show it. I don't know why! Probably because, at the same time, I felt very guilty. She started packing with the music blasting from the speakers. I tried to talk to her, but I didn't succeed because of the music. I was trying to turn it down, but Dana was coming immediately to cranking it up.
- Please! I really don't need sermons and worries! For once in you like, just enjoy yourself and let yourself be happy! Really.
- But Dana...
- No Dana! I'm really not in the mood! And you're not right, because, if you were right, I would have told you not to go. Come on, pack your bags and leave all these dark thoughts aside! It's only three days, that's all I ask!
I had no one to discuss with, so I started to pack my luggage. The truth was that, in the depths of my soul, I really wanted to go. While packing, I was also talking to Tony through texts. He told me that he is very happy and that he could hardly wait to spend more time together. Without wanting it, his father always appeared in my head. Not because I liked him more than Tony, but because I wished the entire story with him hadn't happened and I wished I could go with Tony, to Paris, with an open and pure soul. I had to keep a big secret about him now. And I could not decide, in my mind, whether it was better to tell him, just not to mention anything or simply never to tell him. I also imagined what my meeting with Rwan and Gabi would be like from the position of their son's girlfriend. I'm sure Gabi wouldn't have much to say, maybe just that I came from a poor family and I didn't have his son's education, but what about Rwan? I couldn't figure out what his reaction would have been, certainly not a good one, but would he have wanted to keep this secret of his relationship with me from his son?
We packed, danced, showered, beautified and so 11 o'clock came. We just had only another hour and we had to leave for the airport. Tony had sent me a text and told me they would come and pick us with their driver. I was starting to worry again, thinking that Jo knew about my existence and my escapade to Madrid. I wasn't sure whether he was Tony's driver, but he would be, more than sure. I had not slept at all and, due to the fatigue, I could only think negative thoughts. Or maybe that's just how I knew how to think.
- Oh, my God, what would I do if Jo will come with Tony and Eddie?
- Nothing will happen. You will be totally indifferent. You don't have to pretend that you don't know him, but you must not let them introduce you. Be a smart girl and you'll find a way, I am right there with you. Everything will be fine!
- I just hope he won't come. I insisted that we leave with a taxi and meet us at the airport, but he doesn't want to do this. If I insist again, I think it will look too strange.
- Exactly. Maybe we'll lucky and they don't have the same driver. I mean, though, they both seem pretty busy, I think there wouldn't be time for one person to drive them both.
- I hope you're right!
We sat down in the kitchen and made some coffee. I felt the need to smoke five cigarettes, hoping it would calm me down, but that was just a myth. I liked it and it put me a good mood, but smoking didn't calm me down, nothing could calm me anymore. Dana seemed very excited and could hardly wait to walk the streets of Paris. She kept telling me about Paris, but she had never been there. Well, she did do her research, better than I did.

- Let's go down, they're in front of the building.

- Yaaaaay, we're going to Paris! Smile a little, you're more beautiful when you're smiling, believe me! Come on... don't be so grumpy!

- Oh, Dana, what are you doing to me?

- I'm trying to get you to relax. You're much too serious.

We took the elevator and got down. The two of them, dressed beautifully, but lightly, with their glasses on, waited for us in front of the building. I jumped in Tony's arms and kissed him passionately, I was really happy to be with him and I told myself it was time to leave all my thoughts at home.

- You're very beautiful, Eva!

- Thank you!

- Let's put the luggage in the trunk and go!

I saw that it was not Jo behind the wheel, which calmed me down. I had avoided a major issue and it was just that this trip of ours would not start on the left foot.

I helped Tony get the luggage into the trunk. Dana and Eddie were already in the back of the car. I pulled his sleeve a little before we climbed in, kissed him and smiled at him. I was going to go with the flow and avoid talking about his parents, so I felt less guilty towards him about the situation.

I climbed in the car all smiles, pulled the door behind me and followed Tony with my eyes as he climbed in front of me in the right seat. He put on his belt, lowered his glasses and turned to face us.

- Are you ready, girls? What about you, Eddie?

- Yeees!

- Oh, Dana, Eva, this is Ivan, mu driver.

Dana extended her hand to him, but I felt my blood freezing in my veins when I saw his face. I immediately started to cry. It was Ivan, my father! I tried to pull the door handle, but it didn't budge. I couldn't breathe, I felt I had no air and the world spinning around in the opposite direction than me.

- Open the door, right now. I screamed while I could not take my eyes off the bastard who was driving. I couldn't believe he was sitting in front of me, dressed in a suit, pretending to be a respectable and honest man.

- Eva? They all looked at me surprised and completely confused.

- Now, I want to get out of this car, right now!

Tony opened the door for me and I ran. I went up the stairs of the block, closed the door behind me and threw myself into a corner. I was crying so loud that I had no air. All kinds of unpleasant memories went through my head and I couldn't forget his gaze when he turned to face me in the car. I remembered all the beatings, all my and my mother's tears. I remembered the day they took me to the orphanage. I realised that, during all these years, he lived and never cared what happened to me, his child. That he left me alone and without any hope in a hell, a worse place than my, his and my mother's home. I hated him, I hated him with all my being. This moment created more frustrations and resentments that I had cultivated for a long time. He made me feel fear at the same time, I was afraid of him even now. I was shaking so hard that I couldn't get up and go up to the flat. I was crouching in a corner that reminded me even more of the corner of my childhood home, when I was trying to escape his anger and beatings. It seemed to me I felt the belt strikes on my back and my whole body was stinging. Everything I had left in a corner of my soul was now coming out and it hurt me more than ever. My whole body was aching and I just wanted to die.

Oana Babagianu | **Eva**

A successful entrepreneur in the UK and Romania, Oana Babagianu is part of the "young and restless" generation. Eva is her first published book, a project close to the heart of an active woman, who wanted to share with everyone a piece of reality mixed with fiction about the lives of the lives of the children and teenagers in real Romania. A story that does not hide things, does not mince words and without embellishments.

Often brutal, the action takes the readers out of their comfort zone and carries them through all the social strata in our country. Harsh and captivating, the story of the girl with a primordial name makes anyone daring to enter the universe created by Oana Babagianu experience many emotions

The trip was about one hour long. I didn't know where they were taking me, in what city, for how long... I knew nothing. I cried almost all the way through the trip. I cried in silence, I would wipe the tears off my eyes as quick as I could, so that I wouldn't let them see me suffer. I felt the hate for them and I would have done absolutely anything to disappear. I could imagine mother crying in the house and that made me feel even worse. Even the thought of not going to the same school was destroying me. Why all these? Where had I gone wrong?

ISBN: 978-973-0-29606-8
Barcode
9 789730 296068

www.ingramcontent.com/pod-product-compliance
Lightning Source LLC
Chambersburg PA
CBHW061429160726
47995CB00003B/809